# Ring on Her Finger

# Ring on Her Finger

## Lisa Swinton
## Award-winning Author

Copyright © 2014 Lisa Swinton

All rights reserved

The characters and events portrayed in this book are fictitious. Any similarity to real persons, living or dead, is coincidental and not intended by the author.

No part of this book may be reproduced, or stored in a retrieval system, or transmitted in any form or by any means, electronic, mechanical, photocopying, recording, or otherwise, without express written permission of the publisher.

ISBN-13: 978- 1500879235

Cover design by: Ashley Johnson

Printed in the United States of America

*For Brian,*
*who gave me a ring*

# Chapter One

Face down in the pillow, Amanda's head pounded and her tongue felt like it was covered in fur. She spat out the blond hair that stuck in her mouth and rolled onto her back, but didn't open her eyes yet as her groggy brain tried to process in the quiet morning. Intense sunlight penetrated her lids and opening them would hurt. She was hung over.

What happened to her two drink limit she'd installed after that wretched hangover her freshman year? Usually, she opted to be the designated driver and drank nothing at all.

Her limbs felt too heavy to move as she tried to recall the previous night. She, Alison, and Aria had met up with Sean, Kurt, and Blake in the lobby of the Paris hotel, grabbed some French provincial cuisine with heavy garlic sauce, then headed over to the Bellagio to watch the fountain show. She remembered the taxi ride to the MGM and Blake scoring passes to the night club. Usually, Amanda couldn't stand Blake throwing his status around, but in Vegas it had its perks.

Blake challenged her to do a shot with him and she'd accepted just to wipe the smug expression off his face. On the dance floor he'd dared her to do another, but she'd declined. He'd accused her of being too stubborn to know how to have fun and be spontaneous. She'd gotten mad, taken the second shot, and then grabbed a random guy to dance with to prove him wrong. Three songs later, when the guy got frisky, Blake cut in and kissed her.

Blake kissed her! She cringed. That was bad, really bad. They'd shared a kiss once before, early in their freshman year, when she thought she might be something special to him. But then she'd discovered over shower talk that he was doing a lot more than kissing with the other girls. They didn't seem to mind sharing Blake, if anything they relished competing for him, but she wasn't that kind of girl.

As much as her head protested, Amanda fought to recall what had happened next, but her mind clouded over in a haze. Possibly another taxi ride back to the Bellagio, someone in a dress, and then nothing. Her brain wouldn't give up one more detail. What had happened?

Amanda pulled the sheets up to her chin and noticed her hand brushed over silk instead of the usual cotton tee she wore. Odd. Had she grabbed one of Alison's silk tops by mistake at bedtime last night? Had she been that out of it? Whatever. Alison wouldn't care and they'd get it washed back at home.

Inwardly, she groaned. Alcohol and airplanes were bad separately, but together . . . Amanda wasn't fond of flying. Being that high off the ground made her queasy on a good day, mixed with a hangover equaled barf city. At least only Alison would witness it. Everyone else flew to their homes scattered across the country. Who knew when they'd be together again, now that their week-long graduation celebration was over?

Amanda decided to get the worst of it over and opened her eyes. Above her, the tray ceiling painted like a blue sky with white clouds contained cherubs that smiled down at her. Dimly, an alarm bell went off in her brain. Her hotel room ceiling didn't look like this.

She rolled her eyes to the right. The cream-colored furniture and walls had little gold accents, while embroidered curtains hung at the edge of the wall-to-wall window. Pale pink roses set inside robin's egg blue vases dotted glass tables.

Amanda swallowed down the panic rising in her throat. Definitely not her room. She needed to get back to Alison and find out what happened last night.

She got ready to roll to the right, toward the edge of the bed, when she felt warm breath tickle her left ear. Her toes curled with tension. She wasn't alone. Not wanting to wake the sleeping scoundrel next to her, she ever so slowly turned her head and stifled a shriek.

Blake Worthington's classic good looks mocked her. Oh no! No, no, no, no! It couldn't be! How had she ended up as just another girl on Blake's long list of conquests?

Shocked, Amanda jerked to a sitting position and instantly regretted it. Her pounding head threatened to explode. Bile burned her throat. If she didn't make it to the bathroom, then she could add a puke-covered bed to her list of horrible mistakes. Amanda turned and quietly slid her legs over the side of the bed. The last thing she wanted was to wake up Blake. She'd rather do the walk of shame in private rather than have his smug expression of 'I finally got you' follow her out the door.

She put her toes on the floor and looked down. French manicure? She had come to Vegas with bright pink polish on them. Her eyes traveled up her legs to catch sight of a white silk nightgown. Her stomach lurched. She slid down to the floor and crawled her way to the bathroom. She breathed a small sigh of relief when the cold tile hit her knees. Almost there.

Once clear of the door she gently swung it shut. When she reached the toilet, she pushed up the seat and pulled back her hair, but her left hand snagged. Her parents had gifted her a small sapphire ring at high school graduation, which she wore on the middle finger of her right hand. Confused, she untangled her left hand and stared at the very large Tiffany cut diamond set in platinum nestled between sparkling diamond bands.

The contents of her stomach emptied into the toilet. It was worse than she'd ever dreamed. Amanda's foggy brain might not be running at full capacity, even so, she could put all the clues together to reach one inevitable conclusion.

She had married Blake Worthington.

# Chapter Two

From the floor, Amanda flushed the toilet, and then used the counter to haul herself upright in front of the sink. She winced at the smeared eye make-up and out-of-control hair reflected in the mirror. She eyed the double-sized shower behind her. The less noise she made the less chance she had of waking Blake. Even flushing the toilet had been a gamble but she couldn't stand the smell. She settled for washing her hands and face. The shock of cold water against her skin helped her brain function a little closer to normal instead of zombie mode. Her arms felt like they had lead weights attached as she raised them to pull out all the pins she could find from the elegant French twist she'd paired with . . . what? Her mind blanked out again.

She looked down at her white slip. Or was it a nightgown? What was she going to do for clothes? She didn't relish the walk of shame down the Strip in just a silky slip which could pass as a slinky summer dress as it went to her knees. But, what was the alternative?

Amanda cracked the door open and cringed at the sound. Blake's mass of a body lay still on the bed and asleep, if her assessment of his breathing was correct. Good. She scanned the bedroom. Nothing. No purse, no phone, not even slippers to stick on her feet. She bit her lower lip. She really didn't want to walk barefoot back to her hotel, but she couldn't even call Alison for help and using the white phone on the glass table was out because the sound of her voice would wake Blake. Grr.

One thing at a time, she reminded herself. First, she needed to get out of this bedroom and into the sitting area beyond without waking Blake. She inched the door open and tiptoed across the plush carpet which muffled the sound of her steps. She passed through the French doors and into the sitting area and winced as the sunlight blared into her eyes. She shut them, and then fluttered them open. The penthouse suite gave her a spectacular view of the Bellagio fountain below. She watched the water dance to the tune of Big Spender from Sweet Charity. How ironic. Her gaze lifted to the hotel across the street. The Paris. Only one hotel away. She breathed a sigh of relief, then turned her attention to locating clothes and shoes.

Thrown across the back of the cream loveseat lay her wedding dress. Amanda felt both repulsed and drawn to it at the same time. Her cheeks burned to think she had so casually given away the wedding day she'd looked forward to since her childhood. But her curiosity drove her to see what dress she had picked out to be married in. Was it everything she'd hoped it would be?

Gingerly she picked it up and held it full length. Pleasure warmed her cheeks and she smiled. The stunning white silk gown had Italian embroidered lace on the bodice with a full skirt. Simple and delightfully elegant. Her eyes dropped to the glass table where something sparkled. There sat a tiara like Tiana wore in the Princess and the Frog. She set the dress down and only then noticed the shoes. More like Cinderella's glass slippers with the unmistakable red soles of Christian Louboutin. She vaguely remembered admiring them earlier in the week, but hadn't even had the courage to try them on. A thousand-dollar pair of shoes wasn't practical or attainable for a middle-class girl like her. Tears welled in her eyes. The ensemble was everything she'd ever dreamed of, but knew her family could never afford and she'd wasted them on Blake.

Amanda admired the crystals on the shoes. She'd certainly look like a lady of the night, as her mother called them, if she strutted out of the Bellagio in a slip and those shoes midday. Her pride refused to keep anything Blake bought her. She'd leave the slip on the floor if it didn't mean walking naked back to her room. No, the shoes, dress and tiara would stay here. She refused to be one of those brides walking around town they'd giggled at all week.

Amanda started toward the door when a noise came from the bedroom. She ducked down behind the sofa. Drat! She was on the far side of the room and would have to pass by the French doors in order to get to the hall door. Where was a potted tree to hide behind when you needed one? Her head peeked up over the sofa. Blake had turned over to have a perfect view of the French doors. Thankfully his eyes were still closed, but he'd probably be up soon. She needed to get out undetected now while she still could.

A stealthy mad dash brought her to the door handle. Only a second away from freedom she gripped it and turned the handle.

"You aren't running out on your husband on the first day of our honeymoon, are you?" Blake's voice came from behind her. He yawned.

Caught! With all the dignity she could muster, she turned around to face him.

He leaned against the doorframe and lazily scratched his defined chest, which appeared extra tan above his white silk pajama pants.

She'd been so intent on escaping she hadn't heard him get up. "First of all, you are not my husband and this is not our honeymoon. And second, I am not sneaking out. I am returning to my room where I should have been last night. I need a shower and a change of clothes before I catch my plane." She folded her arms.

"Sorry to disappoint you, Mandy."

She cringed. No one called her Mandy except Blake, and she was pretty sure he did it just to get under her skin.

"But this piece of paper, photo album, and video say otherwise." He picked up a stack of items from another table she'd overlooked and handed them to her.

On top lay a perfectly legal marriage certificate, at least it looked that way. Dread filled her as the color drained from her face. "Is this some kind of joke? Did you have this printed up in the business office or something?"

He smirked at her. "Check the witnesses' box."

Alison and Kurt's signatures filled the lines. Amanda groaned. Alison would never play a cruel joke like this on her. Even Kurt, a known prankster, wouldn't go this far. "That doesn't mean we are staying married." She thrust the pile into his hands. "You are going to get this fixed. Get it annulled, get us divorced, whatever, but get it ended."

"Easy now, wife." He set the items back on the table.

"Don't call me that," she growled. "This was a mistake. It never should have happened."

One side of his mouth curled up. "You were pretty keen on it last night." His slight Texan drawl, which Amanda normally found to be moderately appealing, grated on her nerves at the moment.

"I was drunk last night. I would've married anything male that breathed, as evidenced by my choice." She pointed at him.

He faked a frown while his eyes twinkled with amusement. "That's cutting it low, Mandy."

"Seems pretty accurate from where I'm standing," she huffed.

He untied the drawstring on his pajama bottoms and advanced a step toward her. "Maybe you should come a little closer then."

His obvious enjoyment at her discomfort ate at her all the more as she took a step back. "Don't come any closer."

He pulled the photo album from the pile on the table. "Would you like to see the pictures?"

"No."

"You looked beautiful." His voice took on a reverential tone as he ran one finger over the silver letters of their names on the front cover.

"I'm sure I looked like a drunken idiot because that's what I was. And how is it that you remember so much? Weren't you just as drunk and out of your mind as me?"

"Unlike you, I'm used to alcohol."

Amanda's eyes widened, then narrowed. Anger coursed through her as she got nose to nose with him. "You mean to say you knew what you were doing last night? You got me drunk and tricked me into marrying you?"

"Now, Mandy, that's not—"

The slap of her hand against his bare chest echoed through the room as she pushed him away. "Save it. Let me tell you how this is going to go down. This sham of a marriage never happened. You are going to legally fix that. You've got the money. More importantly, you are going to keep this a secret. Absolutely no one is to know."

"Well, I think my parents will notice when they get the bill."

She snorted. "That's your problem, not mine."

"What about your parents?"

Her breath caught in her throat while her cheeks burned. She knew from experience Blake liked her most when she was angry. But right now she felt like a hurricane about to unleash its fury. She hissed, "I'd rather die than tell them I married you." Blake looked stung by her venomous words, though he tried not to show it, and she felt a modicum of satisfaction at having scored one for a change.

He tried to shrug off her remark. "How are you going to keep the witnesses quiet?"

"They'll keep quiet out of respect and loyalty to me." She pointed at him. "And if they don't, you'll pay them off to keep their mouths shut."

"You're really serious? You really think we can pull off pretending this never happened?"

"Well, I certainly can. I have serious doubts about your abilities, but I'm stuck having to hope you do the honorable thing for once in your life. Now, do we have a deal?" She stuck out her hand. She felt Blake's keen eyes scan her from head to toe for several heartbeats, but she refused to let her cheeks blush.

He sighed and took her hand. "Deal. Now, let's order room service and have breakfast."

She wrenched her hand from his. "Are you crazy? I'm not

staying here to eat with you. I need a shower, clothes and a little chat with my B.F.F. as to why she let me do something so incredibly stupid and didn't stop me."

"You could shower here," His eyes smoldered as he brought a hand to her shoulder.

Amanda slapped it away. "And put on what afterward? All that's here for me is this slip, a wedding gown and some ridiculously expensive shoes."

"Well, it is our honeymoon, you could just—"

"Oh, save it, Blake."

"At least let me call you a cab."

"The doorman can call me a cab. There's a line of them waiting in front of every hotel."

"Fine." He grabbed his wallet off the table from next to the wedding paraphernalia and fished out a twenty. "Here's a tip for the cab driver."

She hesitated. "I don't want anything from you."

He waved it at her. "Don't be so stubborn, Mandy. You wouldn't want to deprive the cab driver's kids of their breakfast or college education, would you?"

"For the kids' sake." Amanda snatched the bill and turned the door handle. "I think it goes without saying, but I'll say it anyway since you seem to be so thick-headed. After we leave Vegas today I never want to see you again." She stepped into the hallway and slammed the door shut.

## Chapter Three

Amanda knocked on her hotel room door, closed her eyes momentarily and prayed Alison was inside. She couldn't ask the front desk for a new room key without I.D. Without her cell phone she couldn't call Alison to meet her. Not that she wanted to be going very far in her current condition. The adrenaline from confronting Blake had worn off, but the hangover raged with a vengeance.

The door opened. "You're back." Alison wrapped her arms around Amanda, who promptly burst into tears. "There, there," Alison sat them both on the bed while Amanda let it all out.

Between sobs Amanda said, "How could I have been so stupid? How could I have made such an awful mistake" She pulled back to look into Alison's green eyes. "And how could you stand there and let me do it?"

"Well, if you'd watched the video, you would've noticed there was more swaying than standing on my part."

"Alison!"

"Look, we all had too much last night and got swept away. None of us were in our right minds. I'm sorry." She grabbed the Kleenex box and handed it to Amanda.

Amanda fished out a few tissues, mopped her face, and blew her nose. The hangover effects had doubled, due to her cry fest, and now her head felt like it weighed a ton. "Well, apparently Blake was in his right mind. He just admitted he got me drunk and tricked me into marrying him."

"No way." Alison gaped at Amanda, horror-struck.

"Yes way. He tried to deny it afterward, but it was too late. He let the truth slip out."

"Why would he do that?"

"Why does he do anything?" Amanda threw her hands up in the air. "Because he's Blake Worthington and he can." She tossed the tissues at the garbage can but missed and they fell in a snowy ball to the floor. "Now tell me everything that happened last night."

Alison cocked her head to the side. "You don't remember anything?"

"No. My brain left off somewhere in the night club when Blake kissed me."

"Oh, wow, you really don't have any tolerance for alcohol."

"As evidenced by my choice to mostly abstain from it."

"Okay, but before I start, take these." Alison handed her three Advil and a glass of water.

"Thanks."

"I figured you'd need them after last night. We'll have to pick up some Pepto on the way to the airport," Alison mused, then took a breath. "So Blake got you mad about something in the club. Don't ask me what; I couldn't hear what you two said over the music. He kissed you. You kissed him. Another drink or two later and we were all headed to the Bellagio."

"The cab ride I vaguely recall."

"First stop was Tiffany's, where you two picked out those gorgeous rings." She pointed at Amanda's hand.

Amanda groaned and tugged at the rings to get them off. "Crap! I forgot to give them back to Blake."

"Well, don't give them back. Those puppies will set you up for a long time."

Amanda braced herself and shut her eyes. "How much?"

"I didn't see the receipt, but I'd say in the twenties at least. Possibly even in the thirties."

Amanda gasped and opened her eyes wide. "He paid thirty thousand dollars for these rings?"

"You may not remember much about last night, but Blake was very generous with your wedding. No cheap drive thru with Elvis marrying you."

Amanda gave up on the rings momentarily, grimaced and sipped her water. "What else?"

"Well, he got the Bellagio to agree to a wedding with all the works in record time. They actually sealed off the arboretum and married you in there with all the flowers and twinkling lights. It was stunning and very romantic." She sighed reliving the memory before she shook her head and returned to the present. "But I'm ahead of myself. Next, we went dress shopping and the guys got tuxes. You have great taste in bridesmaid dresses by the way." Alison stepped over to the closet and pulled out a pale pink dress with intricate embroidery and beading on the bodice. It flowed to the ground and Amanda heard the crinkle of crinoline hidden underneath. "We got shoes and jewelry too." Alison produced a pair of strappy elegant Christian Louboutin shoes and diamond earrings with a matching necklace.

Despite her horror at the expense of what Alison held, she couldn't help admire them too. "They're beautiful," Amanda murmured softly.

Alison placed the items back in the closet before she plopped back onto the bed. "Didn't you look at the pictures or watch the video before you stormed out?"

"No. I was too angry." Amanda finished the contents of her glass and refilled it from the bottle on the nightstand.

"That's too bad, especially since you don't remember. It was definitely the most amazing wedding I've ever been to or will probably ever go to."

Alison's wistful tone made Amanda brave enough to ask another dreaded question. "Was I a mess?"

"Mess?" Alison's forehead wrinkled in confusion.

"You know like one of those drunken prom queen types or like in the movie What Happens in Vegas? I mean, did I sway and stumble around and look utterly pathetic?" Tears threatened to spill again, so she gripped the glass harder to keep them at bay.

Alison laid a reassuring hand on Amanda's arm. "No. You were not like some drunken prom queen stumbling about and slurring your words. You were giddy and giggly, but not embarrassingly drunk."

Amanda leaned up against the headboard, pulled a pillow to her chest and wrapped her arms around it. "Did you even try to stop me?"

Alison's eyes twinkled. "A few times, actually. I kept asking if you were sure this is what you wanted. The third time, you threatened to hit me if I asked again. So, I stopped. You told me to just be happy for you because you were happy and not spoil it."

Amanda chucked the pillow at Alison in frustration. "And you listened? I was out of my mind with liquor."

Alison caught it without missing a beat and gave her best friend a serious look. "Amanda, we've been friends a long time and I know better than to argue with you when you're being stubborn."

"Determined," Amanda corrected automatically. It rankled her to be called stubborn. It sounded close-minded.

"Fine, whatever you want to call it."

Amanda placed her head in her hands and tried to recall more details of the night now that the gaps were filled in, but her brain seemed to be jammed. Maybe a shower and sleep would unwind her brain. She rubbed a hand across her forehead and steeled herself to ask another terrifying question. "Did I say any of that in front of Blake?"

Alison intently studied the fringe on the pillow. "Well, you told him you were happy."

Amanda narrowed her eyes suspiciously. She could always tell when Alison wasn't giving the full truth. "What exactly did I say?"

"You told him it was about time he woke up and realized after four years that you were the one girl worth having." She stopped.

"And?" Amanda pressed her fingernails into her palms.

She raised her green eyes to meet Amanda's and said in a rush. "And that he could spend the rest of his life making it up to you for wasting the four years you could've been together."

"I'm going to be sick again." Amanda bolted to the bathroom

and made it to the toilet just in time.

Alison turned on the shower. "Get cleaned up. I've already packed us both and charged up your phone."

"Thanks."

"I'll run down and pick up some bread from the bakery. Think you can keep it down?"

"Yes. Bread sounds good."

"Okay, I'll see you in fifteen and then I'll answer any more questions you have about last night. Plus, I want to hear about this morning."

"Okay."

Amanda heard the room door close as she stepped into the shower. The hot water warmed her skin, and the steam helped clear her head. As she shampooed, she thought over what Alison had told her. She'd happily married Blake, even threatened physical violence against her best friend if she tried to stop her. Not exactly like Blake had tricked her, she admitted. The truth was, intoxicated or not, she had willingly entered into the marriage with Blake. But, why? The question gnawed away at her insides. She rinsed the shampoo, massaged in the conditioner, then finally lathered her body with soap.

Her hands stopped as realization clobbered its way through her foggy head. "The kiss," she said out loud. Her heart pumped faster. The kiss from freshman year. For four years now, she'd loathed Blake for kissing her and then for not thinking she was special enough to be the only one he kissed. Loathing veiled her true feelings—major attraction. Apparently it only took a few shots of whatever they'd had last night for her to fess up.

With her head pressed against the shower tile she pounded it with her fist once. She wasn't really angry at Blake. She was angry with herself for being vulnerable; for giving him the opportunity to reject her again. Her defense was to play the opposite, just like this morning, before he could say last night was a mistake and he wanted it over.

Her body slowly slumped to the shower floor as her conflicting emotions poured over her, intensifying her headache. Another wave of nausea threatened to spill the contents of her stomach for the third time in an hour, but there was nothing left to give. Several minutes passed as her self-pity and loathing washed down the drain with the soap. Finally, she turned off the water and toweled off. She'd just finished dressing when Alison's red curly head poked through the door.

Alison winked. "Feeling more human?"

"A little. Although, I think I won't feel fully human until after I've slept in my own bed tonight." She combed her hair, while Alison watched her.

"Ready for some breakfast? It should help your stomach by soaking up any of the remaining alcohol in there."

Settled picnic-style on the bed, Alison handed Amanda a croissant and a bottle of Ocean Spray cranberry juice. "I thought O.J. might be too rough on your stomach this morning. Besides, cranberry juice is what you're supposed to drink to prevent honeymooner's disease or whatever you call it."

"What?" Amanda asked mid bite.

"You know, a lot of women get UTI's and stuff from the frequency of sex on their honeymoons."

"Sex!" The croissant fell to the bed while Amanda frantically ran her hands through her hair. The rings snagged again. She scowled as she untangled them. "I didn't even think about that. Did I have sex with Blake last night?" Her expression begged for a negative response.

Alison bit back a laugh. "I have no idea, seeing as I wasn't there. You'd have to ask Blake."

Amanda shuddered. "I'm not about to ask him that." She successfully tugged the rings off her fingers.

"Well, how else are you going to find out?" Alison took the rings and held them up. "They are gorgeous. Are you sure you want to give these back?" She placed them in Amanda's palm.

Amanda's fingers curled around them. "Absolutely. I want nothing from him, but a divorce. I left everything in the room. I'd have left the slip too, but I couldn't very well cross the Strip naked."

"You left the shoes and gown?" Alison turned astonished eyes on her. "I mean really, the shoes?"

"Yes."

Alison shook her head. "I'll support you whatever you decide, but I think you shouldn't be so hasty. Maybe you should give the marriage a chance."

"No way," Amanda flatly refused. "I'm leaving for Africa in July and I want everything taken care of by then. I told Blake that after today, I never want to see him again. The airport is goodbye." She held the rings up. "I can return these before we leave."

"What about your parents? Are you going to tell them?" A mouthful of croissant muffled her words.

"Absolutely not. They are the last people I want to know about this. Their oldest daughter married a billionaire playboy in a drunken haze in Las Vegas." She paused imagining the horrified looks on her parent's faces. "No. It would break their hearts. I'd never be able to look them in the eye again." She took a bite. "And you're not to breathe a word to my family either or anyone else. I'll swear the rest of them to secrecy when we meet in the lobby." Amanda's eyes jumped to the clock. "I guess we better finish up and brush our teeth if we're going to be on time. I do not want to miss that plane."

"You could always have Blake fly us home in his private jet. Your last perk as his wife, so to speak," Alison suggested with a smirk.

Amanda glared fireballs at her. "Don't ever call me his wife again."

Alison rolled her eyes. "Okay. Take it easy. I was just trying to lighten the mood." She chugged the last of her juice.

"I just want to get home and forget any of this ever happened."

The group assembled in the lobby to head to the airport, minus Blake who hadn't shown up yet.

Amanda huddled them together. "Listen, about last night—"

"It totally rocked," Sean interrupted.

"No. That's not what I meant," Amanda said through tight lips. "I meant I want you to forget it ever happened. Blake is going to legally clean up this mess. So out of respect for me, I'm asking you all to keep it a secret. Permanently."

"You're serious?" Aria's skeptical expression mirrored the guys.

"Dead serious," Amanda replied.

"Are we allowed to joke about it just with each other?" asked Kurt with a note of hope.

"No. After we break this circle, never mention it again. Agreed?" Amanda put her hand in the center. Alison added her hand on top, then Aria, then Sean, and finally Kurt.

"I still think it's a perfectly good waste of an awesome wedding, but I'll be quiet," Kurt huffed.

"Thank you," Amanda replied as short-lived relief washed over her.

They released their hands as Blake walked up. "Did I miss something?"

Stony-faced, Amanda turned to him. "No. Just getting our friends to agree about what happened last night." She pulled a small bag out of her purse and put it in his hand. "These belong to you."

Blake looked inside, frowned, then thrust the bag back to her. "I bought them for you. I want you to keep them."

She stepped back. "They don't belong to me and I don't want anything from you except a piece of paper saying we are no longer married. Besides, I'm sure if you explain to the store, they can refund your money. I bet stuff like this happens all the time here."

"Fine." Blake scowled as he jammed the bag into the pocket of his jeans. "Let's get you home, since that's where you are so keen to be." He grabbed her bag from the floor and strode out the door. They piled into two taxi cabs and headed to the airport. When the wheels finally left the tarmac in Vegas, Amanda breathed a sigh of relief. "Thank goodness, that's over."

Alison's curls bounced as she shook her head and chuckled softly. "Dream on, sister."

## Chapter Four

Alison pressed down on the brake and the car rolled to a gentle stop in front of Amanda's house.

Amanda eyed the check engine light. "You really need to get the engine looked at. I wasn't sure we were going to make the last twenty miles."

"Ha, ha. Well, maybe if I had a rich husband . . ." The corners of Alison's mouth turned up as she gave her best friend a sly look.

Amanda glared back unamused. "Not funny."

Alison patted her on the leg. "I'll see you tomorrow, or maybe I'll wait until the next day when you have cooled off a bit."

"Sounds good. I need some rest. See you." She hugged Alison.

"Not if I see you first," Alison replied in their usual custom since middle school.

Amanda grabbed her bags and walked up the flagstone path to her family home. It was a modest two story farm house with white siding and a covered wrap around porch in a typical middle-class neighborhood. She paused at the bottom of the wooden steps to admire the blooms on the rose bushes which dotted the green landscape with shades of red, pink, and purple. But Amanda's favorite flowers were the white daisies under the river birch near the corner of the house. She noticed that Mrs. Franks, two doors down, had put her pink plastic flamingos in the yard for the summer.

She stared up at the front door, both relieved and nervous to be home. After all, she was a temporarily married woman with a secret to keep. She took a breath, formed her mouth in what she hoped was a normal 'happy to be home' smile, and then raced up the steps. Her suitcase bumped on each one announcing her presence to all inside, while her purse bumped her on the hip. She popped open the screen door and called, "I'm home!"

The sound of chairs being pushed across the hard wood floors and feet tromping through the house reached her ears before her family appeared in front of her.

"Oh, Amanda, so nice to have you home. Did you have a good time?" her mother, Jenny, asked as she wrapped her in a hug.

"Here, let me take that for you." Her dad took her bags and gave her a kiss on the cheek.

"Did you bring me something?" asked Amanda's youngest sister Tiffany. Her green eyes gleamed with anticipation.

"Tiffany!" her mother scolded.

"What? It's a legit question, Mom," replied Missy, Amanda's younger sister, as she picked at a hangnail.

"Did you do something crazy?" asked Josh, the older of the twins. He gave her a light slug on the arm.

"Not likely," replied James, the other twin. "Amanda never does anything unpredictable."

"Leave her be, all of you," shushed their mother. Jenny wrapped an arm around Amanda and led her toward the kitchen. "Are you hungry or do you want to rest first?"

Amanda's hangover had subsided to half level. All she'd eaten today were the croissant and the complimentary bag of pretzels on the plane. "I would like to eat first. What did you make for dinner?"

"Mom made your favorite, because you're her favorite," smirked Tiffany. Her high ponytail swished as she sashayed in front of them.

"Tiffany, I do not play favorites," Jenny reprimanded. She swatted her youngest daughter on the bum with a cloth napkin.

"Of course you do, Mom," replied Rich from the doorway to the kitchen as he buttered a roll. "We all know Dad's your favorite." He winked at his mother.

Jenny playfully pushed on his chest. "Go sit down, all of you. Amanda, go wash up and I'll dish you a plate. Goodness knows what kinds of germs you picked up on the airplane."

"Thanks, Mom." Amanda stepped into the bathroom just off the hall. Her mother had redecorated it while she was gone this past semester, so now it was a delicate purple with dark green and lime green accents. With a twist of the knobs, warm water spurted out of the faucet. As she washed her hands, Amanda stared at the picture hanging over the toilet and smiled. All six St. Claire kids were lined up along the side of the pool at the Great Wolf Lodge on a surprise vacation their parents had taken them on eight years ago. She'd been just thirteen. Life sure was different now. With a sigh, she turned off the water, dried her hands on a green fluffy towel, and then joined her family at the large kitchen table.

"Mom, can I have more mashed potatoes, please?" Tiffany asked.

"May I," Jenny automatically corrected.

Tiffany gave a small eye roll. "May I please have more mashed potatoes and gravy?"

Jenny wagged a finger at her. "Don't roll your eyes at me young lady and yes, you may have more. Get them yourself."

"Your legs aren't broken," the other five siblings chorused.

Amanda's dad rejoined them at the table after stowing Amanda's bag in her room. "How was Las Vegas?" he asked cutting into his golden chicken.

Amanda decided to keep her answers to a minimum. "Fun."

"Really?" James arched an eyebrow at her. "That's all, just fun? Aren't you going to share with us some interesting details?"

A pit formed in the bottom of Amanda's stomach. Did her family know? Had someone spilled the beans about her and Blake? It was hard to tell. The twins were notorious jokesters so James could be baiting her for the fun of it. She decided to play it cool. "Okay, you got me. It was more than just fun."

A smug smile settled on James' face as he dug into gravy-laden mashed potatoes. "Thought so."

"We saw the Cirque du Soleil show at the Bellagio, the Secret Gardens at the Mirage, snuck into the wave pool at the Mandalay Bay, where we also saw the Shark Reef and took a day trip to the

Hoover Dam."

"Anything else?" asked Missy.

"We went dancing and got massages."

"Not to mention a sweet manicure." Tiffany pointed at Amanda's fingers. Leave it to Tiffany not to miss a cosmetic detail like that. Her dream was to become a licensed cosmetologist and specialize as a make-up artist to the stars in Hollywood.

"Yes, a manicure too." Amanda sipped at her glass of milk. Milk was served at dinner in the St. Claire household, one of mother's laws.

"And highlights too," Tiffany added.

Amanda laughed hoping to throw Tiffany off the trail. "Okay, highlights too. We took a bit of girl time to primp and pamper while we were there."

"About time you relaxed a bit. You work too hard as it is." Jenny passed Amanda the homemade rolls still warm from the oven.

"Well, I had to keep my scholarship, Mom."

"I know. But college shouldn't be all about books. It's some of the best time of your life. You can cut loose a little. You have all your adult life to be responsible."

"How are things at the yard, Dad?" Amanda changed the subject. Her father worked at the train yard in Des Moines.

"Same as always, busy. A broken locomotive came in yesterday and it was giving Dizzy fits. We had some pretty good laughs when the oil line sprang loose and caught him square in the face."

"Oh, Bill, I hope you helped him clean up." Jenny buttered a roll.

"I handed him a rag, dear." He patted his wife's hand.

"Think you'll be able to fix it?" Amanda asked her dad.

"Of course. They haven't built a train yet I can't fix."

"How's the side project coming along?" Amanda asked him.

"Ol' Belle? She's getting there. I have to make some custom parts for her. I've called my contacts and no one's got the parts for her. She's just too old and rare. I think it'll take me another six months to finish her up. But when I do, the money should pay for the rest of Missy's college. Tiffany will have to wait for the next train to come in for the cosmetology school tuition." He winked at Tiffany, who groaned.

"Dad, really, that line is so old," Tiffany said.

"So am I. It still works though." He dived into his mashed potatoes.

"Rich, where's Rachel?" Amanda asked. Rich had married Rachel six months ago and the whole family adored her.

"She had to work late." He looked at the clock on the stove. "She should be here in half an hour."

The twins stood up. "Thanks for dinner, Mom. We gotta go."

"You're leaving without dessert?" Amanda asked astonished. The twins never skipped dessert.

"Oh, we'll be back for dessert. Don't you worry little sister. But we've got flag football practice tonight. Can't be late and let our team down." James said. The twins cleared their plates to the sink.

As they passed by her on their way out, Josh ruffled her hair. "See ya later."

"Yeah, yeah." Amanda smoothed her hair. "What is everyone else doing tonight?"

"I have a date with Steven," replied Missy.

"Steven?" Amanda asked blankly.

"You know, Steven Winters, my homecoming date from freshman year," Missy said as she cleared her plate.

Before she made it half way to the sink, Jenny called, "You didn't eat your peas."

"Mom, I'm nineteen. Can't I decide what vegetables go into my body?"

Bill smiled at Jenny, but said to Missy, "Not in this house."

"Oh, fine." Missy screwed up her face and downed her peas in three big forkfuls. She hated peas.

"Now, may I please be excused to get ready?" Missy asked Jenny.

"Of course, dear," her mother replied.

"Wait." Amanda turned around in her chair. "Steven Winters was that acne-faced nerd, right?"

Missy's eyes sparkled. "Not anymore. He's quite the hottie these days, and he's even got himself a ride to Texas Tech. Just don't try to steal him from me." Missy wagged a finger at Amanda and then at Tiffany. "That goes for you too, little sister."

"Oh, please, he's totally not my type. He's from here," Tiffany said. It was her dream to escape Iowa.

"What's wrong with being from here?" Bill asked with a trace of indignation.

"Oh, Dad. Nothing's wrong with being from here," replied Missy. "It's just that Tiffany has her heart set on landing a Hollywood heart-throb, like Zac Efron or Taylor Lautner." Missy laughed and escaped to her room.

Tiffany called after her. "Tattle tale." She slouched in her chair, crossed her arms and pouted her lips.

Amanda smiled at her sister's antics. She was sure Tiffany would get her revenge on Missy eventually. Tiffany had a vengeful streak to her, and she was also calculating and patient. She'd wait for just the perfect moment then one up you into the ground. "Try to take it easy on her, Tiffany," Amanda said.

Tiffany arched one eyebrow. "Are you taking her side?"

"No, I'm not taking sides. I'm Switzerland. Just don't go all Carrie on her and dump a bucket of blood over her head while she's on her date."

Tiffany perked up. "A bucket of blood. Good idea, Amanda. Thanks." She grabbed her plate and headed to the sink. "Well, I better get going too."

"Where are you off to?"

"Vegetarian Vampires 3 comes out at midnight tonight. I'm meeting Jazz and Trixie at the theater to stand in line. Rachel got us passes." Tiffany skipped out of the room.

"Doesn't she have finals to study for?" Amanda asked Jenny.

"She does. She spent all day at it too. I made her recite the entire periodic table to your father before I agreed she could go to the movie."

"She studied all day? She must really want to see this movie."

"Well, this opener has been driving Rachel crazy," added Rich. Rachel was an assistant manager at the movie theater. "She's just grateful it wasn't her turn to do a midnight opener this time. Last time she got stuck with The Millennium Falcon and had to be at the theater for two days with all the star geeks waiting in line. It was a nightmare." He picked up his plate and his dad's. "Wanna catch the game?"

"Sure," replied Bill

"What game?" Amanda asked.

"Hockey, baseball, whatever's on," replied Rich with a shrug of his shoulders.

"I'll keep a plate warm for Rachel to eat when she gets here. Just tell her it's in the oven," said Jenny.

"Okay," Rich replied, and then he and Bill disappeared into the den.

"Won't you be here, Mom?"

"Sorry to desert you on your first night home, but no. I've got my book club tonight. We're meeting at Lois' house. It was supposed to be here, but I asked to switch since I knew it was your first night back and I figured after your week in Las Vegas you'd need a quiet night." Jenny turned on the water and commenced rinsing the dishes.

Amanda hugged her mom from behind. "Thanks, Mom. I definitely need a quiet night and since everyone seems to have plans, now I don't have to feel guilty about going to bed early." She took a plate from Jenny's hand. "I'll help with the dishes."

"Thanks, dear."

"What book are you reviewing tonight?"

"*North and South* by Gaskell. Lovely stuff."

Jenny and Amanda worked quietly for a few minutes rinsing dishes and loading the dishwasher. When it came time to do the pots and pans, Jenny asked, "Are you feeling all right?"

"I'll be fine, Mom. I've had a raging headache all day. Apparently I had a little too much to drink last night."

Jenny paused her scrubbing and frowned. "That's not like you, Amanda. You're not usually much of a drinker."

"I know. I guess I did a little too much of that cutting loose you talked about at dinner and you know how I feel about flying."

"Yes, I do. You almost missed coming home for Christmas your freshman year because you were so terrified to get on the plane."

"I'm sure I'll feel better in the morning. Nothing your home cooking, two Advil, and sleeping in my own bed can't fix." She nudged her mom with her elbow. "I'm going to unpack, start my laundry, take a bubble bath, eat a slice of pie, and crawl into bed."

"Don't be up too late, dear. I'll be getting you up for church in the morning."

Amanda smiled and dried the last pot, while Jenny left one pan to soak until morning. Once they'd toweled off their hands, Jenny gave Amanda a big hug.

"I'm so happy to have you home," Jenny said. "Even if it's just for two months. I'm going to miss you when you go to Africa. It's so far."

"I'm going to miss you too. Thanks for being such a great mom." Amanda was tempted to tell her mother the whole truth about Vegas, but didn't.

Jenny kissed Amanda on the cheek. "Good night, dear. Sweet dreams."

"Good night, Mom."

Jenny bustled off to get ready for her book club and Amanda headed to her room. With all the boys moved out of the house, the girls had their own rooms. Amanda completed her to-do list, including a chat with Rachel over pie, and had just crawled into bed when her cell phone buzzed at the arrival of a text. It was from Blake.

The lawyer has started the paperwork, Wife. ;)

Arrogant jerk, Amanda thought, but simply replied with one word.

Thanks.

She deleted the thread from her phone. She didn't put it above Tiffany to read through her texts. For the first time all day the anxiety that kept her body in knots eased. Soon this would all be an unhappy memory and she would be free of Blake forever.

# Chapter Five

The sleek black sedan slid to a quiet stop on the paved drive in front of The Mansion. Blake's mother, Danyelle, had named it Worthington Manor, but the family called it The Mansion because it was so huge compared to their former middle-class colonial home. Danyelle had wanted old world charm and his father, Rex, couldn't have cared less. Rex's greatest concern was the tinker lab set away from the house where he could work in peace. The lab looked like a casita to go along with the Mediterranean look of The Mansion, although the lab was much too large to have such a small moniker.

As Blake exited the car the twelve-foot carved wooden doors swung open. Out of the corner of his eye, Blake saw Duke, the driver, shut the trunk and heft Blake's bags. As he'd been trained to do, Duke carefully stayed three steps behind Blake as they ascended the stone steps to where Horst, the butler, stood at attention in the doorway.

In his immaculate black suit, Horst greeted Blake "How was your trip, sir?" Horst relieved Duke of the bags.

"Eventful." Blake stepped into the two-story foyer, which was large enough to accommodate a sitting area. Their steps on the marble floor rang hollow in the large space. Blake's eyes traveled past the view of the infinity pool through the back windows to the lake beyond where a few long-horned steer grazed lazily. In Texas everyone with money had a pool. The sight of the water helped relax him. But as usual, he didn't feel at home. He'd never felt at home in The Mansion. It was more of a museum he lived in. Home was that long-gone colonial in the suburbs where he played basketball with his brother and friends in the driveway. "Is anyone here?"

"Your father is at work, your mother is attending one of her charity luncheons, and Miss Cici is at her tennis lesson. Miss Vivian is in the solarium. I'll see your bags to your room, sir."

Blake grimaced and peeked around the corner to where a part of the sun room was visible just to the left of the hallway. There he saw Vivian comfortably settled on a white wicker lounge chair, phone to her ear, chatting away. He looked back at Horst. "Thank you. I'll see her in a minute. I need to make a phone call first. I'll be in the study. Please make sure I'm undisturbed."

Horst nodded and departed.

Blake hurried around the corner in the opposite direction from the solarium to the tall double doors just past the foyer which led into the study. He shut and locked the doors, then whipped open his phone. He rested an elbow on the mantle over the fireplace decorated with white tiles of Vermeer scenes outlined in blue. He dialed the law firm that handled all the family's business. Mr. Greene got pulled from a meeting to take his call, but he didn't care. He paced the dark Brazilian wood floors as he quickly explained the marriage situation with Amanda. Mr. Greene agreed to see to it immediately. Blake hung up and tapped the phone against his chin. He'd promised a swift end to their marriage to make Amanda happy, but if he could have his way, the marriage would stand. He finally had the girl he wanted and he needed to find some way to get around giving her up. But right now there was Vivian to deal with. He pocketed the phone down and headed to the solarium ready for battle.

When he passed through the solarium doors, Vivian immediately hung up her phone and launched herself off the lounge chair. She pressed her body against his. "Blake, darling." She coiled her arms around his neck and went in for a kiss, but Blake turned his head. "Aren't you happy to see me?" She pouted her full lips colored red with lipstick.

He unclasped her hands from around his neck. "Of course, Viv." Blake stepped back, unwilling to endure her touch for one moment more.

"Then give me a kiss," she cooed and closed the distance between them enveloping him in her perfume-soaked aura. "I knew your family would be out and I wanted you to feel welcome when you got home. Wasn't that nice of me?" She smiled up at him.

"Always thinking of others now, Viv. Is that your latest trick?"

He stiffened as her crimson fingernails walked up the buttons of his shirt. "Well, I figured with everyone out, we could get in some quality alone time together. It's been far too long." A wicked smile graced her lips and he felt the pressure of her fingers against his skin as she deftly undid the top two buttons of his Oxford shirt. Blake grasped her fingers with his hand.

"Don't." His cold tone held a warning.

"Don't what?" She batted her eyelashes trying to appear innocent but Blake knew her too well to be fooled. "Don't stop. All right, Blake, if you insist. I think the solarium is a rather voyeuristic place for a little afternoon delight, but I've never been one to shy away from attention. I'm more than happy to accommodate your every desire." She moved her other hand to attack the rest of the buttons but Blake caught her wrist an inch from his shirt.

"No, Viv. I told you before; there'll be no more of that." He released her hands and stepped back again.

Her eyes narrowed as her hands rested on her hips. In a shrewish voice she said, "So, you'll do every girl at your university but not take me when I offer? Awfully hypocritical of you."

"I haven't chased girls at the university for a while now."

"Oh, did they just lie down naked at your feet this last year? Or do you mean you had to quit because you graduated? Or did show girls and strippers just throw themselves at you in Las Vegas? Is that your definition of quit?"

"You're right that I've never had trouble with girls wanting to bed me, but that doesn't mean that's what I wanted or did."

Vivian's eyes narrowed to viper slits. "Who is she?"

"Who?"

"Whatever gold digger has got her claws into you this time."

"Why must you assume every girl who wants me is a gold digger? Don't I have any other desirable qualities?"

"Yes," she snapped, "and I'm the only one who knows them, who knows you."

"You don't know me, Viv. You haven't known me for some time now. You're still in love with the sixteen-year-old version of me. He's gone."

"If I don't know you, it's not for lack of trying. It's because you won't let me."

"If you would stop trying, we would get along better."

"Stop trying? And lose you to some tramp? I don't think so."

"It's the manipulating that makes being around you exhausting, Vivian."

It was Viv's turn to take a step back. Blake hadn't used her full name in years and he could see it affected her. Right before his eyes the viper melted away to sweetness and she laced her tones with sugar. "It's just because I love you so much, Blake, and I want you to see how happy I can make you. How great we can be together." Her eyes welled with tears and she flipped her 'just shy of black' tresses over her shoulder.

Blake wasn't fooled. He'd seen this display before. "Nice try, Viv. I have to say, your performances have improved lately. But I've seen all your masks and I know all your tactics. You don't love me. You just want to possess me and keep any other girl from having me. Possession and love aren't the same."

The tears instantly dried up. "You're right, they aren't the same. Possession is an even deeper and more passionate form of love, and I do want to possess you, Blake." She latched her lips onto his.

With his hands on her waist, he pushed her away, then wiped the lipstick from his mouth with the back of his hand. "Don't ever kiss me again."

"Why? Because you might like it? You once craved my kisses,

and my body. You'll crave them again. I know you will. You are a guy after all." Her waspish tone made his skin crawl.

"This is your final warning, Vivian. You and I have history, yes, but we don't have a future. You need to accept that."

"Or what?" Defiantly, she crossed her arms over her chest.

"Or I will let your relationship with Sandy slip out in a very public setting where your parents are present." Blake didn't like resorting to blackmail, but she'd left him without any other options this time.

Fear darted through her eyes, but she kept up a brave front. "I don't know what you're talking about."

"One of Texas' outstanding families' daughter caught in the arms of another girl. That would make a very ugly headline. Even if it was only an experimental fling as you called it."

"You wouldn't." Her sure tone was betrayed by the doubt in her eyes.

"I wouldn't want to. But remember, if you back someone too far into a corner, they will do whatever is necessary to fight their way out, and I'm not any different."

"I shall count myself warned," she huffed. "Well, I can see you are in a foul mood, and I won't make any headway with you today. It's sad to waste such perfectly good lingerie on you. I was looking forward to you ripping it off my body. Get some rest and your head straight, and then call me when you are in a more agreeable mood." She brushed past him, making sure her breast pressed against his muscular arm.

Over the click of her heels on the Spanish tile, he called over his shoulder, "Don't wait by the phone."

## Chapter Six

"Morning," Alison called as she stepped into the St. Claire's house.

"In the kitchen, Alison," called Jenny and gave her a hug when she entered. "Nice to see you, dear. Did you have fun in Las Vegas too? Amanda's told us all about what happened there."

Alison arched an eyebrow at a wide-eyed Amanda, who shook her head behind Jenny's back. "Of course I had fun and I'm glad to hear that Amanda has filled you in so completely." She winked and grinned at Amanda as Jenny returned to the sink.

Amanda brought her plate up to her mouth and scooted the last bite of scrambled eggs into it. "Thanks for breakfast, Mom." She downed her last sip of orange juice and cleared her breakfast items.

"Did you want anything, Alison?" Jenny asked.

"No, thanks, Mrs. St. Claire."

"Well, if you do, you know where everything is." Jenny wiped her hands on the dishtowel, then hooked it around the oven handle. "Amanda, I'm going to run to the grocery store for a bit."

"Okay, Mom. I'll be in my room packing. Could you see if the store has any boxes they don't need?"

"I'll check for you, dear." She shouldered her purse and located the car keys within its depths before bestowing a quick peck on Amanda's cheek.

The friends raced down the hall and a minute later Alison shut the door to Amanda's room behind them before she sprang into an interrogation. "Has Blake called you? Are you still married?"

"Shh!" Amanda cracked the door and checked the hallway.

No one was there. She shut it with a soft click. "Really Alison, you're going to have to be more careful. My room isn't sound proof. What if one of my family heard you?"

"Sorry." Alison flopped down on her tummy onto Amanda's pink zebra striped comforter and propped her chin in her hands. "It's just so exciting you being secretly married to and divorced from Blake."

"If you think it's all that exciting, then you can marry him next time." Amanda grabbed a cardboard box, taped the bottom tight and opened her closet door. "Might as well start here. Time to do the deepest clean ever. I'm not sure of the last time I saw the back of this closet."

Alison giggled. "I think it was ninth grade. Didn't you hide in here after you broke that ugly vase your mother got as a wedding gift?"

"Unfortunately, I think you are right. That was awful."

"Especially as you tried to glue it back together with Elmer's glue and it crumpled when we tried to put the flowers in it like in that scene from A Christmas Story."

Amanda threw a pile of sweaters onto the bed. "I'm not going to need these in Africa."

"You might need them when you get back. Or you could have Blake buy you all new ones when you return," Alison added slyly.

"Ha ha. I better not still be married when I leave for Africa much less when I get back, especially since I don't know when I'm coming back."

Alison's eyebrows scrunched together. "I thought you were coming back in three months. That's what you told your family."

"My job is for three months, in which time I hope to find another job and stay there. I'd like to check out a few more countries and teach in additional areas. Ideally, I'll be there two or three years."

The corners of Alison's mouth turned down and she stopped folding the sweater in her hands. "You're leaving me for that long?"

"You'll be busy living, too, you know." Amanda took the

sweater out of Alison's hands. "I actually don't like this one very much. I'll donate it." She threw it in a large trash bag and grabbed another sweater.

"But, what if I don't get into my grad program, or what if I meet someone and want to get married? What if I need your shoulder to cry on or your advice?"

"I'll make it to a proper town every few weeks and be able to call home. I won't be able to afford an international cell phone. You'll have to save all your crises for when I can call or access e-mail. Besides, it's not like I'll be lost in the depths of Africa. I'll be with other medical staff." She sat down on the bed and hugged Alison. "We won't really be that far apart."

"You'll be an ocean and part of two continents away. How is that not far apart?" Alison wiped a tear away.

"I mean, you'll always be my best friend and I'll always have your back. And I will come home if you get married. Deal?"

"Okay. But part of that means I get to come visit you in Africa, at least once while you're there."

"You got it." The girls shared another hug. "Now help me get through all this stuff. I've got to get this room stripped down."

"Okay." Alison reached for a sweatshirt and sniffed it. "Ugh. I can still smell Williams High sweat in there. Time to retire this one." She threw it in the donate pile. "And you didn't answer my questions about Blake."

"He sent me a text the night we got home from Vegas. He contacted the lawyer and started the paperwork."

"Oh."

Ignoring the note of disappointment in Alison's voice, she asked, "What about you? Anything new?"

"I ran into Sheffield Caulderwood at the gas station." A happy smile returned to Alison's face.

"The debate team captain from high school?"

"Yes. We went out last night."

"Really? What's he up to?"

"He just finished up at Texas A&M and has a job at one of the agriculture companies in Des Moines."

"So, he's here."

"Yes."

"Think that's going to go anywhere?" From the sweater and sweatshirts pile Amanda kept two and moved on to shoes.

"It's only one date, Amanda." Alison laughed.

"Yeah, one date. Look where that got me. A quickie Las Vegas wedding and an even quicker divorce."

"Well, at least you're finally starting to have a sense of humor about the whole thing."

"It beats crying in my pillow at night. Maybe, I'll be ready for standup comedy by the time this is over."

"That or you'll be ready for a tribal wedding in the depths of Africa."

# Chapter Seven

"Blake, on the court in ten minutes, no excuses," Rex commanded from the doorway of Blake's room.

Bleary-eyed, Blake frowned at his father and rolled over groggily to check the clock on his nightstand: just after seven-thirty. "Geez, Dad," he groaned.

"Ten minutes, Blake, and don't be late. It's a family game. Your mom and Cici are already warming up." Rex left without another word.

Blake propped himself up on one arm and scowled at the clock. Great, a perfectly good morning to sleep in ruined by a family game of tennis. He crawled out of bed, opened his blinds, and squinted in the sunlight. Despite the western orientation of his windows, the glaring sun mocked him. He did a few warm up stretches, used the bathroom, then threw on a t-shirt and tennis shorts, laced up his shoes, grabbed his racquet from the closet, and made it to the court just in time.

His mother, in tennis whites with her bobbed dark hair tucked into a sun visor, walked over. "Morning, sugar." Danyelle hugged and kissed him. "Sorry about the early morning wake-up call, but your daddy positively insisted," she whispered in his ear.

"It's fine, Mom." He adjusted his sunglasses and joined Cici on the court. "I suppose we're playing doubles, us versus them." He pointed across the court with his racquet to their parents.

"Yep. And this time, Blake, try not to make us lose. It's wretched to spend all these years in lessons and then watch you screw up all my hard work and strategy with your oafish hits."

Blake rolled his eyes. "Good morning to you too, Cici."

"Just stay out of my way, and maybe we'll beat them for once."

Blake swept his arm out in front of him and bowed. "As you command."

Horst blew the whistle. The parents won the coin toss and Rex served. Cici hit. The ball flew back and forth until Blake missed an easy shot.

"Blake," Cici hissed.

"Sorry."

"Fifteen, love," Horst called out.

"I see you haven't been practicing lately," Rex called across the court.

"I've been busy with school," Blake reminded him.

His father frowned. "You may have been busy at school, but your mind certainly wasn't on your classes. I thought you would graduate higher up, but there you were hanging towards the bottom as usual."

"Sorry to disappoint you, Dad," he replied in a tired voice.

Danyelle served and the ball volleyed back and forth until Blake's shot flew out of bounds.

"Thirty, love," Horst announced and then retrieved the ball.

"Blake," Cici whined, "Get your head in the game."

"Right." Blake wiped the sweat from his brow. Only eight in the morning and he could tell that, even though it wasn't proper summer in Texas yet, it was going to be a hot day.

Rex caught the ball Horst threw him and called to Blake, "So, do you have plans for the summer yet?"

Aware his dad was baiting him, Blake didn't answer.

With pride Rex continued, "Cici has an internship at the office in the international department. She got top grades in all her language and business classes. I'm hoping she'll be able to run the international side in a few more years."

As he practiced his backswing, Blake growled, "Great job, Cici."

"You're doing it wrong," she reprimanded, then demonstrated a proper swing.

Rex beamed at this daughter. "Excellent form, Cici. I'm happy to see all those tennis lessons are paying off."

She curtsied with a big grin. "Thanks, Daddy." Then, turning to Blake, she added, "At least one of us is earning her place in this family."

Blake gave a grunt and tried to keep his anger in check. It wasn't Cici's fault he was a mediocre tennis player and he didn't begrudge her doing well in school. In fact, he was proud of her accomplishments. He just wished his dad would lay off comparing them. They were different people after all.

"Blake, you ready?" Rex called.

He nodded. Rex served one down the line and Cici groaned.

"Nice shot, Daddy," she called but her frown didn't match her words.

"Forty, love," Horst said. "Match point."

"This is so humiliating," Cici said only loud enough for Blake to hear.

"Tell me about it," he mumbled back.

"Here we go," Danyelle said. She served, and Cici lobbed it back. Back and forth, back and forth went the ball. Blake finally hit one down the line and his mom missed it.

"Finally," said Cici. "I thought they were just going to pummel us into the ground on this match."

Rex tossed Cici the ball and then she served.

"Excellent," Rex said as Cici smiled.

Danyelle returned the serve, but Blake missed it.

Horst announced, "Match point."

"Way to go, Blake," Cici grumbled, her face red from frustration and exertion. "We finally get the serve and a chance to score a point and you ruined it."

"Lay off," he warned.

A few more bounces of the ball and Horst announced, "Game over." The parents had won, again. They all gathered at the bench for a water break.

Blake grabbed a towel from the stack and mopped his face, grateful he hadn't showered before coming out to play because he'd need one after tennis. Sweat rings wet his shirt under his arms. "Congratulations, Mom and Dad," he managed in a tight voice. Rex didn't put up with sore losers.

"Yes, well played," added Cici through a half-hearted smile.

"Thank you, dears." Danyelle beamed at her children. She glanced between her husband and son as she took a long drink of water, then pulled her daughter toward the court. "Cici, will you show me your back swing? I think mine is a little out-of-date."

Blake kept his eyes on them and counted just three heartbeats before his dad started in on him.

"So, you managed to graduate after all and had your week of partying in Vegas. Now, it's time to get serious with your life, Blake."

Blake rolled his shoulders and head. "I know what you are going to say, Dad."

"What is that, son?"

"You want me to work at the office."

Rex's reply came fast and clipped. "Well, I'd rather have you at the lab, but your abilities in chemistry and biology are so abysmal you'd likely burn down the place on your first day, and I don't have time to rebuild. So yes, the office is the place for you."

"I don't want to run the company," Blake admitted.

"Based on your history, I don't really want you running the company either, but I will not have all I built pass out of this family just because you're lazy. You'll spend the next three years learning the business, and then I'll send you to get an MBA so you'll be prepared to run this business the way it should be, and I might have some peace of mind about it staying afloat once I've kicked the bucket."

"What if that's not what I want?" Blake jutted out his chin.

Danyelle and Cici rejoined them to get drinks of water.

"Your party life is over. Your mother has given you too long a leash for far too long, and I'm reining you in. Now if Andrew were here, I'd just let you be the black sheep of the family, and write you off."

"But Andrew's not here," Blake said.

"Exactly. He was perfect for this. He knew biofuel as well as I did, and even better, he had a head for business. He would've taken this company even further than I will."

"But instead you're stuck with me."

"Exactly."

Blake's temper flared and his words came out bitter. "Well, I'm sorry to be such a disappointment."

"You're not a disappointment to us," interjected Danyelle gently as she laid a hand on Blake's arm in an attempt to calm him down.

Blake shook her off. "I'm not Andrew, and I'm never going to be Andrew."

"We don't expect you to be," she said and shot a glance at Rex who continued to glare at his son.

With the head of his racquet, Blake pointed at Rex. "Dad does. He wishes every day it was me who went down in that avalanche instead of Andrew."

"Blake!" Danyelle gasped.

Rex shoved the racquet away with one hand, but didn't deny it.

Hurt washed over Blake, fueling his anger. "It's true, Mom. I see it in his eyes every time he looks at me."

"Rex, tell him he's wrong," Danyelle pleaded.

But Rex just turned away and strode onto the court bouncing a tennis ball on his racquet.

"See, Mom, all he has left is a disappointment for a son." Blake hefted his racquet over his shoulder. "I'm done." He headed for the house.

"Rex, go after him," Danyelle urged with a shout.

But he didn't.

## Chapter Eight

"Got your list?" Jenny asked as they buckled up their seatbelts. She'd traded in her old minivan for a used teal green Toyota Camry that Amanda felt much more appropriate for her mom's close to empty nester stage of life.

"Yes. First stop is the outdoor store so I can buy a backpack."

"A backpack? Wouldn't a rolling suitcase be better?" Jenny started the car, backed down the driveway and headed for the store.

Amanda rechecked the list. "The Red Cross suggests a hiker's backpack. Many of the locations are remote with rough roads, which can become impassable during monsoon season when the vehicles get stuck in the mud. The medics have to hike in. So, a rolling bag isn't recommended."

Jenny's forehead creased in concern. "You know, the more you talk about this, the more worried I get." The creases disappeared momentarily as a new idea stuck her. "Maybe you should wait until next summer. Get a job here at the hospital in the NICU or something. I'm sure Nancy would hire you in a heartbeat." Nancy headed up the nursery and NICU at the hospital.

"She would. But, as much as I love you, Mom, I really feel strongly about going to serve those who have less than I do. Think about all the lives that can be saved if the mothers and midwives know how to resuscitate a newborn."

Jenny laid a hand on Amanda's arm. "I'm only thinking about one life. Yours."

Amanda patted her mom's hand. "Thanks, Mom, for looking out for me."

"It's all part of the job, dear."

They pulled into the parking lot of The Great Outdoors store and walked in. It was a large store with lots of taxidermy animals adorning the fixtures and animal heads mounted on the walls. They headed upstairs to the backpack section located next to the kayaks.

A middle-aged man in denial of his receding hairline approached them. He wore the familiar pink shirt worn by all the employees of TGO. "Morning, ladies. My name's Ed. May I help you find something?"

"Yes," Amanda answered. "I need a backpack for Africa."

He studied Amanda's frame and she tried not to blush. The St. Claires were on the athletic side in terms of body size. Amanda had been diligent in her cross country training over the past four years. Her track scholarship coupled with her nursing scholarship had been the only way she'd been able to make it through college. That way, all her parents had to help with were books and rent. She'd worked most of the time to cover the rest of her expenses. She didn't want to leave college with a bunch of debt hanging over her head like so many graduates did.

"Let's see, you'll need something waterproof, light, and built to last. Not to mention just a tad stylish. The Outback 44 should suit you." He grabbed a brown backpack from the opposite side of the fixture next to them. "This is probably what you'll want." He pulled out the shoulder straps.

Amanda looped her arms through them and moved her ponytail out of the way. Ed let the backpack rest on her shoulders. "It feels so light," she said.

"Ah, yes. The framing is as light as they come but very durable. And anything you get on the fabric, like mud for example, just wipes right off with a damp rag. Have you ever done any back packing before?"

"Just once. I was thirteen, but I only made it half the day before I got sent home with food poisoning."

"Right then, a few rules. Put your heavy items at the bottom. Tie your bedroll under the bottom of the bag. Put the lightest stuff on top." He looked her over once more. "And for you, no more than twenty-five pounds in the bag. Do you have a scale at home?"

"Yes," Jenny answered for Amanda.

"Good, pack it and repack it until you've got it just right."

"Thank you." Amanda slid the backpack off her shoulders and looped the straps around one arm.

"One more thing, use the hip belt. I know the young ladies these days don't care much to emphasize that part of their body, but it is essential to carrying the weight of the bag. If you leave it off and carry it all on your shoulders, you are in for a world of hurt."

"Thank you, I'll remember that." Amanda smiled at Ed. Then she and Jenny headed to the other side of the store to find some hiking boots.

"Won't your feet get terribly hot?" Jenny asked. "Wouldn't you rather get a really nice pair of Nikes or something?"

"If the temperature gets hot enough, the rubber soles can start to melt against the earth."

Jenny raised her eyebrows. "You are making that up."

Amanda shook her head. "Nope, it's in the hand book. Boots."

"Okay, I may consider tying you to a tree to keep you home, like in Ella Enchanted."

"Josh and James would cut the rope in two seconds. You know they have bets on when I'll get back on a plane and come running home, don't you?"

Jenny smiled. "Do they? Hmmm. I'll have to join that betting pool."

"Mom!"

"You know, for the sake of mother-son bonding and all. In fact, we'll all put up bets and if you prove us all wrong, then you get the money. Deal?"

"Deal." They shook hands and entered the shoe section.

A young man with shaggy blond hair approached. "May I help you ladies?" He blew the hair out of his eyes.

"I need boots." Amanda pointed to a pair on the wall. "Can I try those in an 8?"

"Sure." A moment later he reappeared with the box.

Amanda's phone rang as she laced up the second boot. "Mom, can you get that? It's probably Alison. She was going to meet us for lunch if we are done in time." Amanda stood up and walked down the aisle to test out the boots.

"Sure." Jenny picked up the phone and called over to Amanda, "It's not Alison. It looks like a Texas area code. Do you want me to answer it?"

Amanda dashed back. "No!" She swiped the phone out of her mother's startled hands. "It's just someone from school. I'll call back later." She tapped a button and the ringing stopped. As she held it in her hands the phone rang again. "I'll just let it go to voicemail."

Jenny cocked her head to the side. "Go ahead and answer it. You need another walk in those boots. You can arrange to talk later if you need to."

Amanda was torn. She didn't want to talk to Blake in front of her mom, but she wanted to know if there was any news. It probably hadn't been enough time to get the matter resolved, especially as she hadn't received any paperwork to sign yet, but she wanted it done so badly she hoped Blake had played the name card this time and freed her. She turned down the aisle and picked up the call just before it went to voicemail. "Hello?" she almost whispered.

"Hello, wife."

Blake's confident Texas drawl came through the receiver and Amanda had a flash of annoyance. She looked nervously back at her mom who smiled at her. "I told you not to call me that," she hissed. "I'm looking forward to the moment when you call me ex-wife." She paced the aisle like a caged lioness.

"Now, Mandy, that hurts."

"No, it doesn't. And don't call me that either. You know I don't like it."

"I can't call you wife. I can't call you Mandy. What can I call you?"

"Call me Amanda like everyone else does. But honestly, I'd rather you didn't call me at all. Now, what is the purpose of this call?"

"Just wanted to check on you. See how you are holding up."

Amanda gave the phone a funny look. Blake was checking up on her pretending like he cared. Weird. "I thought you might be calling to say we'd made some progress on our situation."

"It's going to take a few weeks to get all that cleared up."

"Can't you just play the name card and throw some money at it to hurry things along?"

"A move like that would attract media attention. Do you want reporters showing up at your door?"

"No!" The idea horrified Amanda. Her shout attracted Jenny's attention, so Amanda gave her a smile and turned away again. "I imagine I'm going to need to sign some paperwork in order to clear this up. When will that arrive?"

"Not sure. I'll have to check with the lawyer."

"Well, when you send it, send it to Alison's house. I can't have court papers showing up at my house. Then there will be questions and everything will come out. And I'd rather take this secret to my grave." Amanda peeked around the corner of a display case to check on her mom. Jenny's eyes were trained on her own phone until the sales boy approached and they chatted.

"You know there are a lot of girls who'd kill to be in your shoes."

"Boots," Amanda automatically corrected.

"What?"

"Oh, I'm trying out hiking boots at the moment."

"You hike?" Blake asked genuinely surprised.

"No. I need them for a trip."

"Oh. Are we going somewhere?"

"No, Blake, we aren't going anywhere. I am going somewhere and I need this taken care of before I go."

"When do you leave?"

She hesitated, torn between giving him information and giving him a deadline. "July."

"Well, I think things should be done by then. Where are you going?"

"Doesn't matter. Look, just text me when you have some actual news to report. Don't call me again."

Blake sighed. "Fine. Bye."

"Bye." Amanda hung up and walked back to her mother. "They feel fine. I'll take them," she said to the young man. She sat on the bench and unlaced the boots.

"Amanda, this is Jimmy," Jenny said.

Amanda looked suspiciously at her mother but replied kindly, "Thanks, Jimmy."

He looked back at Amanda with an expression that begged for her phone number. "I'm glad you like them. Come back again." He picked up the boots and placed them back in the box. "Would you like me to deliver your items to the checkout desk so you can look around some more?"

"That would be very nice, Jimmy," Jenny cut in before Amanda could refuse. "We'll be along in just a moment."

He nodded to them and his bangs fell in his eyes again. He blew them away, smiled at Amanda, then took the items downstairs.

"What nice manners he has," Jenny remarked as they trailed after him. "It's so hard to find a young man with nice manners today. And a hard worker too."

"Mom, no." Amanda shook her head.

"What?" Jenny asked innocently.

"I'm not getting set up with a shoe salesman."

"You could just go out once or twice with him. Have some fun. See if there's any potential there."

"Mom, I'm not looking for dates right now, and I don't want any romantic entanglements before I leave for Africa in July. It's not a good time."

"It's always a good time for love."

"Well, as of right now, love can wait and come find me in Africa."

## Chapter Nine

Blake checked his phone constantly for a text or messages from Amanda, but, as usual, he got nothing but silence from her. He walked into the dining room, the first at dinner, again.

Ana Maria smiled at him, and in her Ecuadorean accent asked him, "How are you tonight, Señor Blake?" She was the only one of the staff who ever called him by his name. Everyone else used Sir, which he didn't care for.

"Fine, Ana Maria." He sat down in his spot and set his phone next to his place setting.

She clicked her tongue as she poured water into glasses. Her long black skirt swished with every step. "You don't fool me."

"It's just work. I've been at it for a week, and I'm tired."

She shook her head and a strand of her long black hair slipped from its bun. "No, again. Something else." She wiped a water spot off the cherry table.

Blake laughed. "Well, if you know, then tell me since I seem to be guessing wrong."

She set the silver pitcher down and the ice clinked against the sides. "You have girl trouble."

"I can never get anything past you, can I?"

"No." Footsteps sounded from the hallway. She smoothed her white ruffled apron. "You come see me later. I have cookies and milk waiting, then you tell me." She patted his shoulder, winked, and exited out the far doorway as Danyelle and Cici entered from the other end.

"Your daddy is finishing up something at work and said to start without him," Danyelle informed him as they sat down. "Cici, If you will, please?"

Cici uttered a short prayer to bless the food, and then they passed around the dishes. At Danyelle's insistence, prayer had become part of their meals after Andrew's death. After his funeral, she'd joined the nearest Baptist church and now served on the board. She encouraged the rest of them to attend with her, but she usually went alone. Blake had been a few times, but hadn't really caught the 'spirit'.

"How was your day, Blake?" Danyelle's chocolate brown eyes focused on the ladle in her hand as she spooned extra cream sauce onto her Dijon chicken.

"I spent the day with the accountants going over the company's portfolio."

"Fun," Cici quipped as she cut up her chicken with surgical precision.

"You'll get your turn soon enough, little sister," he replied as he spooned steaming rice onto his plate. When they'd first arrived at the Mansion, Rex had wanted dinner 'served' every night by the staff, but Danyelle had insisted that dinner was family time and the staff had a right to eat too.

"Looking forward to it, while I'm off working our accounts in Japan, Europe, and South America."

"Haven't picked up Arabic yet, huh? You'll have to turn over the Middle East sector to someone else."

Cici prickled at this dig. She prided herself on her linguistic abilities. One hand smoothed her blond tresses into place. An unnecessary gesture, as her hair was well cemented with hair product and bobby pins to sweep it to one side and cascade over her shoulder. "Well, at least I speak a foreign language which is more than you can say. You couldn't even pass a semester of Spanish despite having a tutor."

"Eva turned out to be better at French than Spanish." He smirked at his sister.

"Blake! I won't have that kind of talk at the dinner table." Danyelle's knife clanked against her Wedgewood plate.

Cici looked up at the ceiling. "So uncultured."

"You brought it up, Little Miss Perfect." Blake cut up his

chicken with an angry vengeance.

"Blake, that is enough." Danyelle banged her spoon on the linen table cloth, leaving a cream stain in its wake.

He held up a hand. "Sorry, Mom."

"I'm tired of you two bickering all the time. You used to get along so well until. . ."

"Andrew died," Blake finished for her.

Silence reigned at the table until Rex entered a few minutes later with the mail in his hand. He set it down next to his plate before he kissed Danyelle and sat down. "Sorry, I'm late." He looked at their full plates. "Glad you didn't wait. Pass me the dishes."

In short order the dishes were set around Rex and soon his plate was full of Dijon chicken, rice, and broccoli. He poured ranch dressing on his salad and took a bite of chicken. "Mmm. How did it go with the accountants today?" he asked Blake.

"Long."

"Did you get it all?"

"Well, I think it will take more than nine hours to understand the financial standing of the company, but I think I got the general idea. Make money, not debts. Look for profit and don't gut the workers."

"Don't be smart with me, Blake."

"That would be a change," Cici quipped.

"Cici," Danyelle warned.

Rex sorted the mail. "Postcard for you, Cici." He passed it to Blake who passed it to Cici.

She admired the picture before she flipped it over. "It's from Regina. She's on the Isle of Capri, lucky thing."

Danyelle pointed her fork at Cici. "Did she accept our invitation to go scuba diving in Belize this August?"

"Yes."

"Good. Blake, did you ask Kurt or one of your other friends to come?"

"Not yet." He wanted to bring Amanda, but first he had to convince her he wasn't the worst man on the planet.

"Well, I need an answer by July fourth so I can finish up the arrangements."

"You got it, Mom."

Rex frowned at the papers spread out in his hand. "Blake, what exactly did you do in Las Vegas?"

Blake stared at the lines of purchases and dollars on crisp white paper before he gulped down the bite of chicken in his throat. Credit card statement. Crap! He trained his eyes on his food. "Oh, I covered a few of our excursions. I just wanted us all to have a good time."

"A good time, huh?"

"Yes."

"You seem to have spent quite a bit of money at the Bellagio and Tiffany's, not to mention a few other designer shops."

Danyelle slid another envelope from the top of the stack with the name of their law firm as the return address. "Oh, wait, Mom, that one's for me. I'll take it." He reached across the table for it, but Rex intercepted and ripped it open. The envelope floated to the floor along with Blake's hopes of keeping his family from finding out about the wedding for just a little longer.

Rex's frown deepened and angry red blotches sprang into his cheeks. He passed both the attorney bill and the credit card bill to his wife. "Take a look at these and tell me if you come to the same conclusions as I have. In the meantime, I'm going to count to ten, although I doubt that will be long enough to stop me from throttling him."

Danyelle took the papers and her brown eyes flashed across the lines. Her mouth fell open, and she stared at Blake in disbelief, but responded to her husband by laying her hand on top of Rex's. "I agree, but give him a chance to explain before we dole out punishment. It may not be what we think. Blake?"

Cici made a poor grab for the papers in her mother's hand. "What's going on?"

Blake took a deep breath. "I spent $30,000 on wedding rings, $50,000 on a wedding dress, another $50,000 on bridesmaids and groomsmen, not to mention the $150,000 on the wedding itself in the atrium at the Bellagio. That's what's going on."

"You got married again?" Cici looked as if Christmas had come early.

"Yes," Blake said through gritted teeth.

"Oh, Blake, how could you?" Danyelle cried out.

"Were you drunk?" Rex asked

"I'd had a few."

"Was she drunk?" Rex asked.

"She'd have to be to marry Blake," Cici jibed.

"Cici, shut up." Danyelle said.

Blake bit his lower lip. His mother rarely said "shut up", as she considered it an offensive combination of words and only used it under extreme stress. This situation definitely qualified.

Cici's eyes widened, but she kept quiet.

"She had a few too," Blake answered.

"You are stupid. Really, Blake, when are you going to learn? Is she taking you to court for rape on top of asking for hush money? How much is it going to cost me this time to keep this one quiet? Because your stunt in Monte Carlo cost me enough, but less than this current tab you've run up." Rex's hands curled into fists while his face went from red to blotchy purple.

"There is no hush money."

"What do you mean?" Rex half stood.

"She's the one who wants the annulment, not me."

"What?" Danyelle looked utterly bewildered as she fanned herself with the papers.

"You want to stay married to this gold digger?" Rex's face was magenta now.

"Amanda is not a gold digger. I've known her for four years and she's never asked me for a thing except to get the marriage ended. If anything, she loathes me."

"Smart girl," Cici slipped in. "No wonder you had to get her drunk to marry you."

Danyelle looked sharply at her daughter. "Cici, go to your room."

"No, Cici, stay," ordered Rex, overriding his wife. "It'll be a good lesson for you if you ever decide to do anything so foolish twice." He fixed steely eyes on Blake and stood up to his full six-foot-two height. "I cleaned up your mess once before and I'm not doing it again. I will take care of the credit card bill, but you will have to pay for the lawyer. As of tomorrow, you are cut off. The credit cards will be shut down and your bank access denied. Whatever you've got left in your wallet is yours." He pushed back his chair and it toppled to the floor with a thud.

With tears in her eyes, Danyelle tugged on his arm. "Rex, no. We can sort out another punishment."

"No. The boy needs to learn to take responsibility for his actions. We warned him after the last time he got married. We never would've had this trouble with Andrew." He pointed at Blake. "Pack your bags and get a flight out first thing in the morning."

"Where?" Blake held his hands up to his sides.

"To your wife, if she'll have you. If not, then to one of your friends. But don't come back until you've taken care of this."

"Fine. I'll go." Blake walked around the table to hug his teary-eyed mother then strode across the Brazilian wood floor. He paused in the doorway just long enough to say to his family, "But just for the record, I only regret one of those pieces of paper in your hand."

## Chapter Ten

When the taxi cab pulled up across the street from Amanda's house, the curb in front of it was packed with cars. Blake instantly liked the white farmhouse with the wrap around porch complete with a swing in one corner. It looked charming, inviting, welcoming; nothing like The Mansion.

He counted a few bills out to the driver, hefted his bags and crossed the street. His bag rumbled over the flagstone and moss walkway until he paused at the bottom of the steps. He hoped Amanda might be gracious about seeing him show up unexpectedly at her house, but he knew she'd be furious. He smiled for a moment at the memory of her anger the morning after the wedding. Standing there in her white slip, she'd looked incredibly sexy and beautiful. All he'd wanted to do was wrap her in his arms and kiss her, but she'd have slapped him or worse for sure.

He climbed up the porch steps, then tucked his bags under one of the wicker tables. He heard voices from the backyard and from inside the house. Certainly there was a gathering going on at the St. Claires'. Odd for a Monday. Then he remembered it was Memorial Day. Perhaps with so many people around, he might fare better with Amanda. He rang the bell, and his heart broke into a rapid staccato as he panicked about who might answer it.

Through the screen door, he heard an older female voice say, "Amanda, would you get that? I'm covered in barbeque sauce. I thought everyone had arrived, but someone must be late."

Amanda's voice floated toward him. "It's probably just Mrs. Franks coming to borrow an egg or sugar or something. I got it."

She opened the screen door and let out a little scream.

Instantly her face colored and she hissed, "Blake, what are you doing here?"

From inside came the same older woman's voice. "Amanda, are you okay?"

"Fine, mom. Just caught my finger in the door," Amanda fibbed.

"Well, who's there?" the woman called.

"Uh," Amanda looked at Blake, her eyes wide with panic while he tried to keep a straight face and not laugh. "Just some guy who got lost and needs directions. I'll be back in a moment. He got our housed mixed up with the Rebels."

"People are always doing that," the woman said.

Amanda stepped onto the porch and shut the screen door behind her.

"Who are the Rebels?" asked Blake.

"A family one street over. We have the same house number and a white farmhouse model too. People are forever confusing our houses." She put her hands on her hips. "I repeat, what are you doing here? Do you have papers for me to sign? Cause I want to get you out of here before anyone sees you."

Blake cleared his throat. "Nice to see you, too, Mandy. Don't you have a kiss for your husband?"

Amanda pushed him away from the door, further down the porch. "Do you have papers or not?"

"No, Mandy, I don't. I just wanted to see my wife is all."

Amanda frowned while her brow crinkled. "You took a plane on a holiday just to see me?"

"Well, I've seen you nearly every day for four years. Is it any wonder that I missed you?"

Amanda took a step back and eyed him. "You're acting weird. Look, what is it you want? I have a house full of family and if I don't get back in there in a minute, one of them is going to come looking for me. The last thing I want to do is to explain who you are and what you are doing here. Now talk."

Blake scuffed one foot across the worn white wood floor board. "My parents kicked me out when the credit card and lawyer bills came."

"Oh. So, why are you here? Why didn't you go to Kurt's or something?"

"My dad suggested I go stay with my wife."

Panic and anger infiltrated her eyes. "Here? With me? You've got to be joking. You've pulled a lot of stunts over the years but this is just cruel and ridiculous. Goodbye, Blake." She turned to go back into the house, but he caught her wrist. She pulled free and glared at him. "Don't touch me."

"Amanda, I am dead serious. My parents threw me out and cut me off. All I got was a one-way ticket here and the cash in my wallet. My father is paying the credit card bill, but told me the lawyer stuff was my responsibility. He said not to come back until it was finished. So, I came to you. We're stuck in this together until I can get a job and pay for the fees. If you want this marriage ended, then we are going to have to work together."

She closed the space between them until they were nearly nose-to-nose. "If you're lying, so help me, Blake."

The intoxicating scent of her citrus conditioner was nothing compared to the glow of her green eyes. It took all of his self-control not to kiss her. "I'm not lying. Those are my bags." He pointed under the table and continued in a softer tone. "I need a place to stay. Please, Amanda."

Blake's eyes pleaded with her for help. The fact that he'd called her Amanda twice in the past minute spoke volumes to her. He'd told the truth. She'd be a fool to let him stay, but she couldn't very well turn him away either or they'd never get a divorce. "You can stay, but keep your mouth shut about us. I will talk to my parents after the barbeque and when everyone is gone."

"Thanks, Mandy. You really are one of a kind." He reached to touch her on the arm but she stepped away.

Distance in every way would be key in not getting sucked into falling for his charm, and touching her was out. She motioned to his bags. "Leave those there for now. They'll be safe." She sighed, knowing she must be crazy to allow this. "Come in. I'll introduce you as a friend from school, got it?"

"Got it."

Inside, Amanda steeled herself as she took him through the family room into the large kitchen. The white cabinets stood out from the yellow walls. Cherry-covered white valances hung over the top of the windows with white wooden blinds. When they entered, her mother stood at the sink washing her hands. When she shut off the water and turned around to grab a towel, her eyes widened at the sight of Blake. Amanda cringed as her mother shot her a curious look.

"Mom, this is Blake from school. He stopped by unexpectedly and I invited him to stay for the barbeque. Is that okay?" Her heart raced while she crossed her fingers behind her back. Fibbing didn't come naturally to her and she expected to be discovered at any moment.

Jenny wiped her hands dry on a cherry dishtowel. "Of course it is, Amanda." She came around the island and extended her hand. "Nice to meet you, Blake."

He shook her hand. "Pleased to meet you, Mrs. St. Claire."

"Call me Jenny, everyone does."

"Okay."

Jenny gave Blake a once over and seemed to approve of what she saw, despite the fact that he was dressed in just a polo shirt, khaki shorts, and boat shoes. "Amanda, take the hot dogs out to Dad, please."

"Sure, Mom."

Blake picked up the platter loaded with hot dogs. "I'll carry them for you. Lead the way."

She frowned until she caught her mother looking at her and at once conjured up a weak smile. "Thanks," she managed, then led him out to the back yard.

"Your mom seems nice," he remarked as she threaded them

through the crowd toward the grill.

"Don't talk about my mother like you know her," Amanda said out the side of her mouth. She pointedly ignored all the stares and whispers following them.

"I'm not even allowed to compliment your family?"

She didn't respond. They reached the grill. "Dad, here are the hot dogs."

Bill scanned the platter then paused to notice Blake. "Your mother sent out enough to feed an army."

"Dad, this is Blake, from school. He stopped by unexpectedly, and I invited him to join us. Mom said it was fine."

"Well, she's the boss." Bill turned back to the grill and flipped over the ribs. While he worked, he pointed to a small prep table next to him. "Just set the platter there." He positioned the last rib, then set down his spatula and shook Blake's hand. "Nice to meet you, Blake. So, you went to school with Amanda?"

"Yes, sir."

"Just call me Bill."

Blake nodded. "Yes, Bill."

"What did you study?" Bill loaded hot dogs on the grill.

"Business and history."

Amanda looked at Blake, surprised.

"What?" he asked her.

"I knew you majored in business. I didn't know you also majored in history."

"Minored in history," he clarified.

"Were you on the trip to Las Vegas with Amanda?" Bill asked.

"Yes." Blake shot a grin at Amanda. "Did she tell you about it?"

Amanda fiddled with her earring. This conversation grew dangerous by the millisecond.

"She filled us in on the sightseeing. Perhaps I'll take your mom out there for our next anniversary." He smiled at Amanda.

"When is that?" Blake asked.

"October."

"Great time to go. Not too hot and there are fewer tourists.

You'll have a great time."

"Did you win much?" Bill flipped the ribs again and rolled over the hot dogs.

"I lost plenty, but came out a winner in the end." Blake winked at Amanda.

She'd had enough, time to intervene. "Dad, can I bring you anything else?"

"No, honey. You go have fun for a bit. I'll send Missy for you if your mom needs anything. That girl is no help in the kitchen." He waved his spatula at them. "You two enjoy yourselves."

Amanda was about to suggest Blake get some food; she figured if his mouth was full, then he couldn't talk, when she saw The Wall coming at them. The Wall was made up of her three hulking brothers lined up like a football team ready to crush their opponents into the ground. "Oh, great," she muttered.

Blake followed her eye line. "More family, I take it."

"My brothers. Be warned these might be your last moments on earth."

He chuckled. "Well, at least the last image I'll see will be your happy face."

"Shut up."

Josh overheard her. "We didn't even say anything yet."

"Really, Amanda, that is no way to speak to your guest. What would mom say?" teased James.

Amanda glared at them. "Rich, Josh, James, this is Blake. These are my brothers." The guys shook hands.

"Are you Amanda's secret boyfriend?" James asked, then he and Josh howled with laughter.

Amanda's wished her eyes could throw knives at her brothers. "Blake and I knew each other at school. Really, talk about poor manners when it comes to guests. I'm the one who should be telling mom."

"Settle down, little sister," said Rich. "The boys thought they'd have a bit of fun since you never bring guys home."

Amanda's cheeks grew warm. "There hasn't been anyone

worth bringing home."

"Until now," added Josh in an imitation of Amanda.

Amanda grabbed the front of his shirt and pulled his six foot-three frame down eye-to-eye with her. "Would you like me to tell Marley what you said about her last week?"

Josh looked sideways at a curvy blond in a pink tank top and denim capris. "You wouldn't."

"Try me." The hard edge in Amanda's voice told him she meant business.

Rich put his hand over Amanda's. "Okay. We get the point. No more teasing about Blake."

"Although that certainly puts a dent in our afternoon festivities." James shoved his hands in his shorts' pockets.

She let go of Josh's shirt.

"We just came over to meet Blake and ask if he'd join us in a game of badminton. We need a fourth to play doubles."

"Thanks guys, but I'm not really handy with a racquet," Blake answered.

"Well, then by all means you should play. A little humiliation would be good for you." Amanda gave him a gentle push toward her brothers. "He's all yours, boys."

The three brothers exchanged glances. "Okay," Rich drew the word out. "First we can't tease you, and then you're all for us beating the guy up? What gives?"

"Exactly." Amanda stalked off.

Rich watched her go, then turned back to Blake. "You two must have some kind of love-hate relationship going on."

"It's pretty much hate on your sister's side." Blake shrugged. "So, which one of you unfortunate souls gets me as a partner?"

"Me," said Josh. "We played rock-paper-scissors to decide. I won. I figured with your build you'd probably be a good bet."

"Not when it comes to sports with a racquet," Blake replied.

Amanda stood on the back porch fuming and watched the four guys head off to the badminton net. How was she going to get out of this mess without revealing her connection to Blake?

A hip bumped hers. She turned her head to say excuse me

and then saw that it was Alison. She gave her best friend a fierce hug. "I'm so glad you're here."

Alison drew back with a perplexed look. "Well, I'm happy to see you too. What's going on?"

Amanda pointed across the yard at the guys playing badminton. Blake hadn't been kidding about not being good with a racquet.

"Blake? What is he doing here?"

Amanda filled Alison in on Blake's unexpected appearance and request for housing.

"No way." Alison hopped up to sit on the porch railing.

"Yes way. What am I going to do?"

Alison shook her head. "I have no idea, but your summer just got a lot more interesting."

"As if moving to Africa wasn't interesting enough," humphed Amanda.

Tiffany and Missy rushed up to them. "Amanda, who is your yummy friend out there playing with our brothers?" Missy asked with admiring eyes.

"His name is Blake," Amanda answered curtly.

"He's hot," remarked Tiffany.

Amanda examined her nails. "He's average, I guess."

Tiffany and Missy exchanged a glance. "No wonder she doesn't have dates," remarked Missy.

"Do you need to have your eyes checked?" sassed Tiffany with her hands on her hips. "That guy out there is drop dead, super fine, sexiest-man-alive hot." Her eyes narrowed. "Do you have dibs on him?"

Amanda's head snapped up. "What?"

"Do you have dibs on him?" Missy pressed.

"No," Amanda replied.

"Good, then you won't mind if Missy or I try for him." Tiffany gave her chest a little lift and smoothed her shirt.

"Tiffany!" Amanda looked horrified. She knew Tiffany had done that to give her chest full advantage.

"What?" shot back Tiffany. "Are you going to begrudge your

sister a chance to score a date with a hot guy that you invited but don't want?"

"You are too young for Blake," Amanda protested.

"Thank you Amanda for taking my side," Missy interjected.

"Your side?" Amanda turned to Missy.

"I told Tiffany she was too young for him and that if he wasn't taken then I was the only one who could flirt with him and try to get a date."

The younger sisters dashed off before Amanda could stop them. She turned to Alison. "What do I do now? I can't have my little sisters throwing themselves at Blake's feet. You know what he's like."

"Well, then maybe you should've told them you have dibs on Blake. Most people count marriage as dibs, but if you have a more open view of what that means . . ."

Amanda shuddered. "Don't say that word again." She looked around to see if anyone had overheard them, but no one was close enough. Then she noticed several of her female cousins had gathered at the badminton court to watch the match. It ended a moment later and they rushed toward Blake and her brothers. "This is a nightmare," Amanda wailed.

"Oh, no. Not yet." Alison laughed, highly amused at the turn of events and Amanda's discomfort. "I don't think you've quite reached nightmare status this afternoon. That'll be later when you ask your parents if Blake can stay longer than just tonight and have to give a reason why."

## Chapter Eleven

Night had fallen by the time the last of the family and friends drove away from the St. Claire home.

The screen door onto the back porch snapped shut behind Amanda and Blake as they entered the kitchen. "Here, Mom. This is the last pan. Kitty and Calvin hid in the tree house with it to finish off the brownies." Amanda set the glass Pyrex next to the sink.

Jenny laughed. "Those two are just like Josh and James, always up to something." She set the pan into the sudsy sink.

"I know, and they're only six." Amanda shook her head.

"Were those the towheaded ones?" Blake dried dishes and stacked them on the counter.

"Yes," Amanda replied, surprised he'd noticed.

"Cute kids. Their parents are Gwen and Mark, right?"

"You have quite the memory." Jenny scrubbed the brownie pan.

"Here, Mom. I'll finish that. You go take a break. You've been in the kitchen most of the day." Amanda shooed her mom away.

Laughing, Jenny removed her hands from the sink and dried them on a cherry dishtowel hanging from the oven door. She squeezed her daughter's shoulders. "Thanks. Come to the family room when you're done. And thank you, Blake, for all your help today." She patted his arm as she passed.

"I was glad to do it," he said sincerely.

Once they were alone, Amanda turned on Blake. "What's your game?"

"What do you mean?" He placed another pan on the counter.

"Are you purposely trying to get my family to like you so

they'll be even more furious when I tell them?"

"I think you've got your psychology wrong. If they like me, then they won't be as mad at you and I'll be more likely to be allowed to stay here."

"So, either way it was all a show?"

"You are determined to always think the worst of me, aren't you?" He dried a platter.

"Your record gives me good reason to."

"Actually, I enjoyed meeting all of your family today, especially Grandma Mimi. She's quite the firecracker."

"I didn't think you'd enjoy meeting a lot of common Iowa folk, not exactly your class."

"You know, before the money, my family was very much like yours. It's not very often that I get to be just Blake, like today. It was a relief."

"Yeah, right." Amanda handed the clean brownie pan to him. "Save me the sob story of how money ruined your life."

Blake cleared his throat. "It's getting late. Soon you'll have to ask your parents if I can stay."

Amanda sighed as she dried her hands on the dishtowel. "I don't know how to ask them without telling the truth and I hate lying to my parents. Even those fibs about you at the front door bugged me."

The corners of his mouth twitched. "I'm not surprised. You are a pretty honest person. You don't wear guilt well."

"I know you're secretly enjoying my agony so don't pretend otherwise. Let's get this over with." She threw the dishtowel on the counter and left the kitchen with Blake on her heels. She hovered in the doorway to the family room with Blake just a step behind. She paused to take stock of the situation. One wall claimed the big screen TV set up, another wall boasted a stone work fireplace complete with family pictures along the reclaimed wooden mantle, and beneath the deep bank of windows facing the street sat a cozy reading bench with bookshelves tucked underneath.

In one corner of the large L shaped khaki sectional Bill

massaged Jenny's feet. Rich and Rachel snuggled at the other end under a blanket, which left Amanda's sisters and Alison in the middle. The twins sprawled on the carpet in front of the TV making wise cracks about the hockey players on the screen. Blake remained in the doorway as Amanda moved to perch on the arm rest next to her parents. Her heart sank at the prospect of asking her parents in front of the family.

"Mom and Dad," she began in a low voice not wanting to be overhead by everyone else.

"Hold on honey, I can't hear you," said Jenny. "Boys turn that down so I can hear Amanda."

The volume lowered and all eyes focused on Amanda. She fiddled with her earring. "Mom and Dad, Blake got into a bit of trouble and I wondered if he could stay here." Her face grew warm and her cheeks turned pink.

Bill looked up at Blake. "You in trouble with the law?" he asked.

"No, sir."

"Uh," Amanda stammered, "He and his parents aren't getting along at the moment and he needs a place to stay." She was horribly conscious of everyone listening as the volume had dwindled down to mute.

"Well, the guest room is clean," mused Jenny. "I don't see any problem with Blake staying the night."

Amanda scratched the back of her neck. "It might need to be longer than one night."

Her parents' eyebrows raised in unison. Jenny said, "Amanda, perhaps we should talk about this in private."

With a sheepish look, James spoke up. "Uh, Mom, we figured out long ago how to listen to private conversations in this house without getting caught."

"Really?" Jenny asked.

"Yes," Amanda confirmed.

Bill looked at Blake. "No offense, but you show up out of nowhere, a virtual stranger and now you," he turned to Amanda, "want us to let him stay here for an undefined period of time with no real explanation expecting us to say yes."

"It's not that we don't want to help you out, Blake," Jenny added. "We've always been open with our home, but you are the first guy Amanda has ever brought home and we've only known you a few hours. You seem to be a well brought up young man, but we need to know where all this is coming from."

"I, uh. Blake is my. That is. He." Amanda's heart pounded as she desperately tried to find some way out of the situation without telling her parents the truth. But there was none. She looked to Blake for help. A strained look in his eyes let her know he wanted to say the words for her. No way would she let Blake present himself as her husband. She'd never forgive him if he did and he already had a considerable list of things she'd never forgive him for. Anger forced the words form her lips. She blurted out, "We got married in Las Vegas."

For a moment there was stunned silence filled with blank looks, wide eyes, and dropped jaws, before all her siblings burst into laughter.

"And we thought you had no sense of humor," Josh gasped out as he pounded a fist on the floor.

"That was classic," added James. "You must have taken a secret acting class on the side. Bravo."

Amanda felt her eyes pool with tears.

Her mother and father noticed and exchanged a quick look before she announced, "I don't think Amanda's playing a joke."

The laughter subsided and all eyes refocused on Amanda. "It's true," she whispered.

Unconvinced, James smirked. "Prove it."

"I can do that." Blake passed through the front door, stepped onto the front porch, and when he returned placed three items in Jenny's lap. She opened the velvet pouch on top and the diamond wedding rings fell into her hand. She gasped.

"Those are Amanda's wedding rings." Blake pointed at the other two items. "That is the photo album and that is the video."

"Video!" the twins chorused, then dived for their mother's lap and in seconds had the disc loaded.

"No. Please don't!" Amanda wailed. Her heart hammered in her chest at the idea of watching her shame displayed on a seventy-inch screen for all her family to witness.

Josh pushed play and the screen filled with the atrium at the Bellagio, while soft music glided from a string quartet playing in one corner.

"I can't watch this," Her stomach rolled and she turned to flee the room.

"Stay," Blake said softly, but didn't try to stop her.

"Amanda," Bill called out as she got to the kitchen doorway. "Have you seen this yet?"

"No," she admitted.

"Then stay."

Alison turned her head and gave Amanda an encouraging smile. Unable to disobey her father, Amanda stood behind the couch and watched the whole ceremony unfold. It was beautiful, like the wedding she'd always imagined. She watched her face and Blake's on the screen. Her stomach rolled. She didn't look like a drunken prom queen, which would have made it appear like a big mistake; that she hadn't been in her right mind. Instead she wore a look of utter bliss when they exchanged vows and he slipped the rings on her finger. When they kissed as husband and wife Amanda tore her eyes from the screen and yelped "I'm going to be sick," then ran for the bathroom.

When she emerged a few minutes later, Alison pulled her into a hug in the dimly lit hallway.

"You okay?" Alison asked quietly.

"No," Amanda moaned.

"I didn't think so." She squeezed Amanda's hand. "Come on. They're all waiting for you. You can do this. The worst part is over. They know."

Amanda nodded and they reentered the family room. Alison resumed her seat on the couch, but Amanda lingered in the doorway.

Jenny waved her over.

She scooted around the couch to stand in front of her

parents.

Jenny took her hand. "It was a beautiful wedding. I'm sorry we missed it."

"I," she gulped to clear away the lump in her throat. "I'm really sorry, Mom and Dad." Tears rolled down Amanda's cheeks. "I didn't want to tell you. It's such a horrible mistake. The marriage is getting annulled, but I didn't want you to know because I didn't want to see the disappointment in your eyes. It should never have happened. I was drunk. I'm so sorry." Her sobs made any further speech impossible.

Her mother's arms enfolded her in a hug and a wave of relief washed over her.

"You should know you can always come to us with anything. We've tried to make that very clear to you kids over the years." Jenny pulled back and her eyes rested on each of her children in turn, then on Blake, who sat on the window seat. "Blake, I'd say in light of events you are welcome to stay in the guest room until you two get things sorted out one way or another."

"Jenny," Bill said softly.

She turned toward her husband. "We're not going to turn him out like his own family did. We're a good Christian family. Blake is going to stay while he's a part of us, even if it's only for a little while. We all make mistakes and natural consequences are usually enough punishment."

"Blake, I take it your parents threw you out when they learned about this," Bill rubbed his palms together.

"Yes."

"Uh, I noticed in the video, your last name is Worthington."

"Yes."

"As in Worthington Enterprises?"

Blake sighed. "Yes, my father is Rex Worthington, the biofuel guy."

Josh piped up. "Wait, that's a multibillion dollar company. You mean you're worth billions?"

"Um, yes." Blake looked as if he'd like to apologize for being rich.

Tiffany hurled at Amanda, "Wait, you mean you married a billionaire and you're trying to get rid of him as fast as you can? Are you crazy? He's every girl's dream guy!"

"Tiffany, that's enough," Jenny said quietly.

"Her mistake isn't in marrying him, it's divorcing him! Can't everyone see that?" Tiffany pleaded with Amanda. "Look at the kind of lifestyle he could give you. How the money could change everything about our lives."

"I don't want his money," Amanda said through tears.

Blake spoke up. "Amanda doesn't want anything from me. She was very clear about that the next day."

"She's nuts! Why won't any of you back me up?" Tiffany's eyes scanned the rest of the family and Amanda guessed she searched for support.

"Missy, take Tiffany to her room please." Bill ordered kindly.

Amanda gave her father a look of gratitude and clutched at her mother's hand.

"Why do I have to go?" Missy whined. "I haven't said or done anything stupid."

"You just did," scoffed Josh.

"Why do I have to go? I'm not a child." Tiffany growled.

"Technically, you are," James spoke up. "You're still seventeen."

"For like four more months," Tiffany shot back.

"Tiffany, go," said Bill. "Missy, see that she stays there. We'll see you girls in the morning."

"Thanks for ruining it for both of us," Missy said as she pulled Tiffany off the couch. They left the room bickering.

Amanda's heart rate picked up speed as Blake approached her dad. "Mr. St. Claire," Blake began.

"It's still Bill," he answered.

Blake shoved his hands into his pockets and shuffled his feet. "Right, Bill. You should know when my parents threw me out, they also cut me off. I got a one-way plane ticket here and the money in my wallet. I was warned not to return until I got things legally resolved."

Honesty was paramount in the St. Claire household. Amanda knew Blake scored big points for telling the truth.

Bill nodded. "I appreciate your honesty, Blake. Is there anything else we should know?"

Blake looked over at her but she couldn't read his expression and worry formed a ball in her stomach.

"Just one more thing, but I'd like to speak about it in private, if there is such a place."

"The backyard," Josh piped up. "It's the one place we haven't worked out how to eavesdrop."

"We'll be just a minute." Bill squeezed Jenny's shoulder as he stood.

Amanda followed them to the back door, then grit her teeth knowing she wouldn't hear Blake spill whatever secret he was about to tell her father.

Away from the house with only the porch lights for illumination, Bill folded his arms. "What would you like to tell me?"

"This part isn't easy, and I appreciate if you want to take a swing at me after I tell you."

Bill nodded. "Noted. Go on."

"The morning after, Amanda accused me of tricking her into this marriage."

Bill's eyebrows went up. "Did you?"

Blake took a deep breath. "In a way, I did." He waited a heartbeat. "Do you want to punch me now?"

"Not yet. I'll reserve the right to do so once I've heard the full story."

"I met Amanda very early on in our freshman year, at a time when I was terribly self-centered and drunk on my own self-importance and I did something she won't forgive me for."

"What was that?"

"I kissed her."

Bill leaned back on the picnic table, his brow furrowed. "I don't follow you."

"At the time, she wasn't the only girl I was kissing and when she found out, she ended things between us."

"Ah." He rubbed his jaw. "She does have a hard time forgiving."

"Well, she has the right. I didn't apologize and I've spent most of the last four years kissing other girls trying to find that spark of magic only Amanda possesses. That didn't exactly raise me up her totem pole. The fact is, there is only one Amanda. I realized Las Vegas would be my last shot at her. So, I dared her to drink with me and hoped if I got her just intoxicated enough, then I could convince her to marry me. As you saw, I spared no expense when she said yes." Blake braced himself for a well-deserved punch to the face. He knew he'd earned it, but Bill's hands remained still at his sides, his expression unreadable in the dim light.

The quiet between them dragged on, broken only by the chirp of crickets, light rustle of leaves in the wind, and dogs barking somewhere down the street.

Finally, Bill spoke. "Amanda is one of a kind and I can see how you dug yourself a great big hole over the past four years. Still, a man doesn't like to hear his daughter's been made drunk and tricked into marriage. You do know this could be punishable by law, right?"

He nodded. "I rather hope it won't come to that, though." He cocked his head to one side. "Is this the part where you give me that deserved punch? Because to be honest, I'd feel a whole lot better if you did."

"It's not in my nature to hit people, even if they deserve it." Bill looked up at the stars. "So, now what, Blake?"

Relieved at not being hauled off to jail, words raced out of Blake's mouth. "Well, I need a job to pay for the annulment. I told Amanda I would take care of this, and I will. Of course, that'll be harder and take longer than I originally thought since I've been cut off. Amanda would rather gouge my eyes out than have me here, but here I am. I just wanted you to know my intentions and feelings toward your daughter are sincere, even if she doesn't believe me."

Bill looked his son-in-law in the eyes. "Have you told her that?"

He stuffed his hands in his pockets. "She won't listen to me. She hates me even more than before. I didn't even think that was possible."

Bill gave a low chuckle and slapped him on the back. "Many a man's loved a woman who didn't love him back. He either found a way to win her or to live without her."

"Well, I hope it's the first one," Blake said as they walked back up the porch steps.

## Chapter Twelve

Two mostly sleepless nights in a row took their toll on Blake. He rarely slept well when he wasn't in his own bed. Even his bed at college hadn't seemed as comfortable as home, although he'd eventually come to fall asleep there pretty well.

At least the guest room was peaceful with azure blue walls and a sea foam green comforter on the bed. Jenny had provided him with towels and while the basement had a half bath, he'd need to go upstairs to the second floor to shower.

Blake checked the clock, after eight. He'd woken an hour ago, but he still didn't know what hours the family kept and he decided to wait until eight to shower so not as to wake anyone. In the meantime, he'd gone for a run to clear his head. He always felt better after running and it was a good way to learn Amanda's neighborhood. Yesterday, he'd gotten lost. Today had gone smoother. He gathered up his towel, clothes and toiletries, and quietly made his way upstairs.

As he passed by the doorway to the kitchen, a gruff voice called, "Good morning, Blake."

Blake returned to the doorway and saw Bill at the island with a mug in his hand. The aroma of hot cocoa lingered in the air. "Good morning, Bill."

"An early riser?" Bill drained his mug.

"No, just couldn't sleep much."

Bill nodded. "Understandable, given the circumstances."

Blake pointed a thumb towards the hall. "Will it bother anyone if I take a shower?"

"No, the girls will sleep through it. With six kids and varying schedules, they're all heavy sleepers." Bill set his mug in the sink.

"I'll see you at dinner time. I'm off to work."

"I didn't get a chance to ask you what you do."

"Mechanic at the train yard. Not the most prestigious job in the world or the biggest money maker, but it's kept food on the table and a roof over our heads." He sat down at the table and laced up a pair of work boots. "Don't have any openings right now or I'd take you with me."

"That's kind of you, but I don't think I have any skills you could use."

Bill tied the last knot and looked up. "Well, what skills do you have?"

"Um, that's a good question." Blake ran a hand through his hair.

Bill rose and clapped him on the back. "I'm sure you'll sort something out. I'll let you know if I run across anything."

"Thanks. I'll go get that shower now." Blake headed upstairs and locked the bathroom door. He took a quick shower, unsure of the water heater size or how soon someone else would need the bathroom. Half-dressed, he shaved and had just patted his face dry when a loud knock hit the door.

Through the door Tiffany's voice bellowed, "Open up. I need the bathroom. Like now!"

Blake zipped up his toiletry kit, grabbed his shirt and jammies from off the back of the toilet, and opened the door.

Tiffany's mouth opened and closed as she stepped back in surprise. He watched as with wide eyes she studied his naked muscular chest, abs and arms. Finally, she got her voice back. "Oh, sorry, Blake, I thought it was Missy or Amanda in there. Missy is quite the bathroom hog."

"No problem." He bowed and stepped into the hall.

But instead of stepping into the bathroom, she took a step toward him and traced a finger down the muscle of his bicep. "You work out, I can tell. You're so well built. A guy who takes good care of his body is likely to take good care of the other things in his life." She batted her eyelashes.

Out of the corner of his eye Blake saw Amanda step out of her room.

"Tiffany!"

Tiffany looked unapologetically at her oldest sister. "What? I'm just saying good morning to Blake."

With her hands on her hips Amanda ordered, "Blake, put your shirt on."

"Sure thing, Mandy." He tossed her his jammies and toiletries then slipped the blue t-shirt over his head. "Better?"

"Yes," said Amanda.

"No," Tiffany said at the same time.

Amanda cleared her throat. "Tiffany, I believe you wanted the bathroom."

But Tiffany remained in place with smoldering eyes fixed firmly on Blake.

"Go." Amanda stepped forward, gave her sister a one-armed push into the bathroom and shut the door. Then she pulled Blake into her bedroom and dumped his stuff on her unmade bed. "What were you thinking? You can't walk around my sisters half-dressed, especially Tiffany. She's already scheming in regards to you, I can tell."

Blake took in the sea glass green walls and white furniture before he sat down on the bed and picked up a worn brown teddy bear. "What are you more upset about, my leaving the bathroom without a shirt or her attempts to lure me away from you?"

Amanda ripped the bear out of his hands. "Don't touch Mr. Cuddles." She clutched it protectively to her chest. "You might ruin him like everything else you touch."

He pointed to the bear's missing ear. "I hardly think I can do your bear much harm. He already looks like he's been through the war."

"That's James's fault. He cut off Mr. Cuddles' ear when I was five in retaliation for something I did."

"What did you do?" Blake fingered the crumpled white bedspread.

"Neither of us remembers, but Mr. Cuddles suffered for it." She set the bear down on her nightstand next to a stack of books.

"Now get off the bed so I can make it."

Blake moved his stuff to her desk chair. The bed was centered on one wall, so Blake moved to the opposite side, near the window, and helped her pull up the covers.

She scowled. "I don't need your help. I am perfectly capable of making my own bed. I've had plenty of practice. I don't have maids to do it for me." She set the pillows in neat rows against the headboard.

"I know how to make a bed. Even after we had maids, mom required us to make them every morning. She said the maids had enough to do."

Amanda frowned, sat down on the bed and pulled Mr. Cuddles to her chest. "What do you mean even after you had maids? I thought you were born rich."

"You assumed like everyone else I was born rich, but actually our family lived in a house very much like yours until I was about ten. I really liked that house." He looked around her room. There were the usual soccer, dance, and gymnastics trophies that littered the shelves. A memoir cork board full of pictures and ticket stubs. An IPod doc and CD player combo sat on the desk. A few stuffed animals lined the base of the mirror attached to the dresser. A book case dominated the sliver of wall between the windows. Blake wandered over it to read the titles.

"I didn't think you ever had a normal life. I didn't think you would care for people like us."

He felt her eyes on his straight back. His mother wouldn't put up with him and Andrew adopting the 'I'm so cool' slouch. She found it ridiculous.

Without turning around, he said, "When are you going to notice that I'm not very comfortable rubbing elbows with the rich? I'm far more comfortable with regular people, but everyone expects me to act like a rich snob so that's really all they see when they look at me. How would you like it, if every time someone looked at you all they read were dollar signs?"

Amanda twisted a ring on her finger. He noticed she fiddled with her jewelry whenever she felt confused or uncomfortable.

"I never thought about it like that. I don't think I would like it very much."

Blake moved over to look at her corkboard and unpinned a picture. "Is this you and Alison?"

"Yeah. We were thirteen at that state fair. We'd just eaten blue cotton candy. It took two days for the color to wash off." She giggled.

Blake smiled as he repinned the picture. It was nice to have her relaxed around him for a change. He sat down on the bed next to her legs, which she instantly pulled up to her chest.

"You know, Mandy, I thought it'd take you a lot longer than a couple of days to invite me to your room," he said slyly.

"Believe me, I hadn't planned to ever have you in my room, but I couldn't have you in the hallway like that in front of my sisters, especially Tiffany. She's put more gray hairs on my parents' heads than the rest of us combined. And that's saying something for the twins."

"You could've pushed me down the stairs," he suggested with a glint in his eye and wondered how long the easy banter between them would last.

"Next time, I'll be sure to do that." She cocked her head. "Tiffany's in the shower now and you're appropriately dressed, so I think it's time for you to go."

"And just like that the wall goes back up. You know, it was nice to talk to the real Amanda for just a moment."

Amanda knit her eyebrows together. "What do you mean a wall and the real Amanda?"

"Exactly what I said. You're a smart cookie. I'm sure you'll figure it out. See you downstairs." He huffed, grabbed his stuff off the desk chair and opened the door.

"Wait." She swung her legs over the bed and grabbed a newspaper from under the nightstand. "You've been here two days now. Have you found a job yet? We need to get this marriage taken care of." She shoved it into his hands. "I circled some in red for you."

He took the paper, his cheeks burning with anger and shame.

"Thanks, but there isn't exactly a market for dumb rich kids with few skills, especially ones that have never had a job before and have no references," he said sourly.

"I've never said that about you," Amanda defended, but he saw the guilty look in her eyes.

"No, you've never said it, but it's what you think." He shut the door behind him.

## Chapter Thirteen

After breakfast, Blake waited for Amanda in the kitchen.

A few minutes later, she waltzed in with keys in her hand. "Don't want to be late for work. You ready?"

"Yes." He grabbed his phone from off the kitchen table and nodded to Amanda's mother over at the sink. "Thanks for breakfast, Jenny."

"You're welcome, Blake. I'll be by to pick you up at five as Amanda won't get done at the hospital until six."

"I'll look forward to seeing you."

"You sure will," Amanda muttered. They headed out to the old blue Honda Accord parked in front of the house and climbed in. After Amanda double checked all her mirrors, they left. She headed into town.

"Is this your car? I thought it was Tiffany's?" Blake asked.

"Most of the time Tiffany drives it, being the only one still at home, but we girls share it when we're all here. There are always more drivers than cars at our house."

Blake looked out the window to watch the houses, stores, fast food places and gas stations pass by. All too soon, they pulled up to the animal shelter. "Thanks for the ride, Mandy." He smiled at her to cover his nerves.

"Oh, you're welcome. I think it's the perfect job for you."

He undid his seatbelt. "Why's that, Mandy?"

"Because you get to work with animals and that's right on your level."

"So, I classify as an animal now?"

"Yes. It's a step up from the reptiles, where you've skulked most of the time I've known you."

"Nice to know I'm moving up in the world."

"We'll see if it lasts. Have a good day."

He exited the car and turned around to lean in through the window. "Do I get a kiss for good luck?"

Amanda looked appalled. "No!" She frowned at him as she put the car in drive.

"Just checking. Thanks for getting me the job." He watched her roll away before he strolled into the building and headed to the back office. "Good morning, Madge."

Madge's brown hair, liberally streaked with gray, was styled in a simple ponytail. She wore jeans and a faded t-shirt that looked like it might have been purple at one time but had faded to an odd shade of gray. Her eyes remained on the computer monitor as she waved a hand at Blake. "Morning. Have a seat while I finish this, unless you'd rather have a cup of coffee." She tapped on the computer keys.

"I'm good, thanks." Blake chose a wooden chair with red vinyl cushions that looked like it would support his weight and sat down. The bottom seat cushion sported a tear and someone had carved the words 'you suck' into one of the arms. It was worn out like everything else in the room and at the shelter in general. Blake had noticed the lousy condition of things yesterday during his interview and wondered how they kept the place running. He jumped when Madge slapped her hand on her desk in frustration.

"Stupid thing froze again. Guess I'll have to finish this later." She pushed back her desk chair and took a swig of coffee from her mug.

"May I have a look?" Blake offered.

"Go ahead. This thing is older than the hills. It needs replacing, but I keep hoping it'll hold out just a little longer. Can't afford a new one." She traded chairs with Blake.

He took a quick inventory of the computer's software. Madge was right. This thing was older than the hills. He tried a few trouble shooting tricks and said, "Okay, I got it unfrozen and you should be able to finish now."

Madge wiped a stray hair back into place. "Thanks, Blake. I've been working on that grant application for weeks now and would be very upset to lose it. It's due in three days and I don't have time to redo it to meet the deadline."

"If you'll let me take a look at the computer later, I think there's a few things I could do to clean it up so it'd run better."

"That would be wonderful. Thank you." She stood up. "Let me show you around and give you the duty sheets." She led him to the front desk. "We get animals of all kinds and in all conditions. Every once in a while, we get something strange like a raccoon or porcupine, and then we call animal control to take it back to the wild. The phone number is here." She pointed to a sign on the counter.

"Got it."

"Marlene, or Cheryl, is usually at the front desk to do check-ins and paperwork, but you'll cover for them when they go to lunch." She pointed to another sign. "If you get one that's badly injured, call Doctor Mills. He'll either come right over, or he'll send someone to pick up the animal. Thankfully, he's just a block away." She pointed to a third number. "This is the number for Joe. Call him if any of the animals die."

"Does that happen often?" He wasn't fond of the idea of handling a dead animal. Even remembering when he was eight and held his dead pet hamster made him shudder.

"Yes. He'll pick it up. I don't ask him what he does with them because I don't want to know."

He silently agreed. He didn't want to know either. "Okay."

She opened a desk drawer with labeled hanging folders. "Here are all the forms plus the message pad for the phone. That's pretty much it." She stepped through a doorway into a smaller room filled with different size cages and motioned for him to follow. "This is the holding room. When we get a new animal we put it in an appropriate size cage with food and water. Dr. Mills comes by at the end of the day to examine them."

"Why not just put them with the rest?" Blake asked as he scanned the array of cages.

"They might be aggressive or carry diseases. It's not safe to mix them with the other animals until they've been assessed by the doctor."

"Got it."

"Your first job of the morning, Blake, is to make sure all the cages are clean and have fresh water. Don't put in food until right before you add an animal, otherwise it just goes to waste and that's not something we can afford here."

She led him out of the room to the main part of the shelter, which was the size of a three-bay garage. The dog cages dominated one long wall and were nearly filled to capacity. The cats took up most of the other long wall, while the birds took one short wall, and the miscellaneous animals like hamsters, mice, and snakes took up the last wall. Four central drains ran down the middle of the cement floor with garbage cans posted at each end.

"Your second job is to clean out these cages. We always keep one empty cage for each kind of animal so you can transfer it there while you're cleaning."

Blake did a mental count and concluded this job would take all day and then some. "That's a lot of cages."

"Yes, it is. At first it'll take you most of the morning to get this done, but soon you'll get a rhythm and finish in about two hours or so. Now if you find an animal sick, transfer it up to the front room and write it on the list at the front desk for Dr. Mills."

Two additional doors led out of the room. She opened the closest one. "This is the supply room. Everything you need is here: food, newspaper, mops, cleaner, disinfectant, eye wash station, tools, and such. Supply runs are done on Tuesdays. So, after the morning chores, take an inventory on the clipboard here, and get it approved by me. I'll give you the money and send you to the store." She headed to the last door and opened it. "This is the courtyard, where you bring the dogs outside for exercise in the afternoons." She turned to him. "Any questions?"

"No, I think you covered it."

She looked at him. "I almost forgot. You need coveralls."

She led him back to the hallway off the front desk. "Bathroom is there and the break room is here." Just inside the doorway brown coveralls in various sizes hung on pegs. She pulled down a stained pair. "These should be about your size." She looked down at his feet. "You'll probably want to pick up a good pair of work boots. You'll be getting plenty dirty. I'd recommend leaving them outside your front or back door, or your place will smell to high heaven."

"Thanks, Madge." He looked down at his Adidas runners and wondered what they'd look like at the end of the day.

She checked her watch. "Right, I'm going to unlock the doors. Marlene left a message that she had to run one of her kids to the doctor this morning, and she'd be late. Let me know if you need anything." She headed to the desk.

Blake grabbed a pair of coveralls and layered them over his clothes. He picked up the cleaning tools from the supply closet and started on the front room cages. He heard Madge's voice answering phones and speaking to those who came in to look for a pet. He'd just finished the last cage when Madge called to him. He stepped into the lobby. A not-quite-yet middle-aged woman stood there with a cardboard box. An orange cat peeked out of the top.

"Blake, please take the cat to the transition room," Madge said.

He smiled at the woman as he took the box. Just as he passed the doorway he heard the woman say, "Madge, who's the new guy?"

"Oh, that's Blake, a friend of the St. Claires."

"Is he going to be here long?" Her voice sounded hopeful.

"Not sure," Madge replied.

"Hmmm. Then I might need to go find a few more strays. He's downright handsome."

"Sara Littleton, you go back home to your husband," Madge scolded.

"Easy, Madge. I'm just admiring. See you at the church bazaar."

Blake settled the cat into the cage, only sustaining one scratch in the process. He could identify with the cat. Homeless and frustrated. Sometimes he'd like to lash out and claw at someone but, unlike the innocent cat, his homelessness was his own fault. He gave the little gray fuzz ball food, then washed his hands and the cut before heading through the lobby toward the back room.

Madge waved him over to the desk. "Blake, this is Marlene."

He shook hands with the pretty, curvy blonde now seated behind the desk. Dimples framed her smile lines.

"Pleased to meet you, Blake. Welcome aboard. It's been downright manic around here trying to share the load." She fluffed her curls with one hand.

"Happy to help." He smiled, but shuffled his feet, unexpectedly uncomfortable with the female attention he usually attracted, now that he was a married man.

"I'll come get you at lunchtime." She waved.

The sights and smells of the back room assaulted his senses as he stepped through the doorway. The barks, meows, and tweets threatened to give him a headache. Blake reminded himself to bring his IPod the next day to help drown out the animal noises. He scanned the cages, then decided to start with the birds and work his way around the room ending with the miscellaneous animals. There were definitely some in that section he wasn't sure how to handle or didn't look forward to touching. He picked up the broom and got to work. The morning sped by in a monotonous routine of shoveling poop, cleaning out cages, and supplying animals with fresh food and water. Finally, he was down to the last two miscellaneous cages. One housed a tarantula. He hated spiders and just the thought of touching a furry one made him break out in a cold sweat. In his opinion, the only thing spiders were good for was crushing with a solid-soled shoe. Just as he was about to get Madge's advice, an older man walked through a side door. He wore a pair of coveralls like Blake's.

"Uh, hi," Blake said. "I haven't met you yet. I'm Blake."

The septuagenarian shook Blake's hand. "Moose," he said.

Blake's good manners kept him from laughing out loud. "Pleased to meet you, Moose. Madge didn't tell me about you."

"Oh, I come by each day to see if she needs an extra hand." He held up a hand and one stump. "One hand's all I got." He laughed at his own joke.

Unsure of how to respond, Blake went with the obvious question. "What happened?"

"Table saw when I was a kid."

Blake grimaced, and his stomach did a flip. "Ouch."

"You're new," Moose changed the subject.

"Today's my first day."

Moose looked around at the cages. "You seem to be getting on all right. Good thing too. Madge has been awful stuck trying to find someone to take this job. Most kids your age won't have anything to do with cleaning up poo and taking care of animals."

"Well, I was qualified, so she hired me."

"Good."

He considered his spider problem. "Uh, Moose, you said you help with the animals. Could you give me some advice on how to clean these two cages?" He showed Moose the tarantula and the snake.

"Ol' Grey won't harm you," Moose said pointing to the tarantula. "Just grab that powder box there, scoop him up and rubber band the lid on. Then clean the cage. And Slither there, just grab him behind the head and watch out for the tail. When a snake gets nervous, he'll poop all over you."

"Could you show me today, and then I'll do them tomorrow?" Blake looked warily at the two cages.

"Sure," Moose slapped Blake on the back, then removed both the spider and snake in record time.

"Thanks," Blake said, relieved he'd postponed the inevitable by one day. He'd need longer than that to work his courage up.

"You're welcome. I'll go check in with Madge now."

Blake had just finished both cages when Marlene walked in.

"Are you done already?" she asked in surprise.

"Yes." Blake wiped the back of his hand across his forehead to get off the sweat.

"Usually it takes the newbie a week before they can get it done that fast. Sure hope you stick around. This job is more often vacant than filled."

"Oh." Blake looked at her expectantly. "Is there something you wanted?"

She shook her curls. "Sorry, yes. It's my lunch break so it's your turn at the desk."

"Ok, let me just wash my hands."

"Good thinking."

Blake met Marlene at the desk.

"I'm going to get Subway for lunch. Would you like anything?" She fiddled with the clasp on her purse.

"No thanks," Blake said. "I brought something."

"Okay." Marlene left.

Blake had a pretty quiet hour while Marlene was gone and spent his own break walking around the surrounding blocks while he chewed a turkey and cheese sandwich Jenny made him. He spent the rest of the afternoon exercising the dogs and cleaning up Madge's computer.

"Five o'clock Blake," Madge said. "Time for you to go home. I can see Jenny's car waiting outside."

"Okay. I just need to shut down the computer and then you need to start it up again to update and install the software I put on. It should run much smoother after that, although it would help to have a newer model."

"It would, but when it comes to spending money on a new computer or on food and vet visits for the animals, guess which one wins?"

"The animals."

"Every time."

"See you tomorrow, Madge."

She patted him on the back as he passed by. "Bye."

Out in the car, after the polite greetings were exchanged, Blake asked Jenny, "Is there an outdoor store nearby?"

"Yes," she replied as she pulled into the street.

"Do we have time to stop there on the way to pick up Amanda? I need a pair of boots for work."

"Yes. I've got chicken for tacos in the crockpot, so we have time for a quick stop before picking her up."

"Great, thanks. Will I have time for a shower before dinner?"

"I won't feed you until you do." Her eyes twinkled in the afternoon sun. "You smell, and even though I'm used to it with three boys, the animal stench will ruin all our appetites."

After they'd driven a few blocks, Blake asked, "How does Madge know your family?"

"Oh, all the boys worked there for a couple of summers when they were younger, and everyone knows they are always looking for help. Rich would have ten dogs by now if Rachel wasn't allergic. The twins are still half-puppy themselves, so they aren't up yet for the challenge of caring for another life." She chuckled and made a turn.

"Nice to know that was part of the reason Amanda got me the job. I thought she just did it out of spite."

"I've noticed you aren't on her list of favorite people, Blake."

"That's putting it mildly."

"Rex told me about your conversation."

He tensed. His relationship with Jenny and Bill was important to him, and not just because of Amanda. He wanted to please them. It'd been a long time since he'd cared if anyone thought well of him. "Are you mad at me? Because I understand if you are."

"I was at first," she admitted, "until I thought about it. Amanda has always had very strong opinions. There must be something about you she likes, even if she won't admit it or doesn't recognize it yet. Otherwise, she'd never have married you, intoxicated or not. Keep that in mind."

## Chapter Fourteen

In the back room, Marlene's voice called over the intercom from the front desk. "Blake, we've got a new recruit."

Blake washed his hands and then stepped into the lobby where Sara Littleton stood next to a box on the floor that emitted a low growl.

She smiled and tucked a strand of glossy hair behind her ear as he approached. "Careful with that one. He's been abused or something. We had a heck of a time getting him into that box, he's so aggressive."

"What breed?" Blake asked as he bent down and hefted the box up to his chest.

"Pit bull, bull dog, I don't know. But his teeth are sharp." She admired the muscles in his arms as they strained to hold the shifting box.

"Well, thanks, Sara." He felt her gaze on his back as he took the dog into the transition room.

"Such a nice young man," he heard her say through the open door as he set down the box on a table. Then he leaned back to peer at the two women through the doorway.

"Thanks, Sara," Marlene said as she tried not to laugh at the smitten, teenager-like look on Sara's face. "See you later."

Sara caught Blake looking at them and blushed. "Oh, right. Bye, Marlene."

Blake shook his head and entered the transition room. He balanced the box next to the cage door, then carefully opened the lid. Dog teeth snarled and snapped at him as he wrangled it into the cage. "Easy boy," he soothed and shut the cage. He turned the lock, then realized he'd forgotten to put the food in before the dog. Rats! He filled a bowl with dog chow, undid the lock and eased the door open just enough to put the dish in. The dog watched him and growled. Just as he was about to draw his arm out the dog attacked. His teeth sank deep into Blake's arm through the coveralls. He yelled in pain and tried to pull his arm away but the dog kept his jaw clenched tight.

Marlene ran in. "Oh my gosh, Blake!" she wailed frantically.

Madge rushed in right behind her. "Blake, don't struggle. Hold still." She grabbed a spray bottle full of water from the table behind the door and aimed at the dog's face.

Surprised by the cold water, the dog released its death grip on Blake's arm. Blake pulled his arm out of the cage. Madge shut the door and locked it. "I'll have Dr. Mills anesthetize that dog before he checks it out." She handed the spray bottle to the dazed Marlene. "Let's take a look at your arm." Madge pulled up the coverall sleeve where blood had seeped through already. His arm was a mess of skin and blood.

Marlene took one look and said, "I'm going to be sick." She dashed off to the bathroom.

Madge grabbed the first aid kit from off the wall and wrapped a gauze bandage around his bleeding arm. "We better take you to the ER. Let's get you out of these coveralls first." She unzipped the suit and quickly stripped it off him. "Marlene," she called as they passed through the lobby. "I'm taking Blake to the ER. Call Moose and ask him to come help you."

Madge grabbed her purse from the office, and fifteen minutes later they arrived at the hospital. Thankfully, the ER was fairly quiet. Madge helped Blake fill out the paperwork.

"Thanks, Madge," he said. "I think I can manage from here. You can head back to the shelter."

"Are you sure?" Her concerned expression clearly indicated she didn't like leaving him.

"Yes. I've been worse," he reassured her, even as his face grimaced from pain.

"Is Amanda working today?"

"Yes."

"I'll have her come down to be with you."

"No, Madge. Really, I'll be fine," he protested.

She gave him a 'don't fight me on this' look and spoke to the nurse at the desk, after which she said, "They'll see if Amanda can come down. I'll let Jenny know so she can pick you up when you're done. Don't worry about coming back to the shelter today. I'll call to check on you later." She patted his shoulder and left.

A nurse took Blake back to a curtained area, got his vital signs and told him a doctor would be in shortly. While he waited, he texted Jenny that he was fine and would call her when he was done. He was checking his e-mail when Dr. Shad arrived with a nurse in tow.

"Let's take a look, shall we?" Dr. Shad unwrapped the blood-soaked bandage from Blake's arm and surveyed the damage. "Pretty nasty. Let's soak it first in disinfectant to get off the dried blood and clean it. Then I'll stitch you up." The nurse hurried off to carry out his instructions, while the doctor asked, "What kind of animal bit you?"

"A dog."

Dr. Shad frowned. "Do you know if it has rabies or all of its shots?"

"No. He had just arrived at the animal shelter. The vet hadn't seen him yet."

"Who's the vet?"

"Dr. Mills," Blake answered. The nurse brought in a bowl and lowered his arm into it. Blake sucked in his breath hard and winced as the disinfectant did its work.

"It's a good pain," she said and then left.

Dr. Shad rubbed his chin. "Dr. Mills treats my wife's cat. I'll give him a call and have him do a work up on the dog. In the meantime, we'll put you on antibiotics for infection and you'll need rabies shots until we get the test results back."

"Sounds fun," Blake said grimly.

"The best. I'll be back in about fifteen minutes to stitch you up." He pulled the curtain shut behind him.

A few minutes later, the curtain opened again. Amanda

gaped at Blake sitting on the hospital bed with his arm in the bowl. "What happened?" she said with concern as she approached him. "I got a call saying you were in the ER and to come down."

"It's fine. Just a dog bite. Dr. Shad will be in soon to stitch me up." The fact that Amanda seemed genuinely concerned for his well-being helped him try to ignore the pain.

"Stitches? Let me see."

Blake shook his head. "It's kind of gross."

"I'm a nurse. I've seen gross before." She lifted his arm out of the bowl by holding his wrist and elbow. The corners of her mouth turned down in disgust. "That is not a simple dog bite."

"Well, he grabbed on real tight and wouldn't let go."

"You've probably got torn muscles and stuff. You'll need some physical therapy."

"No can do," Blake's mouth set in a line.

"Why?"

"Because I don't have health insurance anymore. I'm cut off, remember? Everything about the ER, doctors, and physical therapy would have to come out of my paycheck and that money is already ear marked to pay for our annulment. As you have pounded it into my thick skull, that is my only priority; the rest of this will have to wait."

"Blake, you can't put this off. You could permanently damage your arm."

He shrugged, but his heart warmed at her attention. "I promised you I would take care of this and I will, no matter what the cost."

"But, Blake," she protested.

Dr. Shad returned. "Nice to see you, Amanda. What are you doing down here?"

"Blake is staying with my family, Dr. Shad. I heard he was down here, so I came to check on him. It looks pretty bad."

"It'll heal," he told her, then said to Blake, "But you'll probably have a scar or two."

Blake shrugged. "Scars are no big deal. Just means there's a stupid story to go with it that you get to tell over and over again."

Dr. Shad dried off Blake's arm and picked up the sutures and needle. "You ready?"

"Yes." Blake gritted his teeth and used a breathing technique to manage the pain. Still, he noticed Amanda didn't speak or take her eyes off of him while Dr. Shad stitched him up.

Finally, Dr. Shad tied off the suture and said, "All done."

Blake let out an extra-long exhale. "Thanks, Dr. Shad."

"No problem." He handed Blake two sheets of paper. "Here is your prescription for the antibiotics and the information for Dr. Rasner. His office will administer your daily rabies shots."

"Rabies?" Amanda asked in alarm. "Did the dog have rabies?"

"We don't know yet, and until the test results come back, we have to treat Blake for them in case they are positive," Dr. Shad answered her.

Blake spoke up. "Could Amanda give me the shots? She's a nurse, and I'm staying at the St. Claires' house. Is that possible?"

The doctor ran a hand through his black wavy hair. "It's an unusual request, but Amanda is certainly capable of it. We could give you a week's supply at a time, and Amanda can pick them up from the hospital pharmacy. What do you say, Amanda?"

Amanda looked back and forth between the two men and Blake read the discomfort of the idea in her eyes. "Uh, I guess so."

"I'll set it up with the pharmacy. The nurse will be in to give you the first shot. Be sure to change the bandages every day, and don't get it wet for about twenty-four hours. I'll be in touch with you once I receive the results from Dr. Mills. Just check with the discharge nurse on your way out to deal with the paperwork. You're in good hands with Amanda." He threw them a parting smile as he exited through the curtain.

Amanda stood there blinking.

Blake stood up. "I take it you've worked with Dr. Shad before?"

Amanda snapped out of her thoughts by meeting his eyes. "Uh, yeah. The ER was my first volunteer area. Dr. Shad didn't look down on me like some of the other doctors." She pointed to his bandaged arm. "You're lucky you got him today. He's great at stitches. Dr. Kris, not so much. You'd have looked more like Frankenstein." She took hold of the curtain.

"Lucky me." Blake agreed.

"I'll help you at the discharge desk and then mom can pick us up."

"Don't you need to get back to work? You weren't supposed to be finished until later."

"No, I'm good. We worked things out up there."

He raised an eyebrow. "You're going to give up a couple of hours with your precious babies to care for me?"

"I'm more likely to smother you with a pillow and put you out of your misery."

The nurse pulled the curtain out of Amanda's hand as she entered. "Pull up your shirt please," she instructed Blake.

He tugged his shirt up with his good hand. The corners of his mouth twitched up as Amanda blushed at the sight of his firm abs.

"This is going to hurt," the nurse said. She poked a needle into his stomach just above the belly button and injected the liquid.

The smile disappeared as his stomach erupted in a ball of fire. His breath whistled in and out of his clenched teeth.

The nurse removed the needle. "All done." She left the curtain partly open as she left.

Blake grimaced as he pulled his shirt back down. "Bet you're going to enjoy putting me through that kind of pain every day."

"Not really," said Amanda. "I had to get rabies shots when I was seven. They hurt like hell. The first day it took five people to hold me down and I kicked the doctor in the face so hard his nose bled."

"What happened on day two?" He couldn't keep the layer of pain out of his voice.

"The doctor gave me the choice of doing it the hard way like the day before or doing it the easy and quick way if I would just lay still. Either way it was going to happen."

"So, what did you do?"

"I lay still and mom took me out for ice cream after."

Blake stood up. "Let's get out of here."

Once they were done at the discharge desk, they waited outside for Jenny to come.

"So, how did you get the bite?" Amanda asked.

"Like I said, I did something stupid. It's my fault really. Do you know Sara Littleton?"

"Yes," Amanda said.

"Well, this is the second stray animal she's brought in since I got there. Last time it was a cat. This time it was a dog, and she warned me it was aggressive, so I was very careful about moving it from the box to the cage. That part went smoothly, but then I realized I'd forgotten Madge's rule about putting the food in first. So, I had to reopen the cage to put it in. I'd just finished when the dog attacked. You know the rest."

"I'm sorry, Blake."

He looked at her profile illuminated in the afternoon sun. "Well, those are words I'd never thought you'd say to me in this lifetime."

"What do you mean?"

"I was pretty sure you'd be more of the opinion that I deserved it, and it served me right to have my perfect arm scarred to ruin my image. Or that it served me right for doing something dumb and I'd sink back to the reptilian level."

She turned offended eyes on him. "I'm not heartless, you know. I never like to see anyone injured." She stepped toward the opening in the curtain.

Blake caught her hand and she stopped. She turned back and looked down at their hands. Belatedly, he let go. "I didn't say you were heartless. You're generous. Your kind heart is one of the things I admire most about you."

Amanda reeled from the compliment and stepped back. "Thanks."

"I just wish you would extend it to me."

"Well, it's not like you've earned it," Amanda huffed and

crossed her arms over her chest.

"Amanda, I hurt you four years ago, I get that and I am sorry for it, whether you believe me or not. But I was young and stupid. Why can't you see I've changed and let it go?"

"Let it go? You haven't changed, Blake. You're still the rich playboy bedding every girl who walks by. I know because I've been watching you the last four years. And as far as I can tell you're still stupid when it comes to me. Getting me drunk to marry you doesn't exactly earn you trust points, and certainly sank you to a new level of unforgiveable in my book."

Her angry words hurt more than the dog bite or rabies shot.

Jenny pulled up and they headed to the car.

Blake grabbed the handle to open Amanda's door and said, "You know, Mandy, for someone who comes from an acknowledged Christian home, you sure have a lot to learn about forgiveness."

## Chapter Fifteen

Blake pulled his light blue t-shirt up. "Try not to enjoy this too much," he told Amanda.

Amanda raised an eyebrow. "As much as you may think I enjoy sticking a needle in you, I don't." She ran her fingers over his stomach, searching for a place to inject the needle, while avoiding the small bruises from the past four days. Her touch sent ripples of warmth over his skin. However, the impending needle seriously dampened his joy.

She found a spot and asked, "Ready?"

"Ready." Blake took a deep breath and exhaled it through clenched teeth while the needle plunged into this skin and released its fireball of medicine.

"Done," she said.

Blake continued his breathing exercise while she dispensed of the used needle. "Thanks."

"You're welcome. Now, let's take care of your arm." She removed the gauze bandage and examined the skin around his stitches. "It's looking better." She rubbed some antibiotic ointment over it, then wrapped it in fresh gauze. "I still think you should see a physical therapist." She tied off the end and tucked it under.

"We've already been through this. Can't afford it. Your annulment comes first. As it is, it's going to take me six months to pay for that, plus the hospital bill."

With a frown she sank down onto the guest bed next to him. He'd noticed her aversion to close physical proximity with him had eased with the dog bite business, though she still remained 'clinical' about his body as far as he could tell. "You mean the annulment is going to take six months? I'll be in Africa by then."

Shock and disappointment crashed down on him. He'd never asked about her post-graduation plans. He'd been too focused on 'catching' her and living 'happily ever after' to consider what she had going on. This, he now realized, was a major oversight and terribly selfish on his part. He managed to ask, "You're going to Africa? When do you leave?"

"Didn't I tell you?"

"No."

"Oh, well, I leave in July. I'm going over to teach newborn resuscitation in remote areas where infant mortality rates are high. But I'll get back to a city every two or three weeks, so I can call home and get my orders for the next location, not to mention a proper shower."

Blake's mind raced as he tried to sort out logistics. "How long will you be gone?"

"Well, my original assignment is for three months, but I hope by I'll be able to stay a few years. There are so many people I could reach in that time, so many babies I could save."

Her timeline seriously crushed Blake's hopes of making their marriage work. He rubbed the heels of his hands over his eyes, before settling them in a tight ball in his lap. "Do your parents know?"

"Not yet. Please don't tell them." Her eyes begged for him to keep her secret. For one brief moment he felt a prick of hope that she trusted him to keep it. "My mom's freaking out I'm going at all. She worries about my safety. Will I get enough to eat? Will I contract malaria if my mosquito net gets a hole? You know, mom stuff."

"I won't tell them, but I think you should. It's not like you to leave your parents in the dark, nearly dishonest. I know how much you value the truth."

"I just don't want them to worry."

"They're your parents. They're always going to worry."

"Like yours?" Instant regret shone in her eyes.

"Mine are showing me some tough love right now and I've

earned it. My dad's hoping it will help me step up to my responsibilities; be a man. I disagree with his methods but I do see his point."

Amanda cocked her head. "You're not mad at them?"

"I was at first, but I talked to your mom about it and she helped me see it from their point of view. You're very lucky to have her for a mother."

"I know." Their eyes locked, but Blake couldn't fathom her thoughts.

Heavy footsteps pounded down the stairs and Josh appeared in the doorway. "You two ready?"

"Uh, yeah." Amanda stood up and brushed at her jeans.

"Not interrupting, am I?" Josh smirked at her.

"No."

"Too bad," Josh replied wistfully. "I could use some more teasing ammo. Anyways, we're loading up the cars. Blake, do you want to ride with James and I?"

"Sure. I just need to put on my shoes."

Josh thundered back up the stairs.

"See you at the fair then." Amanda disappeared through the doorway.

"Hey, Mandy," Blake called after her.

"Yes?" She poked her head back in.

Blake smiled hopefully at her. "Think you could stand to ride the Ferris wheel with me today?"

She cocked her head to one side. "I think so. But I prefer the whirligig." She bounded up the stairs.

"One step forward," Blake whispered to himself.

The fair was loud with the majority of the crowd dressed in t-shirts, jeans, and cowboy boots. Occasionally, a pretty girl in a dress would go by on the arm of a love-struck fella, while kids raced past squeezing through gaps in the crowd. Without rain that week the dirt paths between the barns, booths, and rides were dry.

Blake hadn't been to a fair in ages. He walked under the welcoming banner that read "Founder's Day Celebration" and paid for his ticket.

Josh tugged on his arm. "Hey, I know you're injured and all, but we were counting on you to be our fourth in the greased pig contest. Think you can manage?"

Blake held in a laugh. "Greased pig?"

"Yeah. Each team has four people and they release the greased pig in a muddy field. Whichever team catches it first, wins the prize and bragging rights for the next year."

"What do you say?" asked James.

"Sure, why not? I'm in." Blake grinned.

"Great. Be at the muddy field by three."

"You got it."

Amanda walked up behind him accompanied by Tiffany and Missy. "Did I just hear you say you're going to help with the greased pig?"

He nodded.

"Oh, that's so exciting," crooned Tiffany as she tossed her hair and linked her arm through his. "I'll come cheer you boys on."

"Me, too," Missy chimed in.

"What about you?" Blake asked Amanda. "Are you going to come cheer on your family?"

She frowned. "You really shouldn't, Blake. You could do more damage to your arm."

"Oh, Amanda, always the party pooper." Tiffany shook her hair again. "Blake is a strong man. He can handle it." She ran her hand up and squeezed his bicep.

"Besides, he's showing his sensitive side and helping out friends in need. Really, where is your sense of honor?" added Missy.

Amanda rolled her eyes. "You two get out of here. Go find your friends or something."

"You aren't going to hog Blake to yourself all day, are you?" Tiffany pouted. "I'd like to show him some of the fair, too."

"You just want to show him off to make all your friends and crushes jealous, more like," Missy blew a bubble in her gum.

Tiffany stuck her tongue out at her sister.

A boy walking by Tiffany called out, "Hey, can I get some of that tongue later?"

Tiffany turned red and yelled back. "Not in this life, Taylor." She swung back to her sisters and Blake. "I swear high school boys are so immature. I can't wait to get to college."

"Sorry to burst your bubble, sis, but the immature high school boys grow up and go to college, too. Then they are just immature college guys." Missy laughed.

"Great. I'll have to look into the grad students then," Tiffany said. "That Taylor. I'm going to go tell him off." She flounced away.

Missy's phone buzzed and she checked the text. "I'll catch up with you later. I'm going to meet Sara at the rides. See ya." She headed off in the opposite direction of Tiffany.

"Well, Mandy. Looks like it's just you and me." He threw his arm around her shoulders. Secretly he was looking forward to spending the day together.

"And Alison and her date." She shrugged off his arm and pointed up the path. "Here they come."

Blake shook his head. "I should've known better than to think you could spend a whole day alone with me. I'm lucky you can even stand fifteen minutes straight."

"That's not true," Amanda said.

"You're right. Your current record is sixteen minutes."

She looked at him. "You've been timing me?"

Alison and Sheffield arrived, cutting off Blake's response. Alison made the introductions and the guys shook hands. "What do you want to do first?" she asked.

Amanda pointed at the barns. "Let's go see the animals."

They headed over to the big red structures where they checked out cows, sheep, goats, pigs, chickens, ducks, and horses and chatted about school, jobs, and their plans for the future. When they were done, they walked through another barn, but this one was full of crafts and baked goods that made their mouths water.

"How about some rides now?" Alison said with a glint to her eye.

"Whirligig," both girls chorused.

"It's best to do it before lunch," Amanda clarified.

"Yes, otherwise, everyone ends up wearing your lunch," Alison added.

Skeptical, Blake asked, "Has that happened before?"

"Oh, yes," Alison nodded emphatically. "It's one thing to wear your own puke, but quite another to wear a stranger's."

"Sounds gross," Blake replied.

"That's why you ride it before lunchtime. Come on." In her excitement Amanda tugged on his hand, then realized what she'd done and let go. That one hand tug along with her blush gave him reason to believe he just might be wearing down her resolve against him.

"It looks like those cow carousels they use for milking," Blake remarked as they followed the single file line to the far side of the whirligig. They stood in their places, strapped on the waist belts and pulled down the shoulder bars.

"Hope you're ready for this." Amanda rubbed her hands together in anticipation.

"You really like this ride, don't you?"

She laughed. "No. Actually, I find it totally terrifying. That's why it gives the best thrill."

He studied the other riders. Some clasped the bars with white knuckles, while others looked elated like Amanda, who kept tapping one foot. On the far side, one girl's skin had taken on a green shade. "Uh oh," Blake said. "I think there's a potential puker over there." He pointed her out to Amanda.

"That's not good, especially if she's up and we're down when it happens. We'll be covered in it."

"What do you mean up?" Blake asked as the buzzer sounded.

"You'll see," Amanda grinned smugly at him.

"Uh." Blake questioned the merits of the ride, but it started spinning.

"Too late," Amanda said with glee.

Blake tried to watch Amanda during the ride but eventually the centrifugal force pinned his head to the pad behind it. Once the ride picked up enough speed, it tilted on its axis so they spun around and around like a hamster wheel. Sure enough, the girl across the way puked during the ride. Luckily, she was on the downside when it happened and their group was spared the puke shower. When the ride made it to a complete stop and the harnesses were released, the girl doubled over and puked again, this time all over her shoes. They heard the ride operator announce to the enormous line that the ride would be closed temporarily for cleanup and the crowd gave a collective groan.

"Looks like we dodged that bullet," Blake nudged Amanda in the side with his elbow.

"Lucky us," she agreed.

"Lunchtime," Alison announced. They headed to the fairway where all the food stands were lined up on both sides from end to end. After a quick walk through to assess the options, they decided on the Lions Club jumbo hotdogs.

Amanda wrinkled her nose when Blake added sauerkraut to his dog already laden with chili, cheese, relish, mustard, and ketchup. "Are you really going to eat that?"

"I like my dogs fully loaded." He took a bite on the way to a free spot at a picnic table that a family had just vacated.

"Well, I like mine traditional." Amanda bit into her dog that was only covered in mustard and ketchup and pickles.

"Wouldn't want you to do anything outside the box. It could be dangerous." Blake winked at her.

Alison snickered.

Sheff's forehead crinkled. "What's the joke?"

"Oh, nothing much," Alison replied. "It's just that Amanda rarely does anything outside the box or spontaneous. She likes to plan and think everything through before she acts."

"I think working in Africa is pretty adventurous," sniffed Amanda. She took another bite of her hotdog.

"It would be if you just decided to do it and hopped on a plane. But you've been preparing for a year. So, adventurous, yes. But hardly spontaneous," Alison pointed out as she munched her chili dog with bacon.

"Okay, picking-on-Amanda time is officially over," Amanda decreed.

Blake checked the time. "I have to get over to the pig field soon. How about that Ferris wheel ride?"

Alison gave Amanda a sly look. "The Ferris wheel? How romantic!"

"It can be, depending on who you're with," shot back Amanda.

Sheff sucked up some soda. "Well, if you're going for romance, then it's better to do it after dark and once the fair is lit up with all the lights from the rides. It's like a regular Christmas display."

"I don't think it's going to be that kind of ride," Blake said. "Besides, after the greased pig contest, I'll be covered in mud and who knows what else. I hardly think that would add to the romance factor. So what do you say, Mandy? Ferris wheel so we can let our stomachs settle before pigs and more rides?"

"Sure." She wiped her face with a napkin. "I'm ready." She stood up. "You two coming?"

"No, I think we'll wait until tonight and take the romance ride." Alison smiled at Sheff. "We'll see you at the pig field. That's something I don't want to miss."

Blake swallowed his last bite of hot dog and grabbed their drinks. "Looks like it's just you and me." He offered her his arm, but she ignored it. He whispered to Sheff, "See, told you it wouldn't be romantic."

Amanda snatched her drink from Blake's hand and stomped off to the Ferris wheel.

Not sure what had triggered her anger, he gave her a little bit of space to cool down on the walk and caught up with her in the line.

She wheeled on him. "Why'd you say that to Sheff?"

"Did you want me to lie to him and tell him we were going to have a disgusting session of P.D.A. in broad daylight?"

"No, but you didn't have to make me look like the bad guy."

"How did I do that?"

"By intimating that you're into me but that I'm not into you. Neither of which is true."

Blake shook his head. "I'm not sure I followed you on that one. Which part isn't true?"

"The first one."

He brushed his fingers against hers and asked in a low voice, "How do you know it's not true?" Her green eyes clouded with doubt and confusion and Blake knew she was questioning what she thought about him.

"Next!" called the operator.

They didn't move until the guy behind them said, "Uh, you two are next."

Amanda glanced at him. "Sorry."

An awkward tension lingered between Blake and Amanda as they took their seats. The Ferris wheel lurched upward to let the next pair on.

"You didn't answer my question." Blake reminded her. "I did marry you after all."

She met his eyes. "Blake, that doesn't count. We were both intoxicated."

He decided to risk her anger and permanently losing her by telling the truth. "Even intoxicated, I knew what I was doing."

She gaped at him. "You knew?" Anger and astonishment played across her face. She gripped the safety bar hard.

"Yes, I did. I chose you on purpose."

Amanda couldn't decide whether she wanted to hear more

or throw herself off the Ferris wheel seat and take her chances with broken bones when she hit the ground. "Why? I can't stand you. Is that some kind of reverse psychology attraction for you?"

"No. I know I haven't been the most outstanding guy in anyone's book, and certainly not in yours. I totally screwed things up between us with my wild ways. But I haven't forgotten the magic of our kiss freshman year. It's haunted me, and I knew Vegas would be the last time I'd get a shot at you. So, I married you."

Amanda searched his eyes for signs of insincerity but came up empty. "If you're lying to me, if this is some part of a game you're playing, so help me Blake . . ."

He held up his hands. "I'm not lying and it's not a game. The only reason this marriage is ending is because you want it. If it were up to me, I'd introduce you to my family and we'd get a cozy place together, just the two of us."

Amanda refused to believe what Blake said was true. It couldn't be. Blake wasn't a one-woman kind of man. Now, she wished she'd jumped off the Ferris wheel and risked the broken bones. Bones mended faster than hearts.

"Besides, you're the only woman I've met who could care less about my money and that is saying a great deal. I thank your parents for that."

"For what?"

"Not bringing you up as a materialistic gold-digging brat. That's usually what I attract. Not exactly what I'm looking for in a life partner and soul mate."

Amanda's mind spun in circles like a whirlpool. Was it just possible that everything Blake had just told her was true? That she had misjudged him all this time?

The carriage swung into place at the bottom of the ride.

"Time to get off," said the operator.

Blake stepped out and took Amanda's hand to help her. Lost in thought, she let her hand stay just a moment longer than usual before she let go, although she couldn't decide whether to look at him or not. She was too busy trying to process their conversation.

"I've got to get over to the pig field," Blake said. "Which way is it?"

Still half in shock, she pointed down a dirt path. "Follow that to the end. Left at the horse barn and you'll be able to see the field."

"Are you coming to watch?" he asked hopefully as he dug his hands into his pockets.

She nodded slowly. "Uh, yeah. I'm going to grab ice cream first."

"Okay." Blake walked in the direction she'd indicated.

Amanda whisked out her cell phone and sent an urgent text to Alison. She tapped her thigh while she waited for a reply. Buzz. She looked at the screen and made a beeline for the ice cream stand. Alison met her in line.

"What did you do with Sheff?" Amanda asked.

"He went to save us a place in the stands. I promised to bring him ice cream in return. So, what's up?"

Amanda quickly recounted her conversation with Blake.

When she finished, Alison smiled and said, "Guess it was a romantic ride after all."

Amanda punched Alison lightly on the arm. "This is serious. I never imagined in a million years that Blake might have actual feelings for me. What am I going to do?"

They reached the front of the line and Alison waited to answer until both their orders were filled and they were headed to the pig field. "I don't think the question is so much of what are you going to do, but how do you feel about Blake?"

"You know how I feel about Blake. I can't stand him. I've loathed him for four years."

Alison gave a lick at her double chocolate cone. "You know, hate and loathing are just the opposite sides of love and passion. All it takes is the flip of the coin and the deep feelings you have can be switched in an instant."

Amanda stopped licking the drips of her mint chocolate chip cone. "Are you suggesting that in an alternate universe I'm in love with Blake?"

"No. I'm suggesting it in this universe."

"No way."

A tutting noise emitted form Alison's lips. "Amanda, have you even paid the least bit of attention to Blake this year?"

"Not any more than usual."

"Then you didn't notice that this whole past year he wasn't sleeping around."

"Of course he did. I saw him go in and out of apartments in my building all year."

"That may be, but he didn't sleep with any of them."

"How do you know?" They'd reached the pig field and searched the stands for Sheff and Amanda's family.

"Because Kurt told me so in Vegas."

Amanda scoffed. "Oh, yeah, because Kurt's such a reliable source."

"Actually, he was complaining that Blake was throwing away perfectly good opportunities to have sex with attractive girls. He even said that if he were in Blake's shoes, he'd nail every girl that came along."

Amanda resumed work on her cone. "Now that sounds more like Kurt."

"Not to mention, he didn't flirt with anyone on Memorial Day at your house and he's been very careful with his attention to your sisters, especially Tiffany. He read her like a book that first day."

"Yeah, well, Tiffany's the wild card of the family."

"That's putting it politely," Alison countered.

They finally spotted the waving arms of Sheff and the St. Claires, and made their way up the bleachers.

"Knowing all of that, does it change any of your opinions about Blake or is he still the scum of the filthy rich earth?"

Amanda's bottom lip stuck out and her forehead wrinkled. "I don't know. It still doesn't erase his past actions."

Alison paused before they got within earshot of the St. Claires. "Are you really that hard-headed and hard-hearted?"

"You think I should forgive him?"

"I think you should've forgiven him a long time ago. I'm your best friend and I love you, but your stubbornness sometimes blinds you to the truth and, in this case, to your feelings about Blake."

## Chapter Sixteen

Any further conversation about Blake was cut off, first, by a voice announcing over the loudspeaker the teams, their members and then, second, by the cheers of the crowd. The two girls rushed to sit down with Amanda's family. Sheff wrapped his arm around Alison before getting to work on his ice cream. Jenny patted Amanda's leg.

Tiffany leaned forward, her eyes riveted on Blake as she spoke, "I bet Blake catches their greased pig."

Amanda gazed down on the quagmire called Pig Field. Six teams lined one end of the field with its own pig to catch. Whoever caught their pig first won. If someone caught another team's pig by mistake, that team was disqualified. There was usually a lot of intentional physical contact between teams to keep members from reaching their pig. Basically it was rugby with a greased pig in place of the ball. Amanda's brothers had won the contest twice in the past and, judging by the teams, they seemed to be in a good position to win again this year too. Normally she would be all for Blake getting a good thrashing as she thought it to be earned punishment for his immoral ways, but given his recent actions, the conversations today, and the dog bite on his arm, worry had snuck in the back door. She nibbled on her cone.

The bull-horn sounded and the pigs were released in squeals of terror with the teams chasing after them.

Rich was the front man for the team. His job was to clear the way for the catcher, this year it was Blake. James and Josh were the bouncers. Their job was to impede the other teams' progress from reaching their pigs before Blake could scoop up his. Elbows flew and legs appeared from nowhere to trip up slippery feet in the mud. Several dive attempts were made, and in a few short minutes, most of the teams were covered in mud from head to toe. It soon became difficult to distinguish one person from another.

Blake finally cornered his pig and just as he was about to try to grab it an opposing team member flew in front of him to block him. Blake leapt over the guy in a spectacular dive, landed hard knocking the wind out of himself, but managed to grab his pig. The slippery beast struggled to slide from his grasp, but enough years of chasing Cici's hamster around the house, along with intramural rugby in the rain, kept it in his grasp. Holding the pig, he flopped on his back and struggled to catch his breath. Rich, James and Josh cheered as a judge blew the bullhorn.

A silver-haired man in jeans, cowboy boots, and a white cowboy hat approached him. "Well, let's see if we've got a winner," he said into his microphone. He took a towel and wiped off the cloth tied around the pig's middle. "Blue," he said, then checked it against Blake's arm band. "Also, blue. We have a winner!"

The crowd erupted in cheers as Rich, James, and Josh hauled Blake to his feet.

"Congratulations to Rich, James, and Josh St. Claire and to Blake Worthington, this year's greased-pig champions. I believe that makes three wins for the St. Claire brothers." He handed them the trophy and they raised it to the crowd who gave another roar.

In the stands Blake saw all the St.Claires, Alison and Sheff, cheering and jumping up and down, except for Amanda who clapped but wore a small frown.

Rich noticed Amanda too. "Not sure if a greased pig is enough to bring Amanda around, but you sure got our vote."

Each of the boys clapped Blake on the back.

The silver-haired cowboy turned off the microphone. "You boys head over there to get hosed off."

"What should I do with the pig?" Blake asked as he struggled to keep it in his hands.

"There's a box over there for him. We'll get him cleaned up too."

"Thanks," the guys said. Blake dropped the pig into the box and joined the brothers at the hose-off area.

Minutes later most of the mud had come off except where it had gotten ground in and the guys were sopping wet from head to toe.

The St. Claires, Alison, and Sheff fought their way through the crowd and joined them. Congratulations were given, but hugs weren't exchanged.

Blake winced with each breath.

Amanda sidled up to him and whispered, "What's wrong?"

"It's just my ribs," he said.

"We're going to go get changed," said James. "We'll meet up with you at the demolition derby."

"Here's your change of clothes." Rachel handed Rich a plastic bag. "I'll wait for you here." She pecked him on the cheek.

Blake looked at Amanda. "I don't have a change of clothes. I didn't know I was doing this today."

"We'll just swing by the house so you can get changed and come back. The rest of them won't want to leave until after the dance tonight."

Blake grimaced. "Sounds good."

"And I think we better swing by the hospital while we're at it," she added.

"No, Mandy, really, I'm fine," he protested, but knew she wasn't fooled.

"No, you're not." She had a 'don't fight me' look on her face. "Mom, can I have the keys to the car?"

Jenny looked at her surprised. "Sure, but what's going on?"

"Blake needs dry clothes from home. Plus, I think he needs to see a doctor, something is wrong with his ribs."

Jenny bustled over concerned. "Which side?"

"This one." Blake laid a hand over his left side.

Jenny pressed her fingers lightly on his ribs.

He gasped. "Ouch."

"Definitely something wrong."

"I probably just bruised them when I landed hard at the end."

"But, they may be cracked or broken," said Amanda. "You need an x-ray."

"Do you want us to come with you?" Jenny fished in her purse for the keys.

"No. Please, stay and have a good time. Really, this is nothing," Blake assured her.

"We'll be okay. I know my way around the hospital." Amanda smiled.

Jenny handed her the keys, hugged her daughter, then moved to hug Blake, but then thought better of it and patted his shoulder instead. "Call us later."

"Okay." Amanda and Blake headed to the car.

"Really, let's skip the hospital. There probably isn't anything they can do. I can't afford it anyways."

She gave Blake a dark look. "We'll stop at home just long enough for you to get clean and then you're going to the hospital and that's final."

## Chapter Seventeen

It was nearly dark by the time Blake and Amanda returned to the fair and located the family in the bleachers just in time to watch the last demolition derby. Everyone picked a different car to cheer for. The sounds of the cars revving their engines, squealing their tires, and crashing into each other nearly drowned out the sounds of the cheering crowd. Jenny's car won after some spectacular smash ups that left cars littered all over the dirt battleground.

Jenny turned to Bill, "I won. You owe me a slow dance."

Bill pretended to look mortified at the prospect, but the twinkle in his eye gave him away. "If I have to."

Jenny swatted him on the arm. "You can't fool me, dear. Come on, I'm collecting now." They led the family down the bleachers. Out on one of the flat grassy fields a make-shift dance floor had been set up and a band played under a white canopy, but the dance floor was open to the stars. The sign on the drum announced the band as the Yellin' Cowboys.

The moment their toes hit the dance floor, Tiffany grabbed Blake's hand to haul him onto it. "I get the first turn with Blake."

Amanda protested. "Tiffany, I really don't think Blake can dance tonight. He's got three cracked ribs."

"I can take a few spins across the dance floor without doing any major damage." Blake turned to Tiffany. "Although, I have to warn you, I won't be in top form."

"I'll try to take it easy on you," Tiffany replied with a gleam in her eye.

"Missy, you're next," Blake called over his shoulder as Tiffany dragged him away.

"He really shouldn't dance," Amanda grumbled.

Jenny wrapped an arm around her. "Blake's a big boy. He knows what he can handle."

"I'm not so sure about that."

"He'll recover and be as good as new in a few weeks. Your brothers have had far worse injuries and they're all fine."

"That's debatable."

Jenny laughed. "Well, maybe so." Bill claimed her hand and led her out to dance.

Amanda found an empty spot along the fence and took a seat. The song changed and Blake swapped Tiffany for Missy. Alison and Sheff, Rich and Rachel, and her parents looked thoroughly happy as they twirled around the dance floor. Amanda's parents had met at a church dance when they were in college, and Jenny had lured Bill into being on the square dance team. They were fabulous out on the dance floor even though Bill always claimed he had two left feet. Amanda's emotions tumbled around like clothes inside a dryer and she couldn't make sense of any of them. The song changed again and Blake sent Missy off to find a new partner.

He sauntered over to Amanda and extended his hand. "May I have this dance?"

"No," Amanda snapped.

Blake stepped back in surprise at her hostile answer. "Okay," he drew the word out. 'What did I do to offend you this time? Because I thought I'd done a pretty good job of towing the line lately, especially today. Your family seems to be pretty happy with me."

"Oh, sure they are. You confide in my parents, win my brothers by getting injured while catching a pig, and capture my sisters' undying devotion with your good looks and charm. Of course they love you."

"You're upset because your family likes me?"

"It would be a lot easier if they didn't like you when this all comes to an end."

"You don't want to look like the bad guy. Is that it?"

Reluctantly she answered, "Yes."

"You'd rather I was the bad guy?"

She squirmed and wouldn't meet his eyes.

"Are you beginning to question my level of badness?" The corners of his mouth twitched up just shy of a smirk.

She nodded and fidgeted with an earring.

"I bet that's a little hard to reconcile with how you've felt about me up until now."

Amanda pressed her lips together.

"Come dance with me." He took her hand and she jumped down from the fence. He led her onto the dance floor. A slow song played. She noticed her mother's head rested on Bill's shoulder, her eyes closed, and a content smile on her face.

Blake's arm wrapped around her waist and she tried to ignore the tingle that shot up her spine. They revolved in slow circles.

Amanda had been in close contact with Blake for almost two weeks now, but this was different from eating meals, or giving him shots, or rides in the car. The intimacy of being in his arms unnerved her. She didn't know where to look or what to say. But worst, she felt that perhaps she'd been wrong. She'd misjudged him and only had herself to blame. She tried to reassemble all the reasons she loathed him but it was like trying to build a castle wall out of clouds; none of it stayed together and everything kept slipping through her fingers. Amanda didn't like feeling out of control, not one bit, which was a big part of the reason she didn't drink, and drinking was what had landed her in this mess in the first place.

Lost in her tangled thoughts, she misstepped and lost her balance. Blake pulled her closer to stop her fall. She looked up at him and was startled by the look in his eyes. She'd seen it in their wedding video right before he kissed her. A rush of adrenaline mixed with panic set in.

"I'd really like to kiss you right now," he murmured in a low husky voice as his hand pushed on the small of her back pressing their bodies together.

Her panic ratcheted up another notch, even as her heart threatened to melt. A soft, "No," escaped her lips.

He surveyed the couples around them. "I don't think anyone would find it odd if I kissed my wife on the dance floor."

"Don't call me that." Her automatic response lacked conviction as her self-control tried to slip away.

"You afraid?" He lowered his head and she caught the scent of wintergreen from the mint he'd eaten earlier.

"It just wouldn't be right," she stalled.

His head moved in until their lips were only a breath apart. "What if I dare you? I've never seen you back down from a dare."

"Don't." She trembled in his arms. The walls were crumbling fast and she knew if he kissed her, then she might not be able to rebuild them again. "I can't." She dashed off the dance floor and escaped into the crowds of the fair.

## Chapter Eighteen

"Smells good, Jenny. Is there anything I can help with?" Blake asked as he walked into the kitchen the next morning.

"Think you can handle toast?" With a fork in her hand she pointed to a loaf of bread next to the toaster.

"Sure."

"Just grab a plate to pile it on."

Blake grabbed a plate and threw four slices of bread in the toaster and pushed the lever down. "Is anyone else up yet?" he fished, wanting to know about Amanda.

"I heard Missy and Tiffany stir when I came into the kitchen, but I think it'll be a while before we see Amanda." She gave Blake a sidelong glance. "She was up half the night pacing around her room."

"How do you know?"

"Her room is directly above ours. I heard her footsteps going back and forth. You've sure got her in a spin."

"Yeah, well, I think I may have overdone it yesterday. She's likely to keep me at arm's length, if not further."

"That's because she's scared."

"I got that part, but I don't think I really understand why."

"Well, don't bother asking her, at least not yet. I don't think she understands herself, but she will." Jenny flipped the ham and then turned to him resting one hip against the edge of the counter. "Let me tell you something about Amanda. She's had occasional dates and even a boyfriend or two in high school, but she is my planner and she doesn't like to let anything get in the way of her plans. Sometimes she is so busy with her plans that she forgets to have fun and live life along the way."

"As opposed to Tiffany," Blake observed.

"Yes. Tiffany is the exact opposite. She could use a little Amanda in her. Missy is almost a happy medium, though she tends to fall just a little on the Tiffany side." She got the eggs and milk from the fridge and set them next to the stove. "I was actually surprised when Amanda asked to go to Las Vegas. Happy to see her cut loose and relax, especially since she is so frugal and not likely to spend money on 'frivolous things' as she calls them."

Blake couldn't help the grin that spread across his face. "I don't think that trip went as you hoped."

Jenny gave a soft laugh as she flipped the ham again. "Well, the lesson certainly turned out more extreme than I had anticipated. But then, Amanda never does anything by halves. Still, I don't have any complaints about the results." She smiled as she patted his shoulder.

Still in her jammies, a white t-shirt and pajama pants with a blue paisley pattern, Amanda wandered in. "Smells delicious Mom, how can I help?" She stretched.

"You can start on the eggs," Jenny replied.

Blake loved how Amanda looked in the morning with her tousled hair. As he stifled the urge to wrap her in his arms, the lever on the toast popped up and Blake turned around. "Uh, oh."

"What?" Amanda came over to inspect the damage.

"I think I burned the toast." He pulled the blackened pieces of bread from their slots.

Amanda giggled through her yawn. "How did you possibly manage to burn toast? Did you check the setting?" They looked down at the knob. It was turned to the darkest setting.

He looked at her, chagrined. "I guess not."

"Well, that explains it. Try again." Amanda reset the toaster.

Blake threw the burnt pieces in the trash, put new slices in the slots, and depressed the lever. "Round two."

"Have you ever cooked eggs?" Amanda asked as she walked over to the eggs and milk.

"Uh, no, and based on the toast I'm not sure it would be wise to trust me with eggs."

"Well, we won't know unless we try. What do you think, Mom?" She pushed a wave of hair out of her face.

Jenny waved her fork. "It's good for a man to know his way around the kitchen, especially if he wants to serve his wife breakfast in bed." There was an awkward pause. "So, um, yes, please teach Blake how to make eggs," Jenny said as she started on the pancakes while still tending to the ham.

Amanda pulled out a large mixing bowl and whisk. She put the bowl and eggs between her and Blake. "Grab an egg and tap it on the counter like this," she demonstrated a few light taps, then held it up for him to see. "See the tiny cracks with the big one in the middle? That's about how you want it just before you open it over the bowl." She separated the halves and dumped the contents into the bowl before tossing the shells in the sink. "You try."

Distracted by Amanda's just-rolled-out-of-bed look, he tapped the egg with too much force and it smashed all over the counter. "Oops."

"No worries." Amanda fished out the egg shell and tossed it in the sink. Then she slid the rest off the counter and into the mixing bowl. "You just have to make sure not to get any of the shell in." She handed him another egg. "Try again."

Blake went lighter on his taps, then checked the egg. He held it up for inspection. "How is this?"

"Good. Now take your egg in both hands, put you thumbs over the crack and pull it apart." Amanda's egg fell neatly into the bowl.

Blake took a breath and hoped he wouldn't be scraping this egg off the counter too. "Here goes." He copied Amanda and his egg joined hers in the bowl. A delighted smile graced his face. "I did it."

"He can be taught," she teased with a smile.

Once they had all the eggs in the bowl, Amanda added some milk.

"How do you know how much to put in?" Blake asked, noting

she hadn't used a measuring cup.

She shrugged. "You just add milk until it looks right."

"Well, that isn't very accurate," he remarked.

"Some parts of cooking are instinctual," Jenny chimed in.

"Great. I think the breakfast in bed idea is a doomed one then," Blake replied as he watched Amanda whisk the eggs.

She handed it to him. "Beat until well mixed."

He tried to copy Amanda's motion with the whisk. Some of the egg mixture sloshed out onto the counter.

Amanda ripped off a paper towel and wiped it up. "Easy there, cowboy."

Pop! Amanda checked the toast. "Much better this time. There's hope that someday you'll be able to pull off breakfast."

"Great. Just don't tell Ana Maria or she'll start making me cook my own."

Amanda gave him a questioning look. "Who's Anna Maria?"

"Our cook. She's been with us since the beginning. She's the one who's kept an eye on me all these years."

"What about your parents, Blake?" asked Jenny as she flipped pancakes.

Amanda sprayed some oil in the bottom of the pan and added salt and pepper to the mixing bowl. "Pour it in."

He enjoyed the crackling sound made by the egg mixture hitting the hot pan as he poured it in. "Dad was usually at the lab or the office. My mom did charity work, or was at the country club, running the PTA, or something. They came to games, and recitals, and stuff, but there wasn't much time to learn some basic life skills or even just chat. Ana Maria made sure we did our homework, ate our vegetables, and stayed fairly in line. But, the best part was she'd just sit there and listen while you poured your heart out about, well, whatever and she wasn't judgmental about it either." His cheeks warmed with self-consciousness at being so open about his family, a rare occurrence. He put in another round of toast.

"She sounds like my kind of woman." Jenny stacked pancakes on a plate before pouring out another round on the griddle.

He watched Amanda as she quietly scrambled the eggs and wondered if she was thinking about him and his family, or if her thoughts were on her lucky escape of being part of such a family, or maybe on her new life in Africa. She sighed. "Are you tired? Do you want me to take a turn?"

"Um, sure." She handed him the spatula.

Jenny finished the pancakes and the ham. "Blake, how are the eggs coming?"

"Uh, almost done, I think." He gestured at the pan.

She peeked over his shoulder and nodded in approval. "Great. Amanda, will you set the table and then go get the girls?"

"Sure, Mom," Amanda replied.

Pop! Blake pulled out the toast and put in the last round of slices.

"Blake, would you like to come to church with us?" Jenny asked.

"Oh, Blake doesn't go to church, Mom." Amanda set the napkins and silverware on the table.

"Oh?" Jenny looked to him for elaboration.

"It's true, I'm not much for religion, mostly because I don't understand it. But, I would be pleased to attend church with your family." He shrugged and smiled. "Who knows, maybe I'll find some enlightenment."

## Chapter Nineteen

Yesterday, Amanda had pondered about what it would've been like to grow up with parents who were too busy for you. She knew her parents had sacrificed many things in order for Jenny to stay at home with the six kids. She'd hardly missed any of it though because they'd made up for it with love and one-on-one time. It seemed she still had a lot to learn about Blake.

"Are you sure you should go into work this morning?" Amanda asked as she inserted the rabies shot. It was getting harder to find spots on his stomach that weren't either bruised or muscle.

Blake exhaled slowly as the medicine burned. "I'll be fine," he said. "Can you wrap me up?"

"Yeah."

A week ago, she'd been indifferent to Blake's half-dressed body. She'd viewed him clinically, like a patient. Now the chisels of his muscles consumed her vision. She picked up the ace bandage and forced herself to concentrate on wrapping it tight around his torso instead of musing over the smoothness of his skin or the light patch of hair on his chest.

Blake grunted.

"Sorry," she said.

"It's okay. I've had cracked ribs before. They take a few weeks to heal, but they're uncomfortable in the meantime."

Amanda finished the wrap. "Done." She straightened up and found herself inches from Blake's mouth. The warmth of his skin begged her to come closer. She licked her lips and stepped back. "When have you had cracked ribs before?"

"Like every season of intramural rugby the last four years."

He pulled his green t-shirt back over his head with another grunt.

"Really?"

"You didn't notice?" He stuffed his wallet into the pocket of his jeans.

"I remember your broken noses, abrasions, and bruises on your face and arms. I just figured you got them from angry girls you'd used, or from their boyfriends when you got caught."

Blake's jaw tightened, accentuating the planes of his face. "Nice, Mandy. You just took that whole immoral Casanova thing and ran wild with it the last four years, didn't you?"

She huffed and felt a spark of anger ignite. "Well, I had good reason to, if you remember our freshman year."

His voice rose in exasperation. "How many times do I have to apologize for being a young selfish idiot before you forgive me?"

"I don't know," she shouted, "Until I forgive you."

She saw her own hurt and frustration reflected in his eyes, as the tension built between them, until Jenny's voice called down the stairs, "Is everything all right down there?"

"Yes, Mom," Amanda replied, her gaze locked on his.

"Okay, then you better get in the car if you are both going to be at work on time."

The quiet ride to the animal shelter carried an undercurrent of hostility that irritated Blake to no end.

Amanda pulled the car up in front of the building and kept the motor running. "Blake," she began.

"Save it, Mandy." He pulled on the door handle to exit, but she laid her hand on his arm and he paused.

"Just..."

He watched as her eyebrows scrunched together while she struggled to find the words she wanted.

She ended with, "Be safe today."

"Okay." He exited and watched her pull away, wondering what she hadn't said.

Inside the shelter, he pulled on his coveralls, which took a little longer than usual due to his ribs. He heard Madge typing madly away in the office and stuck his head in. "Happy Monday."

She looked up and stopped typing. "Blake!" She came around the desk to hug him.

Blake gasped as she pressed against his ribs.

She released him with a nervous look. "Oh, did I hurt you? I didn't think I got your arm. I tried to be careful."

"No, my arm is coming along fine. I hurt my ribs at the fair this weekend catching the greased pig with the St. Claire boys."

She chortled. "You boys take your games far too seriously. Honestly."

"So, this week I'll have a hard time with any heavy lifting."

"I'll ask James to go with you on the shopping run tomorrow. He owes me a few favors."

Blake cocked his head to the side. "For what?"

"Bucky for one." She picked up a ledger from the desk.

"Who's Bucky?" he asked curiously.

"I'll let him tell you." She frowned at the ledger. "You don't have a spare half a million dollars lying around, do you?"

Blake blanched. He'd worked hard not to let anyone know who he was. "Sorry? I don't understand."

"I didn't mean it literally. It's just I can't make these figures work anymore. The shelter has always had to scrounge for money, but I've exhausted every option. If we can't find some more money, I'm afraid we'll going to have to close."

Blake hadn't been here long, but he could see the needs of the animals and how hard the staff worked to fulfill them. "What will happen to the animals?"

"We'll shuttle them off to other shelters, I suppose." She frowned at the ledger.

"But, what about all of you?"

Madge ran a hand across her forehead. "We'll have to find new jobs. That'll really kill Marlene. She's a single mom and barely hanging on as it is."

"But there has to be something we can do." His job wasn't glamorous, but he'd come to enjoy the sense of having a purpose and of belonging somewhere. Not to mention, he could identify with the animals' homelessness, and the feeling of abandonment.

She set the ledger down and leaned back on the desk. "If you've got an idea, I'm happy to hear it."

Blake stroked his chin. "Well, I can go over the books with you and see if there's anything else we can cut down. I have a degree in business."

"Okay."

"Have you talked to the bank?"

"The manager is prepared to ban me and issue a restraining order if I show up again in the next month."

"What about a fundraiser?"

"We've tried those in the past and most of the times have either just broken even or lost money."

"Would you let me try?"

Madge frowned. "I don't know, Blake; I think it's a lost cause."

An idea sparked. "What about Winter?"

"Winter?" Madge looked baffled. "You mean the season?"

"No." He shook his head. "The dolphin. Did you ever see the movie *Dolphin Tale*?"

"No."

"It's about a disabled dolphin that gets rehabilitated at a marine animal shelter which is about to close. They put up a webcam and started a 'Save Winter' campaign; two middle-school-aged kids save the dolphin and the shelter. We just need a Winter."

Madge looked skeptically at him. "Are you sure you didn't crack your skull along with the ribs? We can't house a dolphin here. We're in Iowa."

"No, what I mean is, we need an animal that people can identify with and rally around, or a reason to get excited about the shelter."

Her brow furrowed with concentration. "I've got nothing."

"I think you've been at this too long. Will you let me put together a fundraiser?"

She crossed her arms. "Do you have any experience?"

"My mother has done more fundraisers than the rest of the state of Texas put together. I paid attention. I can do this."

"I don't know, Blake." She bit her lower lip.

"Please, let me try." He begged.

She took a long moment to consider. "All right. You've got until July 4th to raise the money, because if I don't pay the bank by the fifth, then we'll have to close."

"I'm not going to let that happen."

She laid a hand on his arm and said kindly, "No matter the result, thanks for trying."

"I'll be back in once I've got the animals taken care of to look at the books with you."

He stepped through the doorway.

"Blake," Madge called and he turned around. "I don't know what brought you to the St. Claires', but I'm awfully grateful it brought you here."

Confidently he replied, "It's quite a story. I'll have to tell you sometime. I bet it blows the Bucky story out of the water."

## Chapter Twenty

It had been a couple of days since Blake had cracked his ribs, but working while they healed took its toll. After they'd arrived home from work, Amanda watched him grab three Advil and chug them down with water at the dinner table. Somehow he'd taken over Rich's old place at the table between Amanda and Jenny.

"Blake," Jenny scooped up a forkful of homemade mac and cheese, "have you gotten your results from the vet yet about that dog bite?"

"Yes, earlier this afternoon. They were negative, so Amanda won't have to give me any more shots. And, while I appreciate Amanda's help, I'm not going to complain with them being over. Those suckers hurt."

"That's wonderful," Jenny said, then changed the subject. "Madge mentioned you are organizing a fundraiser for her." She cut up her rotisserie chicken.

"That's right. The shelter will close if they can't raise enough money. I asked Madge to let me have a go at it."

"Have you ever done anything like that before?" asked Amanda as she salted her broccoli.

"No, but my mom's a pro at it and I paid attention to her methods. I've already researched which animal companies will donate or fund match for a cause like this, so that'll be a big help, but what we really need is a Winter."

With a forkful of mac and cheese halfway to her mouth Missy gave Blake an odd glance and said, "Um, it's summer time. Why do you want it to be winter? Won't the shelter be closed by then without the money?"

"No, not winter as in the season, but Winter as in the dolphin." Blank looks stared back at him from everyone at the table. "Why is it that no one here in Des Moines has seen Dolphin Tale?"

"Probably because we don't have little kids anymore," responded Bill from the opposite end.

"Well, my six-year-old cousin loved it and made me watch it with him about three times." He filled them in on Winter.

"Shouldn't all the animals be the attraction?" Jenny asked.

"Ideally, yes. But people get numb when it comes to a group of something, but if you can individualize it, personalize it, then the success rate is much higher. For instance, when my mom was approached to do a children's cancer fundraiser, she could have kept it generic, but then people say, "Oh, it's just another fundraiser". Instead, she looked for a child in our local area who needed help and built the fundraiser around Mary, a six-year-old girl with a rare form of cancer. Mary became the poster child. Mary, Mary's mother, and my mom did radio and television interviews. They posted commercials on the local channels and sent information to all the schools in Mary's district. There were bake sales, 5K's, bowling tournaments, discount tickets to the amusement park, and a ton of other stuff. My mom put it all together built around the one, Mary."

"And how did it turn out?" Bill asked, taking second helpings of chicken.

"Originally she was asked to raise half a million dollars. She ended up with one and a half million dollars; more than enough to cover Mary's care and still donate to the umbrella cancer foundation to help other kids."

Everyone at the table froze and stared at Blake.

"That's amazing!" Missy said.

It was difficult for Amanda to reconcile the image of a generous woman who fought for a cancer-stricken child with the tough love/uncaring mother she'd envisioned the past four years. Quietly she asked, "How much does the shelter need?"

"About two-hundred and fifty thousand," Blake responded.

Stunned at that daunting amount, she blurted, "And you really think you can raise that much?"

"I'm going to try. The fundraiser is scheduled at Shay Park for July 3rd." Blake loaded more mac and cheese on his plate, then turned toward the matriarch of the family. "This is really good, Jenny. Even better than Ana Maria's, but don't tell her I said that. Any chance I can give her the recipe?"

Jenny smiled at the compliment. "Sure."

Blake's phone rang and he looked at them guiltily. House rules stated no cell phones at the table. "Sorry, I forgot to turn it off. I'll call them back later." He looked down at the phone and swallowed hard. "Um, Jenny, it's my parents. Would you excuse me, please?"

"Of course," she answered.

Amanda's eyes followed Blake out of the room and heard him answer hello.

"Has Blake spoken to his parents since he got here?" her mother asked.

"Not that I know of. When they cut him off, they really cut him off. Not a word, no money, and they even dropped his health insurance."

"Well, that explains his reluctance about going to the ER." Jenny frowned. "I hope there hasn't been a tragedy in the family."

Everyone glanced at each other, then concentrated on the food on their plates until Blake returned a few minutes later.

"Is it something serious? Is someone ill?" Amanda couldn't help asking.

He shook his head, but the frown on his face indicated trouble. "No. I'll talk to you about it later."

"Okay," Amanda replied, curious to know what prompted Blake's family to call if it wasn't serious.

Tiffany picked up her dishes. "I've got to go study for my finals."

Jenny gave her daughter a sharp look. "Be sure you're studying and not on Facebook or texting your friends."

"Yes, Mom," Tiffany sighed and departed.

"I'll be in my room, too," Missy said. "I start work tomorrow."

"Where are you working?" Blake asked.

She gave a careless wave. "I'm helping with the Bible school this summer and those kids have so much energy, I need all the sleep I can get to keep up. Night." She cleared her dishes and headed to her room.

The rest of them piled their dishes at the sink. Jenny turned on the water.

Bill gave her a hug from behind. "I'll get the dishes tonight."

Jenny pecked a kiss on her husband's cheek. "Thanks, dear. I'll go start folding the laundry."

"I can help, Mom," Amanda volunteered.

"Could I speak to you first?" Blake asked in a voice so low only Amanda could hear. She nodded.

"Be there in a minute, Mom." She followed Blake out onto the back porch. They sat down on the green rockers and listened to the sound of water coming from the kitchen and to the noises of bugs in the yard. Amanda waited patiently for him to speak. She could tell by his body language the phone call had upset him. His elbows rested on his knees as he twisted his hands around. He kept his head bent to the floor so she couldn't see his eyes.

"My parents require my presence. My dad's fiftieth birthday is in a couple of days and there's a huge party. There'll be questions if I'm not there. They'll fly me home for it and then straight back here."

"Oh," Amanda said. Part of her wanted Blake to go, if only to put some physical distance between them. The longer he remained in her home, the harder she found it to keep her heart caged tight and to keep her judgments against him in place. The other part of her felt a trickle of sadness at not seeing him every day. She'd sort of gotten used to him being with her, dangerous as that was.

"I'm not going."

Amanda's brow crinkled as she tried to think of the right way to convince him to go. She fiddled with her earring. "I know things are difficult, but he's still your dad. I think you should be with him on his birthday."

He brought his head up to meet her gaze. The look in his eyes was unfamiliar; one she'd never seen before. "I have responsibilities here. I have work, a fundraiser to get off the ground, and a wife to divorce. Leaving will delay all of that."

"I think it's commendable you want to take care of your responsibilities, but one thing my parents taught us is that family comes first. Perhaps going home for a day or two may help start healing the rift between you."

Blake shook his head. "I don't think my dad's interested in mending fences. He's more worried about appearances."

"Does the reason really matter? They still called you and want you to come home."

He leaned the rocker back and placed his hands behind his head. "That's funny coming from you."

Amanda frowned. "What do you mean?"

"I mean, you sit here telling me to try to make peace with my family and that the reasons don't matter, but you won't make peace with me no matter how hard I try."

An angry retort tried to rip its way out of her mouth, but she held her tongue. His words hurt because they had the ring of truth. She gazed into his eyes for a long moment. "You're right. I haven't been fair to you. I'll try to do better."

"I'll go, but only if you come with me." His words hung in the air, like a dare, a challenge.

Her thoughts tumbled like a Chinese acrobat. She needed to put distance between them, time to rebuild the walls around her heart and secure it from the danger of falling in love with him. And yet, she felt this strange tug to support him, be with him, and to help him reunite his family. Going with him was definitely a bad idea. There had to be a way to convince him to go without her. "I don't think that's a good idea."

"Why?"

Her brain spun for a legitimate reason. "Well, I've got work."

Blake raised his eyebrows. "Lame. You just told me family was more important than work. Besides, you're leaving here in a few weeks anyway. I think the hospital can spare you for a day or two."

She withered under his gaze and looked down at her bare feet. "It would be uncomfortable."

"For who?"

"For all of us." She gathered enough courage to meet his eyes. "If your parents kicked you out for marrying me, then I think it's clear they don't want me around."

"Kicking me out had everything to do with me and nothing to do with you. I think it would help if they see what an amazing person you are."

Her cheeks burned at his compliment. "Is that what you really want me there for or just so you won't have to face them alone?"

"Honestly?" Blake rubbed the back of his neck with one hand.

"Honestly."

"A little bit of both."

She felt secretly pleased that he wanted her there, but that emotion conflicted with her past feelings. She stalled for time. "Fair enough. Can I think about it and tell you in the morning?"

Blake nodded. "Deal." He stood up from the rocker and offered her his hand.

As the warmth of his palm met hers, she felt a spark flicker in her heart. She tamped it down and in an attempt at a normalcy she didn't feel, said, "I'm going to go help Mom fold the laundry."

"I'm going to sit out here for a while." He let go.

"Okay." She went inside to the family room where Jenny sat in the middle of the floor surrounded by baskets of clothes. One basket held Missy's clothes neatly folded and ready to be put away. She had just started on the second basket, which held Tiffany's clothes.

"Really, Mom, you don't have to fold our clothes. We're grown up enough to do it ourselves." Amanda plopped down beside her, grabbed her basket of clothes, and began folding the shirts.

"I know, dear, but it's one of the few ways I have left to show you how much I love you." She paired socks together.

Amanda gave her mom a one-armed hug. "We love you too, Mom."

"So what happened?"

"His family requires his presence at his dad's fiftieth birthday party."

"Ah."

Amanda forced the words out in one quick breath. "He asked me to go with him."

"I see, and what did you say?"

She felt her mother's penetrating gaze on her cheek as she stubbornly folded the t-shirt in front of her. "I told him I'd think about it and give him an answer in the morning."

"Do you want to go?"

She squirmed at her mother's uncanny ability to read her soul and concentrated on getting the folds just right. She hedged. "I'm not sure. His family sounds so different from ours, and I'm not sure how friendly they'll be. I don't want to get in the middle of their family issues. Not to mention they kicked him out for marrying me."

"I think that had more to do with Blake's past conduct than you."

"That's what he said. Still . . ."

With Tiffany's basket completed, Jenny moved on to her own clothes. "It might help you understand more about Blake if you meet his family and see the world he comes from."

Amanda paused in her work and frowned. "I don't know if I want to understand him."

Jenny set down the shirt in her hands. "Amanda," she said softly, "I have tried very hard over the years to teach all of you not to judge another person until you have walked in their shoes and seen the world the way they see it. And while it is impossible to do that literally, I think you get my point. You've seen Blake a certain way for the past four years and judged and sentenced him without hope of an appeal. That's not fair. It's not what your dad and I taught you. You aren't supposed to judge others against the standards you hold yourself to, when they haven't been taught them." She laid a hand on her daughter's arm. "Why is it you are so hard on Blake?"

Her mother's touch pulled the truth from her lips. "I'm scared, I guess."

Jenny picked up a pair of capris and resumed folding. "Scared you may have been wrong about him?"

"Yes, because if I am mistaken about him, then I may have been mistaken about other people and other things."

"We all make mistakes, Amanda. It's part of human nature. But it's our mistakes we often learn the most from if we are willing to look. Do you remember the story about Edison and how many ways he found not to make a light bulb before he succeeded?"

"It was actually Davey who invented the light bulb," she couldn't help pointing out. "What are you trying to say, Mom?"

"Don't be afraid to make mistakes and give others a second chance."

"Like Blake?"

"Yes, and also yourself." They worked silently for a few minutes.

Amanda's mind whirled as she talked herself into going, and then talked herself back out of it again. Her mom's good points went a long way to convincing her, while her stubbornness refused to give up its original verdict on Blake.

When all the clothes were folded neatly in the baskets, Jenny asked, "Any closer to a decision?"

Amanda slowly nodded her head and set her last pair of socks on top of the basket. "I'm going, for all the reasons you said."

"And more importantly for the one I didn't say," added Jenny.

Amanda cocked her head. "What is that?"

She placed the last folded shirt on her stack. "Because for better or for worse, he is your husband and needs your support."

## Chapter Twenty - One

The stress of traveling to the Mansion, mixed with the anxiety of meeting Blake's family, left Amanda on the verge of exhaustion as she paced the blue guest room. She replayed the cold and indifferent greeting she'd received from Blake's family. Rex had pretty much called her a gold-digging whore. Coming had been a mistake and she'd considered several times asking Blake to drop her back at the airport so she could fly home. However, an annoying sense of commitment combined with pity for Blake's dysfunctional family stopped her. The only bright spot in the day had been Ana Maria's warm hug. She could see now why Blake felt at ease with the stout Ecuadorean woman who loved him unconditionally.

She checked the clock, almost show time. It was tempting to plead illness and crawl into the inviting bed to sleep the rest of the bad day away. Instead she steeled herself for the long, uncomfortable night ahead.

A quick once over in the mirror confirmed her ready. Not only had her dress been fitted, but Danyelle had also sent a hair and make-up team to glamourize her within an inch of her life. She looked ready to walk the red carpet at the Oscars and felt utterly ridiculous. The teal gown fit her like a glove, and the heels, which had originally looked murderous, were quite comfortable. But she supposed that three-hundred-dollar heels should be comfortable because she certainly wouldn't spend that much on a pair that tortured her feet no matter how pretty they were. A diamond-studded cuff bracelet woven in an intricate pattern dominated her left wrist. Its matching earrings hung from her ears. Her neck had been left bare so as not to pull focus from her face or gown. When she was complete, Danyelle had come to inspect her and give her stamp of approval. A 'not bad' was all she'd commented before going to attend to the rush of last minute details.

Amanda stepped from the room and made her way to the foyer. As she approached, she saw Blake pacing like a caged lion looking for a way out. He looked sharp in his Armani tuxedo and very much like the inheritor to a multi-billion-dollar fortune. Her heart did an unwanted flip.

When she appeared, he stopped, then his eyes drank in every inch of her. "You look..."

She waited, and when he didn't fill in the blank, then inserted, "Ridiculous?"

He took both her hands. "No! Stunning, amazing, beautiful, rapturous."

Amanda cocked one eyebrow. "Rapturous?"

"I've never seen you look like this."

She cracked a nervous smile. "I don't think anyone has."

Blake fumbled in his pocket for his phone. "Hold on. I want to send your picture to Jenny, or she'll never believe it."

Amanda pasted a smile on her face. With a soft click the shot was taken and sent.

She sighed. "You may as well send it to Alison too."

"Done."

In a moment of clarity, Amanda deciphered the look in his eyes, how he wished desperately they were a happily married couple so he could take her in his arms and steal her away to a bedroom to do what married couples did. A burning sensation ran through her body at the idea, but she couldn't determine if it was from fear or longing.

Danyelle entered in a flowing red dress that swept the ground and made her look as if she were on fire. "Well, at least you're prompt," she remarked to them and double-checked her image in the gilded mirror that hung over a marble-top mahogany table. She turned and straightened Blake's tie.

"It's fine, Mom," he said and pulled away.

"Now, the four of us will form a receiving line. Amanda, you can enjoy the party in the garden and mingle with the guests until we break up the line. Then Blake can join you later after business has been attended to."

Blake cleared his throat. "I'd like Amanda to stand next to me."

After an awkward pause, both women said, "Oh, no, Blake," then looked at each other.

"I don't want to cause any trouble. I'll be fine in the gardens," Amanda assured him.

Danyelle said, "See, Amanda knows her place. You can find her later."

"Mom, it's rude to ask your guest to wander a party alone, especially when she's my wife."

"Blake," Amanda protested.

"Gold digger more like," Cici added as she sauntered in wearing a strapless, fitted cream gown with gold beading.

"Cici, stay out of this," Blake warned. He returned his attention to his mother. "Amanda will stand next to me. I will introduce her as a friend from school and that's the end of it."

"Don't I get a say in this? It is my party after all," Rex proclaimed as he joined the group. He stared at Amanda until she looked away. "Better to have her stand with us where we can keep an eye and an ear on her. Don't want her to spill the beans about your little secret."

"Fine." Danyelle lined them up. "Rex, me, Cici, Blake, Amanda." She tucked a card into Blake's coat pocket. "This is your toast speech for later. Just follow it word for word and don't add any of your extra flair."

"Thanks for the vote of confidence."

Horst entered and took his place at the door. "The guests are arriving, shall I let them in?"

"Yes, thank you, Horst." Danyelle smoothed her skirt over her curvy hips.

The next hour went by in a blur of smiles, kisses, handshakes, nods and greetings before Danyelle announced they could mingle freely in the garden. "Blake, at nine sharp you head to the bandstand to give the toast. Please don't make me come find you."

"I wouldn't want to disappoint you." Blake's surly tone matched his expression.

"It's a little late for that," Rex said and led Danyelle out to the gardens and guests.

Blake turned to Amanda. "Well, that was fun. Can you see now why it was better to elope in Las Vegas than go through a nightmare of a wedding with my Mom running the show? At least in Vegas you got to pick everything out."

Amanda had never seen such a fierce look in his eyes. She said quietly, "I'm sure your Mom is just stressed with organizing the party and sorting things out during this difficult time."

"Nice of you to give her the benefit of the doubt. She didn't do the same for you." He pulled at his cuff links. "Sorry. How about a dance?"

Amanda recalled their last time on the dance floor and a panic of butterflies fluttered in her stomach. "Oh, um, I don't know. Maybe we should get something to eat first."

Blake narrowed his eyes at her. "Are you scared to dance with me, Mandy?"

"No," she said hotly.

"Prove it."

"Are you daring me?" A glint crept into her eye.

"Absolutely."

"Then I accept." She squared her shoulders and threaded her hand through his elbow.

Blake led her onto the dance floor and into his arms. Amanda looked around to see who might be watching them. A feline-looking brunette narrowed her eyes at them. Before she had time to dwell on the hostile look, she noticed the music. "Blake, what kind of dance is this?"

"Waltz."

"Waltz? I don't know how to waltz." Amanda bit on her lower lip fearful of looking like an utter fool in front of everyone.

"It's easy. Just count in threes and I'll lead you through the rest."

"Okay." She took a deep breath and tried to keep time as Blake swirled her around the floor.

The night wore on. Blake gave his toast word-for-word promptly at nine. The cake was cut and passed, business deals were brokered, well wishes given, and the dancing was endless.

Danyelle approached them by the cake table. "Blake, your dad wants you for some business." She looked pointedly at Amanda. "Alone."

"I think I'll go sit down for a bit," Amanda excused herself politely.

"I'll find you soon." Blake walked off with his mom.

Amanda found a seat at an empty table. She reached down and rubbed at an ankle. She wasn't used to wearing heels for such a long time, much less dancing in them. A shadow fell across her.

"Is Blake wearing you out?" asked a female voice.

Amanda looked up to see the feline dark-haired woman from before sitting next to her. She straightened up. "Um, no. I'm just not used to these shoes."

"We didn't get a chance to chat before. I'm Vivian. You've probably heard about me from Blake." She gave a syrupy smile of newly whitened perfect teeth.

"Um, sorry, no." Amanda apologized.

"No." Viv's eyes slid over to Blake across the garden. "I'm surprised. Blake and I go back a long way. In fact, I consider him mine."

Amanda shifted uncomfortably in her seat. There was something about this girl she didn't like. "Yours?"

"Mmm. Blake and I have been lovers since we were sixteen and have had an ongoing arrangement for some time. I expect now that he's graduated and learning to take over the company that he'll be proposing soon."

"Really?" Amanda's face grew hot with embarrassment.

"His family certainly doesn't have any arguments against

me."

"I see." Definitely didn't like this girl.

"Just thought you should know, so you didn't get your hopes up of stealing him away like his first wife," Viv said acidly.

"First wife?" Amanda echoed as her thoughts went into a tail spin.

"Of course it was hushed up, but Blake certainly couldn't keep it from me." She lowered her voice. "He married her in a drunken state in Monte Carlo just after freshman year. His father had to pay her quite a bit of money to keep it from getting into the news. It would've been a big scandal for the company to have a future board member and CEO to have that on his record. Just thought you should know." She stood up with a satisfied smile. "So nice to have met you, Amy."

"Amanda," she corrected automatically but her voice came out hollow. A fissure formed in her heart.

Viv sauntered off and got lost in the crowd.

As Blake approached, she vainly fought down tears.

His smile faded as he took in her face and crouched down in front of her. "What happened?"

Amanda just shook her head and bolted from her chair, through the crowd, and into the dark gardens beyond.

# Chapter Twenty - Two

Amanda sobbed by a fountain. The splash of the water muted the sounds of the party behind her.

"Mandy?" Blake laid a hand on her back.

She slapped it away as she whirled around to face him. "You were married?" she accused.

"Viv told you," he spat out.

"Yes. Is this a habit of yours? Getting drunk and marrying the nearest girl around?"

"No," Blake said quietly. "I know it looks that way, but that isn't how it is."

"Oh, really?" Amanda crossed her arms over her chest and scowled at him. "Then please enlighten me."

"The girl I married in Monte Carlo drugged me."

"You can't really expect me to believe that. I'm not stupid."

"No, you're not. You're smart and beautiful and,"

"Don't distract me with compliments," Amanda snapped.

He sagged down onto the stone bench surrounding the stone fountain. "I met Gia the first day in Monte Carlo and she latched onto me like a tick. She was highly attractive and flattering, and I fell for her whole act. Toward the end of the week, she kept intimating how heartbroken she'd be when we had to part and suggested we should secretly elope. It would be so romantic. I know, I'm not the best at picking up on things, but I refused to agree. I knew my parents would be furious, plus I wasn't in love with her. On the last night, we gambled and drank in the casinos, and at some point she slipped something into my drink. I woke up the next morning married to her and with no memory of what had happened."

Still processing his words, she slowly asked, "You mean the date rape drug?"

"Yes. Apparently it works in reverse." An ironic laugh escaped his lips.

"What did your parents say?"

"Everything, and then some." Blake scooped up some water with his hand, then let it drain through.

"That's why they were so angry and kicked you out after Vegas," Amanda murmured as she sank down next to him.

"Yes." He continued to play with the water.

"They think I drugged you, too?" Amanda's voice was small.

"They haven't said so, but I imagine they're thinking it along with the gold digger they've already called you."

She rested her head in her hands. "This is so much worse than I imagined." They sat in silence for a long moment. Slowly, Amanda brought her head up. "And what's the story with Viv? She claims to be your lover and expects your impending engagement soon."

Blake let out a heavy sigh. "Viv is living in her own little fantasy world. I have no interest in her and haven't since I went to college. I've tried to make her understand, but she just tries to dig her claws in deeper."

"So you do have a history together?" Amanda pried.

"Yes, but do you really want to hear it?"

Amanda thought it over for a moment, then said, "Yes, I think it's best for both of us if we're just honest about things."

He stared up at the stars and in a flat voice related his history. "My dad invented biofuel when I was ten. By the time I hit ninth grade, we'd moved here and every girl in school was after me. So, for tenth grade, dad sent me to an all-boys academy to focus on my studies, except there were problems there too. I spent my junior and senior years at a highly exclusive private school here. I met Viv and her family at the country club the summer in between sophomore and junior year. We lost our virginity together and spent quite a bit of the next two years together. I ended our relationship shortly after the start of freshman year at college, but she persists in hanging on, saying I'll come back around one day and that we belong together. Every time I turn around she's in my face, trying to kiss me and rekindle a dead flame." He splashed some of the water and a few drops fell onto his pants.

Too many conflicting feelings swirled through Amanda and she couldn't make any sense of them.

The silence between them stretched until Blake stood up. "We'd better get back. I need to fulfill my duties."

Amanda stood and wiped under her eyes. "Thanks for explaining things to me."

"There's someone I want to introduce you to." He led her through the crowds and tables as he searched. Finally, they arrived at a table where a brunette woman in a pale yellow gown sat by a little boy with the same hair and brown eyes.

"Good evening, Aunt Janelle."

"Blake! We haven't seen you all night. I told Ben we'd have to go in five minutes whether we saw you or not."

"Blake!" Ben scrambled out of his seat and threw his arms around Blake, who bent down just in time to receive the little boy's crushing hug.

"Easy, big boy! You'll knock me over; you're getting so strong!"

Blake's transformation with his cousin surprised Amanda. Here was another side she wasn't aware of.

Blake turned to her. "Ben, Janelle, this is my friend Amanda from school."

Amanda shook hands with both of them. "It's so nice to meet you. If Blake had introduced us earlier, I'd have come over here to hang out at the fun table."

They sat down and Ben claimed Blake's lap. Ben resumed demolishing the food on his plate.

"So, Ben, how old are you?" Amanda asked.

"Six," he said around the big mouthful of cake he'd just shoveled in.

"Don't talk with your mouth full," Janelle reminded her son.

"Wow!" Amanda widened her eyes on purpose. "You're big for six."

"He's tall," Janelle agreed.

"Does that mean you're in first grade?" Amanda asked.

Ben shook his head in the affirmative.

"I bet you're a whiz at math." Amanda said.

"Two times two is four," Ben said, after swallowing his cake.

"Yep. Definitely a math whiz."

Ben returned her smile, then whispered something to Blake, who looked over at Amanda and said, "Yes, she is."

She gave them a quizzical look. "I am what?"

"Can't tell you." Blake shook his head. "Guy stuff."

Ben beamed up at Blake then devoured a cracker and cheese.

"Blake," Danyelle called as she approached the table. "Your father needs you to speak to a few members of the board." She looked to Janelle. "Having a nice time?"

"It's a grand party, Danyelle. I'll have to go in a few minutes though. It's way past Ben's bedtime."

"You can put him to sleep in my room if you want to stay longer," Blake offered.

"That's sweet of you Blake, but I'll take him home tonight."

Blake gave Ben another hug. "I have to go now, Ben."

"When are we going to play baseball?" Ben said with a pout. "You promised to play with me after your trip."

"I know I did, big guy, but I have to go away again. The next time I come back, we'll play. Okay?"

Ben still frowned, but said, "Okay."

Blake ruffled Ben's hair. "Be good for your mom." Before Blake joined his mother, who tapped her foot impatiently, he whispered to Amanda, "I'll see you when I can get away."

While Ben attacked his cake, Janelle asked, "Have you known Blake long?" She moved the umbrella in her drink out of the way to take a sip.

"Four years."

Janelle set down her drink and ran a finger around the ring. "Hmm. Interesting, He's never mentioned you."

Amanda shrugged. "That's not surprising. We've been part of the same social group, but never close."

"And yet you're here." Janelle raised her eyebrows.

"Um, yes." Amanda wished she had a drink to hide behind.

"Something must have changed."

"Mmm," she said noncommittally.

"Is Blake staying with you?"

Her question caught Amanda completely off guard.

"Don't look so surprised. I know Blake isn't staying here or he would've been at Ben's baseball games and taken him to the park. They're very attached to each other and have been since we both lost loved ones."

"I can see that." She fiddled with her bracelet. "If I may ask, what happened to your husband?"

Janelle's eyes dropped to the table. "Killed in the Middle East; one of the terrorist attacks on the embassy. He was only there for a week to sort out some business and just happened to be in the wrong place at the wrong time."

"I'm very sorry," Amanda said genuinely. "That must be awful."

"It is." A moment of silence followed.

"Mom, what's this?" Ben held up a black oblong object.

Janelle raised her eyes to her son. "It's an olive, dear."

Ben examined it. "Do I like olives?"

"Why don't you try it and find out?"

Ben popped it in his mouth.

"You didn't answer my question about Blake," Janelle gently reminded Amanda.

"Oh, yes, uh, he's staying with my family."

"So, Rex finally threw him out. He's been threatening to for years. I wonder why."

Amanda was spared answering when Ben gagged, sputtered and fell off his chair onto the grass.

"Ben!" Janelle cried and dropped to the ground next to her son with Amanda on his other side.

"He's choking."

Ben gasped for air and attempted to cough. His eyes pleaded with them for help.

"Ben!" Janelle's loud cry attracted the attention of the nearby guests. "Help!" Janelle began to cry.

Out of the corner of her eye, Amanda saw a gentleman whip out his cell phone as her training kicked in. Total calm settled over her. She pulled Ben into her lap in a sitting position, then wrapped her arms around him and made her hands into one fist. Her fist thrusted against his sternum in an attempt to force the object loose. Nothing. She laid Ben back down, did a finger swipe and repeated the process over and over.

By the time Blake reached them, Ben's eyes had started to roll back and his skin was pale.

"Amanda, he's turning blue." Blake's whisper was laced with fear.

"I know. I've got to get air in him." She repeated the Heimlich once more then checked his mouth. "It's moved. I can almost reach it, but if I accidentally push on it, it could fall further down his windpipe." She shifted Ben onto his back, barely aware of Janelle's sobs. She covered Ben's mouth with hers, gave a breath, then started chest compressions. She alternated between those and the Heimlich. Just as the EMT's ran up the object flew out. Blake caught it - an olive pit.

Ben sputtered and gasped. The EMT's quickly assessed Ben's condition in the midst of all the onlookers.

The older EMT asked the sobbing Janelle. "Are you his mother?"

She nodded, too overcome to speak. "He's going to be fine, I think. We'd still like to take him to the hospital; to be sure he's okay. Would you like to accompany him in the ambulance?"

"Yes."

The younger EMT scooped up Ben.

The older EMT looked at Amanda. "You're the one administering to him, right?"

"Yes, I'm a nurse." Amanda shook from the adrenaline rush.

"Good work. If you hadn't, we'd probably have been too late

to save him."

Janelle threw her arms around Amanda. "Thank you, thank you," she sobbed.

Weakly, Amanda patted Janelle's back. "You're welcome. Don't worry. Ben will be okay."

The older EMT spoke to Amanda. "We just need you to come to the ambulance for a minute to do some paperwork, then we can take Ben to the hospital."

Conscious of all the eyes on her, Amanda nodded and followed the EMTs through the crowd. She heard murmurs of appreciation and a few people patted her on the back as she passed by. She wasn't aware of Blake at her side until they reached the ambulance. As they loaded Ben in, Blake crushed her in a hug. She was surprised to see tears in his eyes.

"Thank you for saving him," he whispered in her ear. "I couldn't have—" his voice broke.

"It's okay." Amanda reassured him.

The younger EMT brought her a clipboard. "Just fill this out and we'll be on our way."

"Sure." Amanda scribbled furiously so they could get Ben to the hospital. A few minutes later she returned the clipboard.

"Janelle, please call me later to tell me how Ben is," Blake called to her as she sat in the ambulance running her hand over Ben's forehead.

"Of course," she replied.

"Do we need to treat you for shock?" The older EMT asked Amanda as he shut the doors to the ambulance.

Amanda shook her head. "No, I'll be fine once the adrenaline wears off. I've been through this before. I'm good."

Blake spoke up, "I'll take care of her."

The doors shut, the lights flashed and the ambulance drove away.

Danyelle rushed up all a flutter. "What's going on?"

"Mom, where have you been?"

"I was in the bathroom, then there was an issue in the kitchen, and then Cici came in all upset because she said Ben was being hauled away in an ambulance. Is Janelle with him? Is he all right? Oh, please don't let anything happen to that dear boy. He's all Janelle has left." Tears welled in her eyes. "We can't lose another."

"Mom, calm down." Blake led her into the house with Amanda in their wake. "Sit down, take deep breaths." He seated her on the divan trimmed in gold brocade.

Amanda grabbed some tissues from a box on the hall table and handed them to Danyelle, then took a seat on an overstuffed armchair.

Blake sat down beside Danyelle. "Ben is going to be fine. He choked on an olive pit. I guess he didn't know it had one. We nearly lost him, but thankfully Amanda was there. She saved him."

"Saved him?" Danyelle's eyes shifted to Amanda.

"Amanda's a nurse. The medics said if she hadn't helped Ben, they would've gotten here too late to save him."

Forgetting about clothes and make-up, Danyelle burst into tears and sobbed into Blake's shoulder.

He rubbed her back but kept his eyes on Amanda. "It's okay, Mom. Ben's going to be just fine. They took him to the hospital to be sure and to check his oxygen levels and whatever else they need to do. I'm sure after a good night's sleep he'll be back to his usual bouncing-off- the-walls self."

Amanda watched them and wondered why Danyelle was coming apart at the seams. Yes, the situation with Ben had been dramatic and could've turned out very differently, but everything was fine. Why was she such a mess?

It took Danyelle several minutes to pull herself together. When she did, she stood up and walked over. "Thank you," she whispered and pulled a stunned Amanda into a tight hug. "I apologize for my behavior. It has been quite unchristian of me. I'm grateful Blake brought you."

"It's fine, Mrs. Worthington. I understand your reaction to me given the circumstances and the past."

"That's very kind of you, dear, but I'm afraid it's not. We've been dreadfully unfair. Please call me Danyelle."

There was an awkward pause.

"Mom, you'll have to redo your make-up. Go freshen up and we'll see you outside."

"Oh, yes. Right." She fluttered away.

Amanda watched her go. "Is she going to be all right? She's awfully upset."

"Yes." Blake looked at the hallway entrance Danyelle had disappeared through but didn't elaborate. He got lost in thought for a moment, then returned his attention to Amanda. "Hey, Mandy, are you okay? The medic said something about you going into shock. Do you need to lie down? Can I get you a drink of water?"

Amanda waved at him. "No, I'm fine. The after effects are starting to wear off. But I would like to sit down for just a moment." She sat on the divan Danyelle had just occupied and Blake joined her. A few minutes later, Cici skidded in her heels to a halt in the foyer.

"There you are!" she called. "Everyone is looking for you."

"All right Cici, I'm coming." Blake stood up.

She frowned and waved him away. "Not you. Her!" She pointed to Amanda.

"Why?" Amanda asked in surprise.

"Everyone wants to meet the girl who saved Ben's life, of course! Naturally the story has gotten exaggerated and there are all sorts of rumors flying about what actually happened, but they all want to meet you."

"Looks like you just became the belle of the ball." Blake winked at Amanda.

"Oh, no, they can't possibly want to. I've been around most of the night and hardly anyone has said two words to me."

"That's how it is with the upper crust. You're totally beneath their notice until you do something amazing, and then they all want to rub elbows with you hoping some of your amazing will rub off on them." Blake helped her up.

"Oh, Blake, I can't. I don't do this sort of thing."

"Save lives you mean?"

"Well, no, I mean, I save lives, but –"

"Oh, just come on already." Cici tugged on Amanda's other arm. "Go have your five minutes of fame so they can get on with forgetting about you."

"Cici!" Blake glared at his sister, who glared right back. "That's no way to thank Amanda for what she did for Ben."

"Fine. Thank you." She dropped Amanda an exaggerated curtsy. "Now, can you two get out there?" She turned on her heel and click-clacked her way across the marble floor.

"I guess saving lives doesn't rank very high in Cici's book," Amanda commented as they made their way back outdoors to the party.

"Cici's grateful, she's just mad about having her spotlight stolen for a while. She'll get over it."

## Chapter Twenty - Three

For the next hour Amanda endured handshakes, air kisses and gushing. Finally, she escaped the crowds to a quiet, hedged part of the garden where, heedless of potential grass stains to her dress, she lay down and star gazed until the strains of music stopped.

Grass-padded steps approached. "This is where you've been?" Blake asked slightly out of breath.

Startled from her thoughts, she sat up. "Yes. Why?"

"I've spent the last half hour or so looking for you." He helped her to her feet.

"I'm sorry, Blake. I just had to get away from everyone. It's been a pretty full night."

"I understand," he said as they headed back to the house. "But next time, tell me where you're going so I know where to look. I've probably missed saying good-bye and that's going to put my dad off."

By the time they reached the house, the staff had started the cleanup process.

"Uh, oh." Blake hurried into the house and made it to the foyer to join his parents and Cici just as Horst closed the door after the last guest.

"Where've you been?" Rex growled with his words just a hint slurred. "You missed saying good-bye." He looked at Amanda. "Judging from the state of her dress I'd say you were out getting your kicks on with her."

Amanda shrank toward the wall.

"Dad!" Blake's eyes glinted with anger.

"Don't 'Dad' me," roared Rex. "If you'd spend as much time on this company as you do unzipping your pants we'd be a lot better off."

"Really, Rex." Danyelle said. "I think it's time for bed."

"How could you say that after what Amanda did tonight?" Blake roared.

"Oh, you mean 'saving Ben'? I bet she planned it out with Janelle and Ben ahead of time just to make herself look good to us and all our friends so that if push came to shove, she could go to the media with a sob story of how she's a do-gooder and we treated her like garbage so there'd be even more scandal."

Blake stared dumbfounded at his father before he crossed his arms over his chest. "I think Mom's right. You should go to bed before you make even more of a fool of yourself than you already have. In the morning, I expect you to apologize to Amanda."

Danyelle tugged on Rex's arm. "Come on, dear."

He shook her off. "No, tonight I'm going to speak my mind. He needs to hear this. You are a disgrace to this family. If Andrew were here, then I could tolerate it. But I can't stand by and let you ruin your life and by reflection my company with your actions."

"If Andrew were here, we wouldn't be having this conversation!" Blake shouted. "If perfect Andrew were here, he'd be happily running the company and doing a great job of it. But Andrew isn't here and you're stuck with disappointing, bad-decision-making Blake who can never do anything right and never measure up to Andrew."

"Stop this!" yelled Danyelle with tears in her eyes.

Blake continued. "You know you weren't the only one who lost everything that day on the mountainside. You aren't the only one who wishes I'd been there to stop him. I know you blame me for his death on top of everything else. But you aren't the only one who's been hurting all these years. You aren't the only one who lost a piece of himself that day!" Tears flowed fast down Blake's cheeks as he stormed out of the room.

Amanda stared at the broken family for a moment before she followed after him. He'd headed down the hallway that led to the bedrooms and entered the one room he'd left out of their tour earlier that afternoon. Amanda paused in the doorway and waited, unsure of what to say. Unashamed tears flowed down his face, and he made no attempt to wipe them away as he stared at the framed photograph in his hand.

"Come in and close the door, please," he said softly, his voice husky from crying. Slowly he turned the photo around to face her. "This is my brother, Andrew."

Amanda took the photo in her hands. All decked out in ski gear, the brothers' faces smiled up at her. She noticed they had the same jawline and shape of the eyes and brows, but while Blake was fair-haired, Andrew was dark. She sank down on the bed next to Blake and returned the photo.

"Andrew was my older brother. This was taken on the first day of our ski trip in the Alps. He died a few days later."

"How?" Her voice came out barely above a whisper and instinctively she took Blake's hand.

Blake swallowed hard and his voice shook as he recalled the tragic vacation. "I'd been injured the day before. I'd torqued my knee on a snowboard run and was out of commission for the day, so I stayed at the lodge reading a local history book I picked up in the lobby and watching sports on the big screen TV."

"Reading?" Amanda couldn't help say. She'd never pictured Blake as much of a reader.

His lips formed a tight line. "Yes, Mandy, I do read. I'd have majored in history if dad had let me."

"Sorry, go on."

"Andrew and I went with a couple of friends. I'm afraid we're all a bit daredevils. Anyways, the guys had gotten tired of the mapped-out runs – which as far as slopes go were pretty awesome – and decided to board down the backside of the mountain clearly marked as a danger zone."

Amanda put a hand over her mouth. "Oh, no."

"Seamus went first and Andrew right after him. Seamus's board started an avalanche but by the time Andrew realized it, he'd already begun flying down the hill. They tried to out-run it or get out of the path, but it was no use. Chris came back to the lodge to get help as soon as the avalanche started, while Finn stayed at the top of the mountain to see where they landed so he might be able to direct the rescue team where to find them. They never did."

Amanda's heart broke as she imagined losing one of her brothers in such a way and tears ran down her cheeks. She gripped Blake's hand tighter. "I'm so sorry."

Blake kept his eyes on the photo. "Andrew and I were only eighteen months apart and very close. He was the perfect one to lead the company. He had dad's science brain and understood everything that went on in the lab and had even started some side projects. He also had a head for business. Numbers just made sense to him, and he was great with people." He set the photo back on the nightstand. "Everything I'm not. I wish every day he was here. I miss him so much." He turned to Amanda and cried into her shoulder.

She rubbed his back, stroked his hair, and cried with him. She felt his hot tears soak through her dress and wondered if anyone had held him while he cried after the accident. How long had he been carrying this pain around, holding these tears in? How had she not known about his loss? Her ignorance and judgments of him pressed on her heart. She didn't have just a lot to learn about Blake, she had a lot to learn about herself too.

Eventually, their tears all spent, Blake raised red-rimmed eyes up to her.

"When did he die?" Amanda asked.

"Between our sophomore and junior year."

"Blake, I'm sorry, I didn't know." He'd been grieving over a lost brother while she'd been busy hating him. The thought made her sick to her stomach. How could she have been so blind?

"I didn't talk about it. Even now, we rarely mention his name. It's like a raw wound too painful to touch. It seems like it will never heal."

She wiped a tear off his cheek with her thumb. "Some wounds can't be healed and leave a scar behind on your soul, but they can be diminished and accepted, which helps to ease the pain."

"Where did you learn that? From your parents?"

"Actually, at church."

"Ah, yes, church. Mom started going to church after Andrew died and tried hard to get us all to join her. I tried a few times, but just couldn't wrap my head around a God who would let my brother die."

"God didn't let your brother die. God allows us the freedom to make our own choices."

Blake pulled back from her. "You're saying Andrew's death was his own fault?"

"No, Blake. Andrew died in a tragic accident. Unfortunately, those happen for no reason and that's the hardest thing to try to accept. But don't you think if Andrew was a good person, doing good things on earth, that he's busy doing good things in heaven too?"

"I never thought about it like that."

"Well, maybe if you go to church you will."

"Do you think I'll ever see Andrew again?" Blake's voice was filled with desperate longing.

"Of course I do," Amanda said with conviction. "I believe we get to be with our loved ones when we return to heaven. I believe love endures even after this life."

"How can you be so sure?"

"Because I feel it." She rested her hand over her heart. "In here."

Blake rested his hand on top of hers and Amanda didn't pull away. She looked at their hands and then into his eyes. Her heart started to pound as Blake moved closer, his gaze unwavering.

"I think Andrew would've really liked you."

"You think so?" Amanda knew that if she didn't move Blake would kiss her. Part of her wanted to let the kiss happen, but a stubborn part of her wanted to get up and leave as fast as possible.

"Yes."

Before she could decide, Blake's lips joined hers and the

magic rush from four years ago passed between them. He kissed her cautiously, tenderly, slowly, holding back the passion she knew he felt, the passion that would make her run. She couldn't ignore the warmth that instantly spread from her lips to her toes, or her response. She surrendered for a moment, before panic catapulted her back away from Blake's kiss. Frantic words tumbled out of her mouth. "We can't. You can't. You're confusing me. We are getting this marriage annulled. I'm going to Africa. This can't happen," she stammered. She pushed herself off the bed and propelled herself to the door.

Only a half-step behind her, he grabbed her wrist. "Why are you so afraid?" he said softly.

"This wasn't supposed to happen," she said between breaths. "We weren't supposed to get married. I didn't like you then. I'm not supposed to like you now. Learning about you and your family is changing things. I shouldn't have come here. You shouldn't have come to Iowa. This is messing up all my plans."

"Didn't you ever plan for love, Mandy?" He turned her to face him and ran a finger along her jawline.

She tried to ignore the tingling sensation his finger created. "No. Yes. In about two or three years."

He cupped her chin with his hand. "That's not how it works."

"Well, it has to wait. Right now it's not in the schedule."

He gave a low laugh. "You are so sexy when you are being stubborn." He moved in to kiss her once more.

The small fissure in her heart threatened to explode, leaving her heart entirely exposed and vulnerable to breaking. "Please, Blake, I can't," she whimpered.

He pressed his forehead to hers and ran his hands up and down her arms leaving goose bumps in their wake. "Okay, Mandy, but just so you know, no matter what we're doing or what we're talking about, I'm going to be thinking about kissing you."

## Chapter Twenty - Four

After breakfast Amanda packed up her bag and met Blake at the door. "Can we say goodbye to Ana Maria before we go?"

He smiled. "Absolutely."

They found Ana Maria in the kitchen. "You are going?" she asked.

"Yes. I'm going to take Amanda to the ranch before we leave tomorrow to return to Iowa." He hugged her.

"Then you take these," she said and handed him a grocery bag.

"What's in here?" He peeked inside the bag.

"Cookies and a few of your other favorites, plus lunch. Not sure what'll you'll find up there for dinner. The cook is on vacation this week."

"No worries, Ana Maria," Blake said. "Amanda is good in the kitchen. She even taught me how to scramble eggs and make toast the other day."

Ana Maria beamed at Amanda. "Good for you. I've been trying to teach him how to cook for ages, but he just wasn't interested. He said it didn't matter because I'd always be around to cook for him."

"That reminds me." Blake took a card from his pocket. "This is Amanda's mom's recipe for macaroni and cheese. I think it just might be better than yours."

Ana Maria raised her eyebrows. "Hmm. I'll have to try it then." She grabbed a blank recipe card from a drawer and scribbled hastily on it with a pen then handed it to Blake. "You return this to her mother."

Blake looked down at the card. "Your cookie recipe? Are you

serious?"

"It is only fair to trade one favorite recipe for another."

"Thank you, Ana Maria." He put it in his pocket and gave her a hug.

"Will you be back soon?" she asked.

Blake shook his head. "I was only invited back for dad's party. I'm still banished for now, until I straighten things out with Amanda."

Ana Maria turned her soulful brown eyes on Amanda. "It was a pleasure to meet you, Amanda. I hope I will see you again." She gave Amanda a hug.

"I'm not sure." Amanda said, sorry to disappoint the kind woman who had been the only welcoming person in this house.

"I heard about last night. You'll be back." Ana Maria patted her arm.

"Master Rex still has a very low opinion of me," Amanda said.

"Maybe. But I'd say he's more likely embarrassed about what he said and the way he behaved. He's very proud sometimes." Ana Maria took Amanda's hand. "Blake, may I have a word with Amanda?"

"Sure. Bye, Ana Maria. I'll miss you." He stepped outside the kitchen door.

"I know you have to make your own decisions, but I'm going to put my two cents in and tell you that I wish you'd stay married to Blake." Ana Maria patted Amanda's hand.

That was the last thing Amanda had expected her to say. "Why?"

"You are good for him. I can see the difference in him that being with you has made in just a few short weeks. He is almost like he was before Mister Andrew died, but with more maturity. He seems more ready to do the right thing and accept his responsibilities. Blake has made a lot of mistakes in the past, even some very big ones, and I won't make excuses for him. I never have, but I fear that if your marriage ends, we may just lose him completely."

"I'm sorry Ana Maria, but I never would've married Blake if

I'd been in my right mind. I have plans and this just doesn't fit right now."

Ana Maria sighed. "I understand. Please know that inside, Blake has a good heart. I think that's why the money and Mister Andrew's death have been so hard for him. His desire to please those around him and make them happy has often overcome his morality and often caused him pain and regret. This family has been very lost for some time now. I have hoped and prayed for them and sometimes despaired that things can't be repaired and made better. Blake is the biggest reason that I stayed."

"I don't understand."

"Success changed their lives. Mister Andrew and Miss Cici managed to adjust to the change of lifestyle well enough, but it was the wrong age for Blake to do so, and being the middle child, well – he just got lost."

"May I ask you a question?"

"Yes."

"Was Blake really married before?"

A dark look creased Ana Maria's features. "Yes. I try not to judge others, but she wasn't an honorable person and did very wrong by Blake."

"Thank you. Just one more."

"Are you sure there's just one more?" A smile played at the corner of Ana Maria's lips.

"Yes. What's the story with Vivian?"

Ana Maria's smile faded. "Miss Vivian and Blake have history, but he ended it some years ago, yet she still chases him and frightens away any other girl who invades her territory, so to speak. She has some nasty claws."

Amanda hugged Ana Maria, relieved that Blake had told her the truth about everything. "Thank you so much."

"You're welcome. Now, go and enjoy the ranch. It's far more cheerful than here."

Amanda and Blake nibbled on cookies on the way to the ranch. An hour later, they pulled into the Worthington Ranch, a log-cabin-style building about a third of the size of The Mansion.

Amanda studied the place while Blake and Duke got the bags and made arrangements for their trip to the airport the next day.

Blake called, "Come on, Mandy. I'll show you the ranch."

The interior was done in the typical Texas southwestern style. Lots of leather, steer skulls, Indian weavings, statues of cowboys, and the like adorned the ranch. Blake led them straight to the kitchen where they put away the food Ana Maria had sent with them.

"I'll show you the bedrooms," Blake said. He retrieved their bags from the front hall as they passed through.

"I can carry mine," Amanda offered.

"I got it. I think I can carry my wife's bag." He smiled at her and for once she didn't snap at him for calling her his wife. "Besides, your bag is light, especially for a girl. Cici would've needed at least three bags for this trip."

"Sounds just like Tiffany."

"Man, I wouldn't want to put them in a room together. Talk about a cat fight."

They walked up a staircase that opened onto another living room area with comfortable chairs and a great view of the flat land and sky that surrounded the ranch. Amanda paused for a moment to take it in.

"I never knew Texas looked like this."

Blake smiled at her. "This is your first trip to Texas, isn't it?"

"Pretty much. The first time I visited Texas I was a year old so, of course, I don't' remember it. My parents came for some reason." Amanda stared out the floor-to-ceiling windows as this area looked over the two-story living room below. "It's quite a view."

"Wait until you see it at sunset." Blake led her to a bedroom on the left. The southwestern theme was toned down in here. "Is this all right?" he asked as he set her bag on the bed.

"This is great," she said.

"This one gets sun in the morning, so you can watch the sunrise if you want, or if you'd rather sleep in, you can have the one on the other side of the wall that faces the sunset."

"This is fine. I'd like to see the sunrise." She looked at him. "Where will you sleep?"

"Well, I think it would be too much to presume to share a bed with my wife, so I'll be across the hall on the sunrise side too. Usually I'd pick the sunset view, but we have to catch a plane in the morning and it'll be just as well to get up early." Blake went to put his bag in the other room.

Amanda walked to the window and thought over what Blake had said about sleeping in the same room. It bothered her, but not for the same reasons a remark like that in the past would've done. What bothered her was that the idea didn't seem so foreign to her. There was so much more to Blake than she'd ever imagined, and what she'd learned about him and his life in the past twenty-four hours put her in a tailspin. How could her feelings be changing so rapidly in such a short amount of time?

Blake popped his head in and studied Amanda lost in thought at the window. Her actions and behavior toward him since arriving in Texas had given him hope that perhaps her opinion of him was changing. She seemed just a little softer toward him. At least she wasn't biting his head off all the time, and she seemed better able to abide his presence instead of automatically going the opposite direction. He hoped she would still change her mind about ending their marriage. There was still time to call off the paperwork, at least he hoped so. He wasn't sure he'd be able to convince her to marry him a second time if she was sober.

"Hey," he called softly from the doorway.

Amanda startled and turned to him. "Hey."

He stepped just inside the room. "Sorry, I didn't mean to surprise you."

"No, it's fine. I was just thinking."

"So, I saw. Any chance you want to share those thoughts?"

She shook her head.

"Okay. Well, how about we pack a picnic lunch, saddle up some horses, and go for a little ride?"

"Ride?" Amanda gulped.

"You have ridden a horse before, right?"

"Well, just around the paddock at the county fair when I was a kid."

"Oh. Well, it's just like that, only the horse will be a bit bigger and we'll ride a bit farther." He pointed to the bathroom. "You'll probably want to make good use of that jet tub later though."

"Won't it be dangerous though?"

"No. I'll put you on Ol' Bess. She's about the gentlest horse that ever lived."

Amanda bit her lower lip. "Okay."

Down in the kitchen, they assembled a picnic lunch, then Blake led her out to the stables. He handed her a pair of boots from off a shelf. "Here, these should fit you pretty well. They're Cici's extra pair. I think you're about the same size."

Amanda slid them on. "They're fine."

Blake pulled down his pair and pulled them on. "Jed?" he called into the stable.

"Back here," called a voice from the far end of the barn.

They walked toward the voice. Amanda noticed half the stalls were empty and admired the horses that remained. She especially liked the look of a cream-colored horse.

They found Jed in a workshop repairing a saddle. He looked like a cowboy out of a storybook: weather-beaten face, salt-and-pepper hair, faded jeans, boots, and his hat rested on a hook just over the tack table.

"Hey, Jed," said Blake. "This is Amanda."

Jed shook her hand. Then with a true Texan drawl said, "Nice to meet you."

"And you," she replied.

"You going for a ride?" Jed asked.

"Yep." Blake said.

"To the shack?"

"Yep."

"Shack?" Amanda asked.

"It's not really a shack," Blake explained. "Jed just doesn't like to use fancy words like pavilion or gazebo."

"Shack's good enough," Jed put in.

"We're going to take Rascal and Ol' Bess."

Jed shook his head. "Can't take Ol' Bess. She threw a shoe yesterday. Blacksmith can't get here until tomorrow. Weddin'. You'll have to take Carousel instead."

"Oh." Blake lowered his head and Amanda saw him ponder the change of horses for a moment. He said, "Well, I guess that'll be okay. It's not very far."

A little red flag waved in her head at Blake's reaction. "Is Carousel a gentle horse?" Amanda asked Jed.

"She's gentle, just skittish sometimes. You should be okay. Just use a firm hand with her."

Amanda looked at Blake. "Maybe this isn't such a good idea."

"No, it'll be fine. I really want you to see the ranch."

With misgiving, Amanda watched Jed and Blake saddle the horses and secure the lunch.

Jed called her over. "Time to introduce you to Carousel. Put your hand out like this and let her get a good whiff of you, then feed her this lump of sugar. Next, slowly work your way down her head and neck to her shoulder and give her a gentle pat. Talk to her all the while so she can get used to the sound of your voice. She'll respond better to your commands that way."

Amanda followed his instructions all the while feeling nervous and self-conscious.

"That's good. Time to get on." He bent over and cupped his hands together to help her up.

Amanda placed her foot in his hands and he boosted her onto Carousel. She slid her feet into the stirrups and Jed adjusted them to fit. Jed quickly walked her through how to command Carousel to go and stop.

"You won't need to trot or canter or gallop on her today, and with you being a new rider. I wouldn't recommend it. So, don't get any crazy ideas about doing so."

"I won't," Amanda was vehement.

"Blake's an experienced rider. He'll take good care of you." Jed led Carousel out of the barn while Amanda tried, without success, to find the right position to sit in so she wouldn't bounce so much and be too sore later. Once outside the barn Blake pulled alongside her.

"Ready?" he asked.

"As ready as I'll ever be," she sighed. Inside she was a mixture of fear about being up on a horse and exhilarated at having her first real ride. "Thanks, Jed."

He tipped his hat to her, and she and Blake set off. Blake talked to her about the ranch and told her all about how to hold her reins, and sit in the saddle all the way to the picnic spot at the shack. When they arrived, he dismounted first, tied his horse to the hitching post and then tied Carousel.

He walked around to Amanda and stretched up his arms to her. She hesitated a split second before swinging her leg over the horse. She grasped his shoulders and a moment later her feet touched the ground.

"Now, was that so bad?" Blake's hands lingered on her waist.

"No, Carousel was a well-behaved horse. But I see what you meant about the jet tub." She let go of his shoulders and felt his fingers slowly slide away from her body. Butterflies erupted in her stomach.

A few minutes later they settled onto the red-and-white checkered blanket spread across the wood-plank floor of the gazebo and spread out the food in between them.

Amanda slathered a thick slice of homemade wheat bread with boysenberry jam and took a bite. "Mmm," she said. "That's good."

"Well, we were lucky. Cecilia's baking day was yesterday and the hands are all out on the range right now or it would've been all gone. I bet Jed already went through half a loaf on his own."

"I can't blame him."

Blake reached for a cookie.

Amanda swatted his hand. "You can't have that. You have to eat your food and fruit first. Ana Maria's orders."

"Really?"

"Really." She flashed a smile at him.

"Fine then. You're the boss." He bit into his sandwich.

"Hardly." She gazed out over the plain. "You can see for miles out here. It just keeps going and going."

Blake looked in the same direction. "That's what I love about coming out here. No one around. No one to nag. No one to be disappointed with me." He glanced over at her. "Well, except you're here today, so I guess there's still someone to disappoint."

Amanda frowned. "That's not fair, Blake. It's already been several hours since you last disappointed me."

"Really? Guess I'm making progress."

"Maybe we both are."

Quiet fell between them as they munched and took in the beauty of the golden plain and the brilliant blue sky.

When Blake finished his sandwich and reached for a cookie, Amanda asked, "Do you come out here a lot?"

"Tons since Andrew died. I'm here unless I have to be at the Mansion. It's too depressing there and well, you saw how it is."

"Yeah, I did." She waited a moment before timidly asking. "Did you and your dad ever get along?" She tucked a loose piece of hair behind her ear.

"Um, yeah, actually we did. But once I went to college things sort of fell apart. He wanted me to major in science and be like him, but I'm just not. I didn't get his brain. I barely made it through high school biology and chemistry and needed tutors for both just to get that far. So, he said I had to go into business or pay my own way. At least with business I'd be able to run the company even if I couldn't run the lab."

"And how did that go?"

"Fair, I guess. I mean, business I can wrap my head around, although the serious accountant and econ stuff is over my head. But I'm good with people, so that's one advantage. Dad isn't the best people person; in case you hadn't noticed. He'd rather be hanging with test tubes and getting covered with muck in the lab than sit through a board meeting or meet with investors."

"What about Cici?"

"She's going to be supreme ruler of the international affairs department. She has a talent for languages and people, and she loves to travel. So, she's happy there."

"I meant, were you two ever close?"

"More than we are now. Andrew and I were tight because we were so close in age. Cici got left out a bit because of that, I suppose. But we looked after her and protected her like big brothers do for little sisters. She and my mom were really tight. Everything fell apart when Andrew died. We haven't been the same since. We can't even communicate properly, as you saw. There's just too much pain, but instead of it bringing us together like it would for most families, it's driven us apart. The gulf just seems too wide to cross anymore. I don't think we're ever going to heal from it." He stood up and walked to the edge of the gazebo.

Amanda followed him debating whether to take his hand in hers. In the end she chickened out. "I don't think you can heal from a wound like the loss of a loved one, but I think perhaps you can come to a place of peace."

"Peace." Blake clasped his hands behind his head. "That would be nice." He looked at her out of the corner of his eye and stifled the impulse to wrap an arm around her shoulders. She was still too skittish when it came to physical contact with him, like a new horse who had to learn to trust him before he could ever get in the ring with, much less ride. "You're asking a lot of personal questions today."

"Sorry. It's just . . . I'm trying to figure you out. You're not what I originally thought you were."

"You mean a rich playboy with no moral center?"

Amanda gasped at his direct hit.

"Don't look so surprised, Mandy. I've known what you and so many other people have thought about me for a long time, and most of the time I let people just go on thinking it. Mostly because I just don't care enough to bother with the time and effort needed to correct them. But it's burned the past four years to know that's what you thought of me. Not that it was undeserved. I have plenty of history to support that label, but I've grown up a bit since Andrew died, and I've outgrown that title. At least I hope I have." He dropped his arms down to his sides. "Besides, it's a pretty empty life."

Amanda wasn't sure where all this was coming from. Was it all sincere? His eyes certainly indicated honesty. Or was it a very calculated ploy to suck her in, win her affections, and then dump her in the end? She took a tiny step away from him. "Well, you certainly acted convincingly that it was a fulfilled life you were leading. You should've gone into theater with those talents."

His studied her with narrowed eyes. "You think I'm acting now?"

Another direct hit. "I don't know what to think about you anymore."

He took a step toward her and she took a step back. He stopped. "What is it going to take to convince you that I love you?" The words hung in the air between them.

Shocked at his declaration, Amanda spoke without thinking. "An act of God."

Blake stared at her a moment, then crossed his arms over his chest. "Well, he and I aren't exactly on friendly terms right now. But I think you're right. The only person who could convince you is Him, because I certainly can't."

"Does that mean you're giving up? Because I hardly think if you were in love with me as you say that you would give up on me so easily."

"No, Mandy, I'm not giving up. I figure I have until the annulment comes through or until you go to Africa to convince you."

"Why only until then? Why not until your dying day?"

"Because I don't want to be the kind of person who traps you into loving me anymore. I want you to love me because you simply love me, and because you don't want to live without me. Not can't be without me. There's a difference. And I'd love you until your dying day if you'd let me. But, you've set a deadline. After that, there's no hope anymore."

Amanda stood where he'd left her unable to move and tried to process everything he'd said. Blake wouldn't meet her eyes as he cleaned up the remains of their lunch, but she could read the angry expression on his face. Was he angry at himself for having laid his soul out on the line? Was he angry at her for not returning his affection? Questions pounded in her brain, but one conclusion was obvious: he really did love her. But that was impossible. Elation and fear battled within her with fear on the winning side.

# Chapter Twenty - Five

Blake risked a glance at Amanda. Her expression indicated an internal battle in which he'd certainly come out on the losing side. Why had he declared his love for her now? He'd finally made some progress with her and now he'd ruined it for sure. He clenched the root beer bottle in his hand. Pain shot through him as the bottle shattered. "Crap!" Blood trickled off his skin and onto the floor.

Instantly Amanda was at his side and opened his hand.

"It's fine, Mandy. Just leave it."

She gave him a 'don't mess with me' look. "Open your hand." She poured water from her bottle over his palm to wash away the blood, then she flicked his palm with her fingernail to remove any bits of loose glass. "I don't think there are any shards in there."

"I told you, it's fine. Just a stupid accident is all."

"You seem to have a lot of those lately."

"Yeah, well, maybe it's your turn." He grabbed a cloth napkin to wrap his hand.

"Let me." She took it from him and soon had it wrapped and tied in a neat knot. "I'll finish clearing up. You've done enough. Are you going to be okay to ride back?"

"I'm fine."

With the picnic things stowed back on the horses, Blake cupped his hands for her to step in.

She pointed at his bandaged hand. "That's going to hurt if I step on it."

"It's just a scratch. Go on. How else are you going to get on?"

Amanda frowned, but stepped on his hands, and swung up

into the saddle.

A moment later, Blake was on his horse and leading the way back. "Do you want to see more of the ranch or just head straight in?"

"I'd like to see just a bit more, but not too much. The jet tub is calling me."

He felt the corners of his mouth turn up a little. "Okay, this way then."

The horses ambled along through the tall grass, surefootedly stepping around rocks. The green grass of spring had transformed into summer gold. Blake admired the horizon line where gold met blue.

Amanda's horse lurched, whinnied, then reared up on its hind legs. Amanda screamed, scrambled to keep her hold on the reins, and then plummeted off the horse. She landed hard on the ground and screamed again. Her horse landed, backed up, just missing stepping on Amanda, and then took off like a shot.

Blake's heart lodged in his throat. Then his horse shook its head wildly from side to side and gave a whinny too, but Blake kept it under control. He looked after the runaway horse and then down at Amanda. Her eyes were closed. An icy fear washed through the insides of his body. He got ready to dismount when he heard it, the sound of a rattle. "Amanda," he said, "There's a rattlesnake. Don't move."

Amanda didn't respond.

Blake's fear and panic escalated. He desperately wanted to jump down and help her, but knew if he scared the rattlesnake it could attack her or him or both in defense. He didn't want to add a rattlesnake bite to their list of injuries. He waited and tried to quiet his breathing so he could hear, but the pounding of blood in his ears made it difficult. There was the rattle again. His horse shifted a few steps to the side. "Whoa, boy. Easy now." The horse flicked its tail. The rattle sounded again, but this time fainter. Blake watched the blades of grass around Amanda for signs of movement from the snake, but they only ruffled lazily in the wind. He waited one more tense minute before he jumped down and raced to her side.

Urgently he called her name, "Amanda." He held his breath and prayed she was okay.

Her lashes lifted as she opened her eyes, blinking rapidly before they focused on his face.

A small wave of relief washed over him. "Amanda, Are you okay? Is anything broken?"

It took a moment before she said, "Nothing's broken, but my head sure hurts. What happened?"

"Carousel got spooked by a rattlesnake and threw you." He slid an arm under her shoulders. "Can you sit up?"

"I think so." Working together they maneuvered her into a sitting position. Amanda clutched at her stomach. "Oh, that's not good."

"What?"

"Dizzy, nauseous. I must have bumped my head when I landed, as well as getting the wind knocked out of me. Will you check?"

Blake shifted around to look at the back of her head and reached up to the spot where she'd hit. Blood came away on his hand and alarm shot through his body, fueling his adrenaline. "You hit it. You're bleeding." He showed her his palm. "We need to get you to the hospital."

"It's probably fine. Head injuries always bleed terribly no matter how small they are."

"Well, I'm not taking any chances. Can you walk?" He helped her to her feet.

She immediately doubled over and wretched her lunch into the grass.

He refused to let panic engulf him. He needed a clear head to help her. "That's a no on the walking. I can carry you back to the house, but it will be faster to ride. Think you can make it?"

Pale-faced, Amanda nodded. Blake muscled her onto the horse then swung up in front of her. She leaned against him and wrapped her arms around his waist. Despite the circumstances, Blake found her touch exhilarating. "Don't fall off back there, and don't throw up on the horse. He won't like it." Blake urged the horse into a fast walk. He wanted to gallop Amanda to safety as quickly as possible, but worried that would put her in more danger.

When they made it to the stables, he called out, "Jed! Amanda's hurt."

The old man came out with his usual bow-legged shuffle. "What happened? Where's Carousel?"

Blake swung down and then helped Amanda down. He cradled her in his arms. Her lack of protest frightened him. "Rattlesnake spooked her. She took off. Threw Amanda. I have to take her to the hospital. She's got a gash on the back of her head."

Jed noted the blood and nodded. "I'll find Carousel and bring her back." He grabbed a horse blanket from the barn and tucked the blanket around Amanda despite the Texas summer heat.

Amanda blinked up at him. "Warm," she murmured and then her eyes closed.

Blake bolted for the car, belted Amanda in, then grabbed the keys from the bowl inside the front door before he buckled himself into the car. All the way to the hospital, Blake tried to keep Amanda talking, and while she stayed mostly awake, she only gave one-word answers. It was with relief that he carried her through the Emergency Room doors to the triage nurse. Moments later, Amanda was settled into a bed having her vital signs checked while Blake attempted to fill out the paperwork.

A doctor appeared, assessed Amanda, and stitched up the gash. "Only two stitches," he said when he finished. "But as you have a concussion, I'm going to send you up for a few quick tests to be sure there isn't any internal bleeding or other damage."

"I'm sure I'll be fine." Amanda's protest sounded weak.

"Let's just be sure." He signaled to a nurse, who grabbed another medic and they readied Amanda for transport.

"Can I go with her?" Blake asked. Worry lined his face.

"It's better if you wait here," the doctor said.

"I hate waiting." Blake ran a hand through his hair.

"You are hurt as well?" The doctor pointed to the napkin tied around Blake's hand.

"It's just a scratch. I broke it on a glass bottle."

The doctor looked from Blake to Amanda and back again. He motioned at the nurse who wheeled Amanda away. "Let me take a look," the doctor said to Blake.

Blake sighed and offered his hand to the doctor, who unwrapped the napkin.

"A glass bottle, huh?" The doctor adjusted his glasses and wiped a cotton ball over the surface of Blake's upturned palm to check for glass shards.

"Yes."

"Was it a domestic dispute?" The doctor continued to examine Blake's palm.

"What?"

"Did you hit the lady in the back of the head with the glass bottle?"

Blake wrenched his palm away appalled. "No! Whatever would make you think that?

"Given your injuries it isn't an unlikely conclusion. She has a gash on the head and a concussion. You have cuts from a glass bottle on your hand. It isn't' so far a leap."

"I would never hurt Amanda." Blake was appalled at the suggestion.

The doctor shook his head. "That's what they all say."

"I broke the bottle cleaning up our picnic lunch. She hit her head on a rock when her horse threw her because of a rattlesnake."

The doctor calmly folded his hands. "Were there witnesses?"

"No. We were alone."

The doctor nodded. "Alone. Always alone. Of course it's no use asking the young woman because she will deny the abuse as they always do. They make up so many excuses to stay and then, one day, they wind up dead."

"I didn't hurt her!" Blake's face blazed with anger.

"Well, it will be your word against mine unless you persuade me otherwise." The doctor gave Blake a pointed look. "I'm sure you have the means, Mister Worthington."

Through clenched teeth, Blake said flatly, "I don't have any money."

The doctor guffawed. "No money. That's very funny coming from you."

"I don't. My parents threw me out and cut me off, so I have nothing to give you."

The doctor thought this over a moment. "Well, even if you don't, I'm sure your parents will be happy to persuade me to keep quiet, or change my story, once you've been detained by the police and the press find out."

Blake wanted to ram his fist down the doctor's throat, but knew that would only make things worse. "I don't have any money for you."

The doctor shrugged. "Suit yourself." He left the room.

Moments later two security guards entered with a nurse. She was a young red-head. "I'm here to bandage up your hand," she said apologetically. She worked quickly and silently, then slipped out.

Blake looked at the guards, one of whom pulled out a pair of cuffs. "I will cooperate and walk out quietly. You don't need those."

"Sorry, Sir," the tall one said. "It's procedure."

Blake closed his eyes while they snapped them on. Then he squared his shoulders, held his head up high as they led him out. Sure enough, outside the hospital a few reporters had managed to gather with cameras and microphones. They fired questions at him, but he ignored them all, knowing his face would be all over the place in a few hours on trumped up domestic dispute charges. He was deposited inside a police cruiser, after which he looked up at the hospital windows wondering where Amanda was and if she'd think he'd abandoned her. The cruiser started up, pulled out, and the hospital disappeared into the sunset. Coming home had been such a bad idea.

## Chapter Twenty - Six

Blake leaned up against the gray cinder block wall and stared at the wall opposite. He had no idea what time it was, how Amanda was, where she was, and no way to find out. He'd been dumped alone in this cell hours ago and hadn't been given his phone call yet. His worry moved in a never-ending circle between Amanda and his parents' reaction to the 'news' of his arrest for beating a defenseless young woman. He was sure the press was having a field day with this ridiculous untrue scenario.

Finally, he heard a noise down the hallway. Footsteps, then a guard came into view. "You're being released." He unlocked the door.

Blake rose, a little bit stiff from sitting on the wooden bench for so long, and stepped out. He followed the guard down the hall, used the bathroom, then picked up his personal items along with signing the necessary dismissal forms.

"Your court hearing is set for July fifth," the woman behind the window said. The bad red-hair dye job didn't do her middle-aged face any favors. She poked a crimson fingernail at the document she slid through the gap to him. "Sign there."

Blake signed, then braced himself for the onslaught of fury from his parents and for the questions from reporters he knew awaited him on the other side of the doors. He walked through the doors and stopped in surprise. Bill stood there twisting his baseball cap and waiting for him.

"Bill! What are you doing here?"

"Bailing you out, of course."

"But my parents . . ."

"Cut you off as I recall. Did you want to stay in there?" Bill pointed back at the security door Blake had just passed through.

"No! But how did you know I was here?"

"Amanda called us once she got her head back in some semblance of order and found out what was going on. It wasn't hard. It was all over the TV."

"I'll bet. Did you believe it?"

Bill shook his head. "Not for a minute. I know how you feel about Amanda, and I'm starting to see how your situation in life makes people assume a lot about you when they don't even know you."

"How is Amanda?"

"Let's catch up in the car. The longer we stand here, the bigger the crowd gets out there." Bill jerked his thumb at the exit doors.

"Right."

"You ready?" Bill asked Blake.

"Yep. I've done this before."

Bill raised his eyebrows at Blake.

"I meant, I've had to muscle my way through the press before. Are you ready?"

"Just like going to the fair."

They opened the doors and immediately cameras and microphones were shoved in their faces. Bill led Blake silently to the car. A couple of police officers held back the reporters so they could pull the car out and finally they turned into the street.

Blake checked the horizon where a faint glow outlined the rim of the earth. "It's dawn? I didn't think I'd been in there that long."

"Time does funny things when you're in a cell."

Blake looked sideways at Bill. "May I ask how you know?"

"Got into a little trouble one night when I was young. I declared my love to Jenny with some spray paint on the side of a barn. Not my best idea. She still teases me about it from time to time."

"How did you get here? Where are we going? How is

Amanda?" Blake couldn't hold back his questions.

"We drove down from Iowa as soon as Amanda called us."

"You drove?"

"Couldn't very well fly at the last minute. Besides there weren't any flights out until this morning anyways." He pointed at the road. "We're headed to a little motel outside of town. Amanda is there with Jenny. She just got released a few hours ago. She took a pretty good knock to the head, but she'll be fine. Just needs to rest for a few days, and I'd say no more horseback riding lessons for a while." He gave Blake a small smile.

"I'm really sorry, Bill. I just wanted to show Amanda the ranch, and we were headed back when it happened."

Bill raised a hand momentarily from the steering wheel. "Thanks for the unnecessary apology, Blake. But it was an accident. The horse reacted naturally to the snake. Nothing more to say. As for Amanda, I'd say that whoever created this story is lucky she doesn't know who it is. If she wasn't injured and knew, heaven help that poor soul."

Blake couldn't help but grin. "She does have a fiery temper when she gets going about something."

"She's got a passionate soul. She hides it quite a bit of the time, but she's a deep one. I think that's why she's so keen to go to Africa."

"What do you mean?"

"I mean it breaks her heart every time she hears about a baby dying. She thinks it's her responsibility to save them all if she can, and she is certainly going to give it all she's got trying. I think it's because of the one we lost."

"I'm sorry Bill. I didn't know you'd lost a child."

"We had a seventh; one after Tiffany. It was a very difficult pregnancy for Jenny, so unlike the rest. The doctors told us the baby was likely to have issues if it made it to full term and survived delivery. We explained it to the kids as best we could. Amanda was only six at the time. Anyways, the baby came a bit early. She took one breath, gave one cry, and died a few minutes later in our arms." Bill rubbed at the side of his jaw.

"We came home from the hospital empty handed. It's hard to know just how much your young children can understand when something like that happens. For Missy and Tiffany, the world just kept rolling along. The boys were sad of course, but they were old enough to be able to wrap their heads around it and moved on. It seemed to have the greatest impact on Amanda. She just saw an empty cradle that should've been full." Bill pulled into a parking lot and turned off the engine. He walked them to a door marked number three and swiped his key card through the slot. The tiny lights on the pad turned green and with a flick of the handle they entered the room.

It was a modest motel that had certainly seen better days, but it was clean and comfortable. Amanda sat propped up on pillows against the wooden headboard with her eyes closed. Jenny sat next to her and held her hand. At the sight of Blake, Jenny squeezed Amanda's hand and swung herself off the bed. She wrapped Blake in a hug.

"Are you all right?" Jenny asked him.

"Yes, Jenny. Thanks. I still can't believe you guys are here."

"Where else would we be in your time of need?" Jenny sat at the foot of the bed.

"At home, taking care of the rest of your kids, and working, I would suppose."

"Not with a daughter in the hospital and a son–in–law in jail."

"About that," Blake said.

"It's a complete lie and we all know it," Amanda spoke up. "You should sue the hospital for slander."

"I've had my name dragged through the papers before," Blake reminded her.

"I meant slander against me." She attempted a smile.

Blake smiled back. "I see Carousel hasn't knocked the spirit out of you."

"No, but she gave it a good try."

Blake stood next to her and tentatively took her hand. A warm feeling wrapped around his heart when she didn't pull away. Slowly she ran a finger across the bandage on his hand.

"How's your hand?" she asked.

"Fine. I told you it would be."

Amanda let go of him and ran her hand across her eyes. "We need to stop being married. I can't take any more trips to the ER. I haven't spent so much time in there since I was a volunteer, and we just keep ending up there. It's a bad omen."

Unsure of what to say, Blake stepped away. He looked at Jenny and Bill, who held hands, and wondered if he and Amanda would ever be that way. "I had better go pick up our stuff from the ranch."

"Already got it." Bill pointed to their bags on the floor. Amanda's was unzipped.

"How?"

"Ana Maria," Amanda answered.

"Ana Maria?"

"I called her after my parents arrived and we checked into the motel. She called Jed and he delivered the bags here to us. She even made him bring the cookies." She pointed to the grocery sack on the table next to the window.

"God bless Ana Maria." He took a cookie out of the sack and scarfed it down.

Jenny said, "Perhaps it's time we all had some real food. There's a Denny's across the street and while it's not the Ritz, I'm sure we can get a hot breakfast."

"That sounds great." Blake wiped the crumbs from his mouth.

"We'll go right after you shower," Amanda said to Blake.

"I can shower when we get back," he protested.

She gave him a pointed look. "No, you can't. I'm barely keeping the nausea to a minimum as it is. Go shower. You reek."

Blake looked at Jenny and Bill. Jenny cleared her throat. "A shower might be wise after a sweaty horse ride and a night in jail."

Blake laughed. "Fine. I'll be quick though." He grabbed his bag and disappeared into the bathroom. After a quick shower, they crossed the street and were soon seated at the restaurant.

It didn't take long for their orders to arrive. Blake dived into his food and didn't come up for air until he'd cleared all his eggs, bacon, sausage, and hash browns. He slowed down a bit once he started in on his stack of pancakes and asked, "So, what's the plan now?"

Jenny swallowed her mouthful of eggs. "Well, Amanda needs to rest for a few days and then we can all drive home."

"I want to go home now," Amanda said firmly.

Jenny and Bill exchanged a concerned look. "I'm not sure that's the best thing in your condition, dear." Jenny said kindly.

Amanda reached across the table and took Jenny's hand. "I know you're trying to do your best and take care of me, Mom, but right now I just want to go home and rest in my own bed. I'll be much more comfortable there. Besides, everyone needs to get back to work." She looked down at the maroon napkin in her lap. "I just want to get out of here and forget the last twenty – four hours."

"I agree with Amanda," Blake said. "I'd rather put Texas at my back as fast as possible. Plus, the longer we stay here the more likely it is we'll be found by the press and I really don't want to put Amanda through that – or you." He looked at Jenny and Bill.

"What about your plane tickets?" Jenny asked. "Can you still make it to the airport in time to make your flight? At least then Amanda wouldn't have to bump around in the car for hours."

Blake pulled out his phone to check the time, but it was dead. "Um, what time is it?"

"Eight fifteen," Bill replied checking his watch.

"Nope. The flight leaves in forty-five minutes and we're over an hour from the airport." Blake sighed. "Besides the press could be lurking at the airport to catch me leaving town."

"Who cares about the press?" Amanda grumbled.

"You will very much if I don't protect you," Blake replied. "Look, I've been dealing with them since about the time I was ten. They don't respect boundaries, and the last thing I want is your family and home splashed across the tabloids and TV screens of America. Why do you think people tend to recognize me no matter where I go?" He looked at Jenny and Bill. "I'd rather spare your family from all that and leave you in peace in suburban Des Moines than deal with the three-ring circus of the press that will be there if they follow me."

"What's your idea then?" Bill asked as he scraped the last of his over-easy eggs from his plate and washed them down with orange juice.

"I still have time to rearrange the tickets. We'll put you two on the flight to Des Moines, and I'll drive Amanda home in your car."

"It would be better if Amanda and I flew and you and Bill drove. That way Amanda wouldn't have to ride in the car for eleven hours with her concussion. She could be in her own bed much sooner that way," Jenny pointed out.

Blake grimaced. "You have a point. But doesn't Bill need to get back to work?"

"Don't you?" Amanda said. "If you're worried about work schedules, then why don't you fly home today with Dad while Mom and I drive?"

"But that doesn't get you home sooner." Bill said.

"It's up to you Amanda," Blake said. "We're all trying to do what's best for you here, but you're the one who knows best what that is."

Amanda bit her lip as she thought hard. Blake imagined he could read her mind weighing the pros and cons. He knew she wanted to be home badly, but the more days he missed work the longer it would take for him to earn the money for annulment. Also, her dad needed to be at work too and someone needed to be at home watching over Tiffany. Jenny was the best person for that. But Amanda also had her fear of flying to combat, and the fact that even on her best days she fought air sickness. She wasn't sure she could make even the short flight concussed without going through half a dozen barf bags. Was there even any hope that she wanted to spend some time alone with him, even though she was injured and miserable?

She rubbed at her eyes while the other three patiently waited for her to make a decision. She blurted out, "I want to drive home with Blake."

"Okay," Jenny said, her expression clearly indicating being a little taken aback by her daughter's abrupt outburst.

"If it gets to be too much, then we'll stop at Aunt Sue's in Kansas City," Amanda added.

Jenny nodded. "I'll give her a call to let her know."

"Bill, can I borrow your phone?" Blake asked. "Mine's dead and I need to call the airline now so I can rearrange the tickets for you and Jenny."

Bill passed him the phone just as the waitress arrived with the check. Blake picked up both but Bill took the check from his hand. "I'll get this. You go make that call."

"But you've already done so much," Blake protested.

"I'm getting a free flight home. We'll call it even." He grinned at Blake.

Blake headed outside the front doors thinking that Amanda was definitely blessed with good parents. He wondered whether his family would have been like this if his father wasn't a scientific genius. He remained on the phone with the airline until they arrived back at the motel room.

"Okay. There's a flight in just over two hours. I got the tickets switched, but that means we need to leave A.S.A.P. to get you there on time. Once we drop you off, Amanda and I will start heading for Iowa. Does that sound good?"

"I better go jump in the shower then," Amanda said. "I take the longest to get ready."

There was a flurry of activity as the St. Claires showered and packed and everyone brushed their teeth. Within thirty minutes, they'd checked out and set off for the airport.

# Chapter Twenty - Seven

"Amanda, wake up," Blake said softly.

Her eyes fluttered open. She glanced at the clock on the dashboard, and realized she'd slept off and on for the past ten hours, intermittently having Blake pull over while she'd puked next to the highway. He'd been kind, held her hair, and supplied her with saltines and Gatorade. She even remembered leaning on him to get in and out of the gas stations for rest room breaks. He hadn't even said anything when she gave him a long hug and silently wept on his shirt. What a disaster of a drive. She'd meant to ask questions about his life to clear away all her misconceptions, but the concussion and the nausea had thwarted her. Disappointment trickled through her at the lost opportunity. It was dark out, but she squinted in the glare of the oncoming headlights from the opposite side of the highway. She yawned. "Where are we?"

"Coming up on Des Moines, but I don't know which highway to take or which way is best to get to your house. I've never driven here before, and I didn't pay the best attention in the cab ride from the airport. I need you to give me directions. We're coming up on a split."

"Oh, okay." She checked the sign as they whizzed past. "Go around on the west side. It's closer."

"Got it." Blake signaled and changed lanes. "Do you need the bathroom or anything?"

"No. I'm good. Just happy to get home and into bed. I'm glad we didn't have to stop in Kansas City. Not that I didn't want to see Aunt Sue, but then it's one more person I have to explain to who you are and why you're with me. No offense."

Blake gave a little chuckle. "Sounds like you're feeling better. You certainly seem to be getting back to your old self."

"What does that mean?" A note of defensiveness crept into Amanda's voice.

"Just that I seem to be back in my familiar position of being the thorn in your side."

"Pull over!" Amanda commanded.

Blake signaled, moved onto the shoulder and stopped as fast as he could. Amanda hopped out and threw up into the tall grass lining the shoulder, then climbed back into the car.

"Sorry," she said quietly as she buckled.

"Are you okay?"

She swallowed. "I'm fine. I wish this concussion would hurry up and go away. The last time I was sick like this I had the stomach flu."

"Well, you've done pretty well considering how long we've driven." He eased the car back onto the highway and followed Amanda's directions until they finally pulled into the garage of her parent's house.

"Home sweet home," Amanda said with a pleased sigh.

Blake grabbed their bags and followed Amanda in.

"You're here." Jenny threw her arms around both of them.

"Mom, I thought you'd be in bed and asleep by now." Amanda said.

"With my baby on the road with a concussion, not a chance." She smiled at Blake. "Thanks, Blake."

"Mom, I'm hardly a baby," Amanda protested with a weak laugh.

"Well, I don't care how old you are, or how big you all get, you are always my babies."

Amanda grabbed at her stomach. "I'm going to be sick." She ran for the bathroom.

Just as she walked up the hallway to rejoin the group she heard her mother's voice. "Blake, how many times was Amanda sick while you drove?"

"Quite a bit. Why?"

"I just wondered if she was doing better or not. She doesn't travel well. Never has. Car sickness, air sickness."

"Boats?"

"No idea. She's never been on one. The car sickness got better once she passed age eight, but the first semester of college when she was supposed to fly home, she nearly didn't get on the plane, it was that bad. Even the wrong kind of roller coaster can trigger it."

Not wanting to appear like she was eavesdropping, Amanda reappeared.

"Honey, you look pale," Jenny remarked and put an arm around her shoulder. "Do you want something to eat?"

Amanda shook her head. "No thanks, Mom. I think I'll just shower and go to bed."

"Okay."

Before she could stifle the impulse, Amanda threw her arms around Blake. "Thanks for bringing me home."

"You're welcome."

She slid away and off to her room unwilling to look back to see Blake's reaction. Would he understand her offering of gratitude?

Puzzled, Blake looked to Jenny for an answer for Amanda's behavior.

Her lips twitched up into a smile. "Well, she seems to be thawing. Are you hungry?"

"Starving," Blake admitted.

"Come into the kitchen, and I'll make you a sandwich."

"That's okay, Jenny. I can make my own."

"Of course you can, but I'm still going to make it."

Mulling over Amanda's 'hug', he followed Jenny into the kitchen where he felt as at home as he did with Ana Maria. Life was definitely more comfortable at the St. Claires'. He let his mind wander to his parents in Texas and wondered just how badly it was going there with the press making a mess of their lives again. Often, he seriously contemplated selling the company as soon as he was put in charge, just so he could hopefully regain some semblance of normality again. No company, no money, no one to care what he did, good or bad, and, best of all, not to have his picture in the paper again until it hung over his obituary.

Jenny set a plate down in front of him. He immediately grabbed the sandwich to take a bite, then remembered where he was and stopped. He looked at Jenny. "Should I pray over the food first? I mean, it is the custom in your house."

Jenny looked pleased with him. "Yes, it is the custom, but it's up to you. I'm certainly not going to force you to pray."

"Just a moment then." Blake said a silent prayer over his food, then dived into the turkey and cheese sandwich in his hand that brimmed over with lettuce and fresh tomatoes. "I like following the rules of your house, because I know you made them for the benefit of the family instead of some strict regime to dole out punishment when the line isn't towed." He wiped some mayonnaise from the side of his lip, grabbed a napkin from the holder in the middle of the table, and wiped his hands before he attacked the sandwich again.

Jenny got him some apple juice. "What happened down in Texas?"

Blake gave her a funny look. "You know what happened. That's why you came to get us."

"No, I mean before that. What happened between you two that softened Amanda up?"

Blake looked at the sandwich. "I wish I knew. Really, I do." He looked up at Jenny. "I think it helped her see the difference between the world I come from and here." He gestured to the kitchen. "I'm afraid she didn't receive a gracious welcome from my family. Then she saved Ben from choking to death and that went a long way to softening my mom."

"What? Who's Ben?"

Blake explained what had happened at the party.

"How very like her. I'm glad she was there."

"Me too," Blake said quietly.

"Then I told her about my brother, Andrew. He died two years ago. She didn't know. To be honest, I didn't really make it known at school. It's been hard." He choked up and set down his sandwich.

Jenny covered his hand with her own. "It's hard to lose a loved one."

"Bill told me about your child. I'm truly sorry."

With misty eyes she replied, "Thanks, Blake, but I know I'll see my baby again. He was just too precious for this world and was called home to Heaven." She squeezed his hand.

"Do you really believe that you'll see your baby again?"

"I do."

Blake couldn't hide the emotion from his voice or the tears he held back. "Do you think I'll see Andrew again?"

"Yes. Absolutely, you will. I bet he'll be the first one to greet you in Heaven when you get there."

"How can you be so sure?" One tear escaped.

"Faith. Trust in God. That's how."

"I wish I had what you have." Blake swiped the tear away, then finished up the last few bites of his sandwich.

"You can if you want to. But faith is earned one piece at a time, and it can only be lost if you allow it."

"Like love?" He wiped his face and hands with his napkin.

"Yes, like love." She cleared his plate and washed it.

He chugged down his juice and handed her the glass. Once it was rinsed, and the dishwasher shut, Blake gave her a hug. "You're a great mom, Jenny. Thanks."

"You're welcome."

He made it to the doorway before the question that burned inside of him couldn't wait to be answered burst out. "Do you think Amanda could ever love me?"

She cocked her head. "It's hard to know another's heart, even my own daughter's, but I'd say there are seeds already planted there and every reason to hope they will bloom."

"Seeds?"

"Yes, and hope. Good night, Blake." She turned out the kitchen light and passed him on her way to the stairs.

"Seeds and hope. Not a bad start," he said to himself.

## Chapter Twenty - Eight

Blake raced into the house in search of Amanda, but instead found Tiffany on the couch eating popcorn and watching a chick flick. "Hey, Tiffany. Where's Amanda?"

"Not sure. Her room or the backyard maybe." Her eyes unglued from the screen and she turned around. "Why? Is there something I can help you with?" She batted her lashes at him.

"No, thanks Tiffany. I need to talk to Amanda about it."

"Fine," she grumped and returned to her movie.

Blake checked Amanda's room. The bed was made, although the covers were rumpled from being sat on, but she wasn't there. She hadn't been to work the past two days because of the concussion. He stepped outside onto the porch. Not there either. He stood frustrated. He had good news he really wanted to share with her, and now he couldn't find her. Then he heard a whimper from above. He looked up.

On one side of the yard stood a large tree with a tree house in it that Bill had built for the kids when they were younger. The whimper had come from there.

"Amanda?" Blake called out. He put his foot on the bottom rung of the ladder to the tree house. "Amanda, are you up there?"

Another small sob.

He climbed up and poked his head through the floorboard entrance. Amanda sat on a little three-legged stool with her head in her hands and a small package at her feet. He hoisted himself through the opening and knelt down beside her. "Amanda?" He put a hand on her knee.

She shifted away. "Don't touch me. It's bad enough without you touching me."

Blake removed his hand. "Sorry. What's wrong?"

"You!" she screamed at him and took her hands off her face. "You and everything you touch in my life gets ruined. I'm ruined."

"What?" Blake backed away.

"Why did this ever happen? Why did I say yes? Why was I ever stupid enough to marry you?" The tears fell fast and her chest heaved with sobs.

"Amanda."

"Now everything in my life, all my plans, will be ruined because of your selfishness. You just take what you want and don't even think about the consequences or how they affect others. Why did you have to do this to me? Why couldn't you just leave me alone?"

Totally lost, Blake tried to find out what was going on. "Amanda, I don't understand."

She flew at him and screamed, "Ahhhh!" She beat her fists against his chest.

Blake knelt there and let her rage until she was worn out and sobbed against his chest. Tentatively he eased his arms around her loosely. Ready to drop them in an instant if she decided to beat on him again. Very softly he whispered, "Amanda, please tell me what is going on? We can find a solution together."

She cackled, part laugh, part hysteria. "Solution. That's funny. There is no solution." She pointed to the bag. "Look in there." Her arms dropped limply to her sides in defeat.

With a glance at her, he picked the bag up from the shadows where it lay against the stool leg and looked inside. He drew out a box. "What are you doing with a pregnancy test kit?"

Her hands swung up to her hips. "What do you think I'm doing?"

"You think you're pregnant?" Blake looked at her, his insides a strange combination of confusion, surprise, disbelief and, oddly, fear.

She slumped against the wooden wall. "I don't know. I got the kit to find out, but I'm too afraid to take the test because what if it's positive? I just can't deal with that. I'm not ready to have a baby. But I'm stuck because I need to know." Tears ran down her cheeks again.

He looked from the box to her. "What makes you think you're pregnant?"

"Well, I've been throwing up at all times of the day and night, and I just haven't felt normal the past few days."

"You had a concussion. Those take a while to recover from."

"I know, but then there's that night." Her voice was so low that Blake barely heard her.

"That night?"

Amanda nodded but refused to meet his eyes.

"Who's the father?" Blake asked abruptly.

Amanda's head flew up. "What?" she asked dumbly.

"Who's the father?" Blake repeated. He put the kit down on the floor, and stood directly in front of her so that she had no choice but to look at him.

She scowled at him. "What do you mean, who's the father? You are." She poked him hard in the chest with her finger.

"That's not possible." Blake crossed his arms over his chest.

"Not possible?" Her voice level rose again. She glared at him. "You're low enough to get me drunk and trick me into marrying you but refuse to take responsibility for getting me pregnant? How dare you? You're even worse than I thought!" Her fists flew at him again, but Blake caught her wrists and held them tight in his hands.

"If you are pregnant," he tried not to growl at her, "then it is not by me."

"What? You think I had sex with someone else?"

Blake took a step back. "It is none of my business who you have sex with Mandy, although my observations of you the last four years tell me that you're pretty guarded on that front. I only know that if you are pregnant, it's not mine."

"What are you saying?" her lower lip trembled.

Seeing that she wasn't going to attack him, he released her wrists and slid his hands up to her shoulders. "Mandy, it's a universal rule that you have to have sex to get pregnant and as we've never had sex, if you're pregnant then it isn't by me."

"We haven't?" Her mouth hung open.

He rubbed her upper arms. "No, Amanda, you and I have never had sex."

She ran a hand across her eyes. "But, we got married. We had a wedding night."

"We did get married, and yes we spent the night in the honeymoon suite, but what do you remember about that night?"

She slumped back against the wall again and this time slid down to the floor. "Not very much. I remember the limo ride, the fight out on the dance floor, and you kissing me. That's about it."

"You don't remember anything else?" He couldn't keep the disappointment out of his voice. He slid down next to her.

"No," she apologized. "The video of the wedding and the pictures are all the proof I have that it did happen and that I was happy to be a part of it. But I don't actually have any memories of it."

"Would you like to know what happened after the wedding?" Blake's voice was soft as his hand crept into hers. There was no mistaking the dread in her eyes or her determination to hear the truth.

"Yes."

"I sent the other four back to the Paris in the limo. Then you and I took the elevator to the top floor. I carried you over the threshold of the doorway, and you giggled. We danced by the windows to the fountain show below. Then I helped you undress down to your slip, had you wash down two Advil with a glass of water so your hangover wouldn't be so bad in the morning, and then tucked you into bed. I kissed you, held you, and whispered to you until you fell asleep in my arms. Then I listened to you breathe until I fell asleep."

A moment of silence passed between them while Amanda processed the tale. "That's it?"

"That's it."

She put her hands on his cheeks and pulled his eyes to hers.

"You promise?" her voice trembled. "You're telling the truth? You didn't try to take advantage of me? We didn't consummate the marriage?"

"I promise."

She held his face a long time as her eyes searched his to see if he spoke the truth. When it seemed she was satisfied she let go and laid her head back against the wooden planks.

Blake stood, brushed the dust from his jeans, and handed her the kit. "You can still take this if you want, if it will make you feel better. That is, if you still think you have a reason to take it other than me." He walked over to the ladder hole and descended until just his head stuck through. He fought to keep the tears at bay. "I never knew, until now, how little you thought of me. What kind of scum you thought me to be. I've made a lot of mistakes in my life, but I have never ever taken advantage of a woman when she was drunk, and I'm sorry to know that you think I would. Especially that you think I would do that to you. I would've told you sooner how things were between us if I'd had any idea you thought otherwise. Thanks for letting me know your opinion of me. I can see now why you're so keen to have this marriage over and go to Africa and forget me and all of this. I can see now, that no matter how much I may love you, you're never going to feel the same." He descended the rest of the ladder and slunk toward the house, dejected and heartbroken. All hope of reconciliation had vanished.

"Blake, wait!"

He turned and saw Amanda's head sticking out from the ladder hole. Her eyes pleaded with him but he wasn't sure what she wanted. When she didn't say anything more, he headed up the porch steps and into the house. He managed to make it back to the guest room in the basement and onto the bed before the tears broke through. Nothing he could do would ever convince her of his love. Time to face the truth and let her go. It was over.

## Chapter Twenty - Nine

In the kitchen, Blake sat at his laptop working on the animal shelter fundraiser.

Jenny took off her rings and mixed the dinner meatloaf with her hands in a bowl. "Are things coming together?" she asked him as she shook in the bread crumbs.

"I've got a few sponsors together, and the schools are all notified about the pet parade. We've had several volunteers sign up to run the parade, the booths, and the bake sale. I'm waiting for the auctioneer to get back to me on his availability. But the important thing is now I have Whiskers."

"Whiskers?" Jenny asked as she added in ketchup.

Amanda listened silently as she peeled the potatoes. It'd been an awkward few days now with Blake. He'd been formally polite, and she felt the distance between them. To her surprise and dismay, she found she didn't like it.

"Whiskers is going to be the Winter of our animal shelter and the highlight of the fundraiser."

"What is Whiskers?"

"A cat. She came in badly abused, and Doctor Mills had to amputate her hind legs. She's also missing part of an ear."

"That's terrible!" Jenny patted the meatloaf into the pan. "Blake, wouldn't it be more humane to put the cat down instead of leaving her the way she is?"

"There is certainly an argument for that. Should Winter have been put down for losing her tail because a fisherman was careless, and she got tangled in his net? Do we believe the same for humans who are missing limbs?"

"I see what you mean." Jenny popped the meatloaf into the

oven and commenced cutting the potatoes Amanda had already peeled. "But there are many who would argue that a human life isn't the same as a cat's or a dolphin's."

"There are," Blake agreed. "And that argument over life and when it begins and why, and should one be valued more than another, has been going on for ages. I'd rather not get into it. The point is Whiskers will be mobile again with the help of a specially rigged harness that will allow her to move around without human assistance. That's part of the promotion for the fundraiser."

"Well, I hope it turns out to be a success and that the animal shelter will remain open. You sure have worked hard on it."

"Thanks, Jenny. I hope so too." Blake tapped away some more on the computer.

The front door banged open, and a moment later Rich, James and Josh appeared in the kitchen.

"Smells good, Mom." James wrapped Jenny in a bear hug from behind.

"Your fridge empty again?" She teased him as she unloaded half of the potatoes into the pot on the stove.

"Ah, come on Mom," Josh said. "Our fridge doesn't have to be empty for us to come and visit the best mom in the world, does it?"

"It's empty," Amanda said as she finished peeling the last potato.

"Actually we stopped by to kidnap Blake," Rich said.

"Really?" Blake shut down the laptop. "Where to?"

"Paintball. We need a fourth to take on the Nelson gang," James said as he poured a glass of orange juice.

"Nelson gang? Aren't they pretty cut-throat?" Amanda asked from the sink where she washed her hands.

"Yeah, but we figured with Blake we could take them," Josh said.

"More like use Blake as the bait for the Nelson's target practice," Amanda rolled her eyes.

"That hurts, Amanda," James said, pretending to be

wounded by a knife through the heart.

"Aren't busted ribs enough for you guys?" Amanda asked.

"Blake is fine. See, he's all better," Rich pointed at Blake. "Even his arm is healed from the nasty dog bite. We promise to return him in the same condition we take him in. Okay? Now can he have your permission to go?"

Amanda sniffed. "He doesn't need my permission."

"Well, you're certainly acting like he does." Rich turned to Blake. "How fast can you be ready? We're supposed to meet them in half an hour on the field to suit up and establish the ground rules."

"Which they'll break," James pointed out.

"Five. Ten at the most." Blake tucked the laptop under his arm. "I'll meet you on the front porch.

"Don't dress up," Josh called after him. "Chances are you'll just have to throw the clothes away afterwards.

"Got it," Blake replied from half way down the stairs.

Jenny slid the rest of the potatoes into the pot and turned to face her boys. "I'll keep some dinner warm for all of you when you get back."

"Thanks, Mom," said Rich and kissed her on the cheek.

"Will Rachel come looking for you here when she's done with work?" She put the cutting board in the sink and soaped up the sponge to wash it.

"Yes. I told her to meet me here." Rich knelt down and retied the laces on his worn sneakers with dots of paint splattered across them.

"That's fine. I'll feed her dinner too. You boys make sure Blake doesn't need another ER trip this afternoon. It's about time one of you took a turn. That boy has been in the ER more times since he got here than all three of you in the past four years."

"Well, that last one was Amanda's fault," James quipped.

"Yeah," Josh agreed. "How's the head, little sis?"

"Fine," Amanda replied. "But I second what Mom said. Keep Blake in one piece today."

"Aw, but it's so much fun to watch you experience the

Florence Nightingale effect when you nurse him back to health." Josh gave her a sly look.

"Not funny," Amanda glared at him.

"The only time you're nice to him is when he's hurt," Rich pointed out. "At least from what we've seen."

"That's not true," Amanda defended.

"Boys, leave Amanda alone," Jenny warned as she set the clean cutting board on the counter to dry. "Amanda has to work through Blake on her own. Now, you boys go wait on the porch."

The three brothers filed out, and the front door banged shut behind them.

A moment later Blake poked his head in long enough to say, "See you later," then dashed out after them.

Quietly Jenny asked, "You want to talk about it?"

"About what, Mom?" Amanda said playing innocent.

"About why you and Blake have been tiptoeing around each other the past few days?"

"Is it that obvious?" Amanda brushed some hair off her face.

"I am your mother," Jenny pointed out. "So, yes, it's obvious to me."

"We just had a misunderstanding, is all."

"A fight, you mean," Jenny clarified.

Amanda sighed, "Okay, a fight."

"And you were wrong, weren't' you?"

"I wasn't. Why would you say that?"

Jenny took Amanda's hands in hers. "Amanda, I know how you get when you realize you have done something, or said something wrong, but don't know how to admit it and how to apologize or how to be forgiven."

"It's just complicated, Mom."

"It always is dear, but I'm sure you'll sort it out eventually." She let go of Amanda's hands.

Amanda's phone buzzed in her pocket. She pulled it out and checked the text message. "Alison is waiting out front. Not sure what's up. I'll be back in a bit." She hugged Jenny.

"I'll keep your dinner warm too, and tell Alison she's

welcome to join us. Seems like we'll be feeding the masses tonight anyways." She waved goodbye to Amanda from the front door.

Amanda jumped in the car. "So, what's up?" she asked Alison.

"I need to talk. Let's go get a pedicure."

Amanda raised an eyebrow. "Pedicure serious?"

"Yep." A few minutes later the girls were seated in massage chairs at Cher's Nail Salon.

With her feet soaking in a mini jet tub, Amanda asked, "So?"

"So, I think things are taking a turn for the serious with Sheff." Alison fidgeted with the bottle of electric pink nail polish she'd picked out.

"Why?"

"Well, Karen Boswell, do you remember her?"

"Mousy brunette from biology?"

"Yes. She saw him at Monique's jewelry shop yesterday afternoon."

"So?"

"So, he was in the diamond ring section."

"He could've been picking something up for his mother or a friend," Amanda mused.

"Maybe. But Karen didn't seem to think so."

"And what do you think?" The nail techs started working the calluses off their feet.

"I think he might ask me," Alison whispered.

"Ask you what?" Amanda tried to ignore the tickling sensation in her feet.

"Don't be obtuse," Alison remonstrated. "You know, THE question."

"But you two haven't been going out that long," Amanda protested.

"I know," Alison agreed.

"What are you going to say?"

"Well, that's the thing. I'm not sure."

"You mean you're considering it?" Amanda asked surprised.

"Well, yes. I am. I could do a lot worse than Sheff."

"But we're so young."

Alison laughed. "Well, that's the pot calling the kettle black."

"My situation is totally different, and you know it."

"Still, you took the plunge first," Alison taunted. "A bit hypocritical of you to tell me not to."

"Fine, then. What's on the pro side of your list?"

"He's smart, has a good job, he wants to go places, and he makes me laugh. We have loads of fun together. Not to mention he's easy on the eyes, can take me around the dance floor, and kisses well."

"The con list?"

The techs slathered their legs with lotion and massaged their feet and calves.

"It is fast, and we don't know everything about each other, but I figure we have our whole lives for that, so getting started early isn't a big deal in the grand scheme of things."

Amanda thought hard and fast. She genuinely wanted Alison to be happy and get married and live out her dreams, but she didn't want her to rush into things with Sheff, make a mistake, and have regrets after. "Have you seen him cry?" she asked quietly.

Alison looked at Amanda for a long moment. "Yes. We caught Titanic at the drive in over the weekend. He cried from the time Rose let Jack slip into the water all the way through to the end. Then he held me for a really long time, and said he couldn't imagine having to live his whole life without me."

"Wow."

"Yeah."

The sound of their toe nails being clipped suspended their conversation momentarily.

"What about where to live?" Amanda asked as the filing and buffing commenced.

"Good question. We both have jobs, although mine doesn't start until August, but they are in different places. I guess we could try the long distance thing or one of us could choose to move."

"Tough choices. Have you talked about it?"

"Not really. We're both a little too scared to have that conversation because what if we can't come up with a solution and have to break up?"

"Would that be so bad?"

Alison looked down at her toes that were half-covered in the bright pink. "I think it would be," she said softly. She looked over at Amanda with misty eyes. "I really think he could be the one."

Amanda inhaled. "Where have I been while you've been busy falling in love?"

Alison laughed. "You've been a little busy with your own love life."

"Life, just life," Amanda corrected.

Alison raised an eyebrow. "Pretty anxious about it not being love, huh?"

"Mmm," Amanda said noncommittally.

"I think there's a lot more to that story than you're telling me."

Amanda looked down at her feet. The last layer of top coat had just been applied. She looked at the techs and then at Alison. "How about we go get ice cream, and I'll catch you up on what's been happening?"

They paid and left. Soon they were seated at Smiley's Ice Cream Parlor – the best ice cream in Iowa – or so the sign proclaimed.

Amanda dug into her mint brownie sundae while Alison started in on her waffle cone full of chocolate chocolate chip cookie dough.

"So, spill," Alison instructed.

Amanda recounted the events from Texas.

Alison leaned back in her chair and tapped the end of her spoon against her lips. "He told you he loves you."

Amanda grimaced. "Yes."

"And you didn't have the courage to say it back." Alison shook her head. "Poor Blake."

Amanda stopped the spoon that was halfway to her mouth.

"You think I love him?" she asked incredulously. A drip of hot fudge landed on the table.

"I think you could if you would let yourself." Alison resumed her ice cream vigil.

"Have you gone crazy? This is Blake we're talking about."

"That's right. But as you said yourself, this Blake isn't the same one you thought he was for the past four years. You've been carrying that grudge about him since early freshman year. Don't you think it's time you let go of it and accept Blake for the man he is now?"

"But history and experience tell me it's wrong to trust him. He'll just do what he did before. I won't be hurt by him again." Amanda gouged her brownie with her spoon.

"Amanda, none of us are the same person we were four years ago. A lot of growing up happens between age eighteen and twenty-one. Are you that same girl you were the day we walked into college four years ago?"

Amanda wiggled her shoulders. "No," she said with a sullen tone.

"Well then, why are you condemning Blake to be the same guy today he was then?"

Amanda scowled at her glass dish. "I don't know."

Alison tapped her on the hand with her spoon. "You can be too stubborn for your own good sometimes."

Amanda's head came up. "What's that supposed to mean?"

"It means that sometimes you miss out on opportunities in life that could bring you joy just because you are too stubborn to open up your mind and let go of past conclusions."

"You just want Blake and I to be together because you're happy with Sheff," Amanda challenged. "Isn't that what all couples happily in love do? Hurry up to match up all their single friends?"

"You know I would never push you at someone you didn't like, or rush you to pair up with someone, just to sacrifice your happiness for the sake of my own. I thought you knew what kind of friend I am." Alison pushed back her chair and folded her arms across her chest.

"Ali," Amanda said, using Alison's nickname, a rarity for her. "I'm sorry. I do know what kind of friend you are. You're the one who always tells me the truth even when it's tough for me to hear, and even when you know I'll get mad. And you're right, I am too stubborn for my own good, and yes, it is hard for me to let go. I just think I never really learned how. And this Blake thing has me more twisted up inside than I want to admit, even to myself. I'm terrified to examine my thoughts and feelings about him because of what I may discover. It's just so much easier to ignore them and pretend that they aren't there and stick with my conclusions about Blake than to draw new ones."

Alison's posture relaxed. "Well, that at least is a step in the right direction." She took another bite of her sundae. "And I accept your apology."

"I just think it's best to keep Blake at arm's length and not give him any hope for a future together. I don't want to mislead him or hurt him. It will just be better to get this marriage finished and for me to go to Africa. Then his family will accept him back and he can go run his dad's company."

"Lies, lies, lies. Is this what you tell yourself all day?"

Amanda dropped her spoon into the empty glass dish and said in a small voice. "I don't know what else to do."

"You could try living, for a change."

Amanda looked at her, confused. "Living? I am living."

"No, you are sticking to the plan."

"There's nothing wrong with focus and goals," Amanda retorted.

"There is when they come at the expense of living a life full of joy and happiness."

"Look, what are you trying to tell me?"

"I'm saying sometimes you need to throw out the plan and receive the gifts life brings you. Sometimes you need to get messy."

"I don't do messy. That's why I stick to the plan. Besides, Blake's family hates me."

"No, they don't."

"Were you not listening to what happened in Texas? His dad thinks I'm a scheming gold-digging whore, his sister loathes me, and his mother just barely thinks I may have some redeeming qualities."

"I did hear you, and I don't think Blake's family hates you so much per se as what you represent."

Amanda gave Alison a totally lost look. "And what is that?"

"The family life they lost when they were thrown into the upper echelons of the rich and famous from the comfortable middle class."

"Huh?"

"If Blake's dad hadn't invented biofuel, they would still be living the middle-class family dream in their cozy suburban cookie cutter house, his brother would still be alive, and if Blake brought home a girl like you his parents would be thrilled that he had found such a catch. Instead, they're stuck in the nightmare of the rich with everyone coming after them for money, or support of their charity, or waiting for them to make another groundbreaking discovery, or have their claws out to rip them to pieces when they make an epic fail. And then you walk in on Blake's arm embodying all that they've lost and can never get back. That's what they hate, not you."

Amanda just stared at Alison. "Did you change your major there at the end to psychology? Did I miss that too?"

Alison crunched on a piece of waffle cone. "No. But I did take philosophy and anthropology and you didn't. It gave me a better understanding of the world at large."

"Fine, Dear Abby. Any last words of advice?"

"For just this once, would you try to follow your heart instead of your head?"

Amanda looked up at the stars, and let out a long sigh. "That's like asking for the moon."

"No, the moon would be easier."

Amanda smiled at their inside joke. "I'll try."

"That's all I ask. And remember it's for your benefit, not

mine."

"If this all goes wrong, there's going to be an awful lot of blame laid at your feet," Amanda warned her.

"I'll be sure to wear sensible shoes and have my shoulder to cry on available."

"More like a punching bag."

"Try?"

"Try," Amanda agreed.

"Pinky promise?" Alison held out her little finger.

Amanda locked her own around it. "Pinky promise."

## Chapter Thirty

Blake sank into the padded rocking chair on the back porch and closed his eyes. The shower had helped relax him. He was tired from work and from putting together the fundraiser. But even more exhausting was keeping the polite cool distance from Amanda. Dimly, he heard the sound of children playing in the neighborhood, and a dog barked from a few houses down. He was just dozing off when the screen door opened and shut with a little bang. He opened his eyes to see Amanda take a seat in the rocker next to his. He drank in the line of her profile, the length of her lashes, the one lock of hair that always fell into her face no matter how recently she had put it up into a ponytail, the light sprinkle of freckles across her cheeks and nose, and the summer glow her skin had taken on in the past few weeks.

Amanda broke the silence between them. "I've come to broker a truce." She turned to face him. "I haven't been fair to you. I'm sorry." She bit her lip as she waited to see if he would accept her apology.

"Is that all?"

Confusion flitted across her eyes. "Is that not enough?"

"Oh, I accept your apology, and I know that it wasn't easy for you to give. I'm just curious as to why, and why now?" He linked his fingers together.

"It's all Alison's fault," she blurted out, then blushed.

"Oh. Alison put you up to the apology. In that case, tell her thank you for the good intentions, but I'm no longer going to accept it." He rose and went to step around Amanda to go inside.

She grabbed his wrist. "That didn't come out right. Please stay and I'll explain. Please."

Blake heard the plea in her voice and was surprised when he looked down to see that she was on the verge of tears and struggling valiantly to hold them back. He didn't like to see her cry. It made him feel helpless but at the same time like he wanted to protect her. He stepped back.

She released his wrist, and he sat down. "I meant my apology. It is thanks to Alison that I was able to give it to you. She pointed out how unfair and, well, pig-headed I've been when it comes to you. She forced me to see you for who you are, what you are, not what I've thought you to be. It's hard for me to let all that go. To let the hurt go."

"I'm sorry I hurt you Mandy, but I was young and stupid at the time," he apologized again.

She held up a hand. "I know, and it's been foolish of me to hold it against you all this time. We are both different people now, and while I've been more than willing to accept that about myself, I haven't done the same for you and for that I'm sorry. I will try to do better."

"Does that change anything else?" In the back of his mind, he hoped she'd agree to cancel their annulment.

"No, I still think it's best to end the marriage and go on with our lives," she said as if she'd known his unasked question. "But in the meantime, I will try to treat you like a kind human being should and not constantly dwell on the past and put you down."

"Well, I guess that's all a guy can hope for from his soon-to-be-ex-wife." The smile on his face didn't reach his eyes.

Amanda twisted her earring, a clear sign of her agitation that the conversation wasn't going according to plan. "How is the fundraiser coming together?" she asked, grasping at straws.

"Pretty well. I've got the sponsors lined up. I've committed every rotary club, church committee, and city program to take part by manning booths or doing bake sales or just straight donations. The 4-H club is going to oversee the pet parade, and we hope to get the majority of the animals adopted that day. I think it may just be enough to save the hospital, but I'll just have to wait and see at the end of the day."

"You've worked really hard, and I'm really proud of how you've stepped up and put this together to try to save the shelter. Whether you succeed or not, you should be proud too."

"Thanks."

From inside Jenny's voice called to them. "Amanda, Blake, time for dinner."

"Be right there," Blake called back and scooted to the front of his chair.

Amanda tapped her foot against the floorboard. "There's one more thing."

Blake raised his eyebrows. "Yes?"

Amanda licked her lips. "I wondered if you would be willing to go on a date with me?"

Blake's eyes raked hers. "Are you asking me out?"

She licked her lips again. "Yes. Will you come?"

Blake decided to string her along for a moment. "When is it, and where are we going?"

"Tonight, if you aren't busy. I thought since you'd been working so hard all week, and since we're both mostly recovered from our injuries, maybe we'd have some fun."

Blake looked at her with curiosity. "Are you sure your head's recovered? Because you aren't acting like you."

She swallowed and nodded. "I understand why you think that. But, yes, it's me."

"In that case, I accept."

A smile crept across her face. "Good. We'll go after dinner. Wear your dancing shoes."

"Dancing? You're taking me dancing?"

"If you think your arm and ribs can handle it. You'll be responsible for not dropping me, and for making sure my head doesn't hit anything. I'll be busy being responsible for my heart."

Blake gave her a genuine grin. "Where would be the fun in that?"

"Baby steps, Blake, baby steps."

"You got it, Mandy."

The table was loaded with baked chicken wings, homemade ranch dressing and biscuits, and Jenny's famous raspberry summer salad, but Amanda could hardly eat. She kept catching Blake looking at her, and after several days of them barely making eye contact, she found it unnerving. Plus, she was already a bundle of nerves. Letting go, giving up control on the reins of life were already prompting her stomach into an acid rage. She managed to get down a bit of chicken, a biscuit, and about four bites of salad before she thought she'd have to bolt for the bathroom.

The brothers barraged Blake with questions about the fundraiser, while Tiffany kept up a running diatribe with Missy about the High School Musical marathon they'd planned for the night and all the scenes they were looking forward to. Her sisters had seen them so many times that they sang along with all the songs and even got up and did the dances. They also had a game to go along with it that had to do with Troy and M & M's that Amanda didn't understand. In that respect she was glad she'd asked Blake to go out tonight.

Finally, dinner was over. The twins headed off for a game of Frisbee football, while the sisters donned their HSM gear and laid out the M&M's. Blake met Amanda at the door after they'd brushed their teeth.

"You ready?" he offered his arm to her and she took it. "Lead the way then."

In the car, Amanda changed the station about ten times as they left the neighborhood before Blake took her hand away from the radio.

"How about we just listen to whatever is in the CD player?"

She nodded, still a ball of nerves, and punched the button. It turned out to be Edwin McCain, and as Blake sang along with "I'll Be" Amanda felt her heart melt just a little. Her head angled to stop it, but she remembered her promise to Alison and slowly turned the tide of fear back away from her heart. She'd forgotten that Blake had a good singing voice, and she was so busy being entranced by it, that she nearly missed the exit. It turned out he knew the CD, because he sang along to every song. Halfway through the disc they arrived.

Blake looked out the window at the neon sign on the barn-like building in front of them. "Trudy's?"

"Trudy's," she confirmed and hopped out of the car.

Blake followed her into the building. The roof went up two stories and turned out to be a converted barn with a stage at one end, a bar at the entrance, tables and stools along the walls, and enormous fans that whirled above. Most people were dressed in jeans, t-shirts, and cowboy boots.

"Want a drink?" Amanda asked.

"Maybe later."

"There may not be time later. The band is getting ready for the next set. You won't get another chance for a while once they get started. You'll be too busy."

Blake looked at Amanda and was happy to see that the paleness that had been on her face during dinner had faded away. In fact, she looked energized. "What is this place?"

"Trudy's."

"Thanks, that clears everything up."

"Just try to keep up, don't get stomped on or stomp on anyone else or get in a fight."

"What if I decide to get a ride home with another girl?" He teased her but was alarmed at her reaction.

Storm clouds raced across Amanda's face. "Well, maybe I haven't misjudged you at all then. Perhaps you are still the spoiled, rich playboy I've always thought you to be. So, go ahead and find another girl to take you home, but don't ask her to bring you back to my house." She spun on her heel and headed for the far side of the dance floor.

Blake sped after her and caught her by the elbow. "Hey, Mandy."

She whirled around to face him and threw out her free hand to shove him in the chest, but caught him in the nose instead.

Blake let go and clutched at his nose.

"Oh, Blake, I'm sorry. I didn't mean to."

He waved a hand at her to stop her protestations. "I know. I need to remember how dangerous it is to be around you." He took his hand away from his nose and a trickle of blood ran down to his lip.

"You're bleeding," she said. "Crap."

"Like I said, dangerous, especially when I make you mad."

She grabbed him by the elbow this time and dragged him to the bar. "Mike," she called down to a guy who looked to be in his early thirties with a towel slung over his shoulder. "I need a towel and some ice."

Mike looked up at her and saw Blake. "Not again, Amanda."

"Uh, yeah."

Mike passed a bottle to the guy in front of him, pocketed the cash and brought over the ice and towel. "Here you go."

"Thanks, Mike." Amanda used the towel to mop up Blake's hand and face then wrapped it around the ice. She pressed it against Blake's nose. "Hold that there."

"Who'd you nail this time?" Mike asked just as the band started up.

"This is Blake," she answered.

"Innocent bystander?" Mike asked as the bar area cleared out and the dance floor filled up.

"No, not this time." She licked her lips. "My, uh, date."

Mike raised his eyebrows and gave Blake a nod of approval. "Date, huh? Well, congratulations." He reached over and shook Blake's hand. "Amanda's been chased by nearly every guy in this place, and she turns them all down. Nice work finally landing her."

"Mike." Amanda swatted his arm.

"Yeah, well, seeing as how I'm bleeding at the moment, I'd say perhaps the other guys were better off." Blake pulled the ice pack down off his nose. "Has it stopped bleeding yet?"

"Just about." Amanda dabbed at it again.

"Do you make it a habit of hitting people on a regular basis around here?" Blake reapplied the ice.

"Amanda's had a few mishaps out on the dance floor. You're not the first bleeder she's brought over to the bar," Mike answered.

"Thanks, Mike. Just share all my embarrassing secrets, why don't you?" Amanda gave a small scowl.

"I can do that." Mike grinned at Blake.

"No, thanks." Amanda grabbed the ice off Blake's face. "Good enough." She handed the towel and ice back to Mike. "Thanks." She tugged Blake toward the dance floor.

"We'll talk later," Blake shouted back to Mike over the surge of country music.

At the edge of the dance floor, Amanda looked for an opening in the crowd of dancers. "There." She pointed to a spot near the center.

Blake looked sideways at her. "I don't think we'll fit or even get out there without more blood."

"Sure we will." She counted the beats in her head and watched the dancers' footwork. "Okay, in four counts we'll have an in. Follow me. Ready?" Before Blake could respond she shouted, "Now!" She hauled him through the throng and made it to the tiny patch of clear dance floor just in time to yell, "Turn!"

All the dancers on the floor turned to face the wall to their right, and Blake had no choice but to follow or risk getting his nose swatted again. "What do I do?" he yelled over his shoulder to Amanda.

"Follow the girl in front of you, and try to keep up. I'll give you a heads up when to turn again."

"I don't know this one," Blake called back.

"That's obvious," she replied. "You'll catch on." He felt her gaze slip down to his feet. "Or you won't."

"Very funny. Did you catch on the first time you did this?"

"No, it took me a few times. Turn!"

They faced the next wall and were now side by side.

Blake had a few beads of sweat on his forehead. "How long is this song?"

Amanda laughed. "Halfway. But this set just started, so it'll be a while before we can take a break."

"You're kidding, right?"

"Turn!"

Now Blake's view was of Amanda's backside, and he couldn't help admiring how smoothly her feet followed the steps and how well her jeans fit. He tried to relax and let his feet take over instead of letting his head try to direct them. He'd just started to figure out the sequence of steps when he heard Amanda yell at him to turn again.

Side by side again she said, "I told you to have a drink before we came out here."

"Well, there wasn't time after you clocked me."

"Save your breath," she said as a small blush crept up her cheeks.

The song blended seamlessly into another and then another. Blake had just entertained the thought that he might pass out and be trampled in the middle of the dance floor if the band didn't take a break soon, when the tempo slowed, and one of the band members began to sing instead of calling out patterns. Blake looked around to see couples pairing off.

"Thank goodness, finally a slow one." Instinctively, he pulled Amanda into him and rotated them in a slow circle. Conscious of Amanda's proximity and the heat radiating off their bodies, Blake worked to keep his thoughts from straying into dangerous territory.

"You're doing pretty well for a first timer, I thought you might pass out soon," Amanda remarked.

"Without this slow song, I just might've." He held her close with his hand in the small of her back.

"I take it you've never been country line dancing before."

"Nope, this is a first."

Amanda shook her head. "How did you grow up in Texas and not learn to line dance?"

"By the time I would've, we'd moved into The Mansion and I was sent off to cotillion to learn more refined dances like waltz, fox-trot, and rumba."

Amanda giggled. "I can't imagine you in a tux fox-trotting around the dance floor."

"I'll have to remedy that. I do a mean fox trot, but what you should see is my salsa."

"Salsa? You know how to salsa?"

"And cha cha, merengue, samba, bolero, cumbia, among others."

"How did you learn all that? I didn't think they taught that at cotillion."

"They don't. But Ana Maria said I needed lessons in real culture and real dancing, so she'd take me to her house on weekends to learn."

"Ana Maria taught you all that?"

"Ana Maria, her sisters, nieces, cousins. She has a very large family, and they get together nearly every weekend to fiesta. It's just their way. She has one niece who is a salsa instructor who saw to it I knew what to do."

"What about Andrew and Cici? Did they learn too?"

A shadow of pain crossed Blake's heart as it always did at the mention of Andrew, but passed as quickly as it came. "They didn't come as often but they both learned, too."

After a moment, Amanda asked, "Could you teach me?"

Blake looked down at her. "To salsa?"

"Yes." She looked back at him with her blue eyes.

"You don't know how?"

"Nope. We Midwesterners line dance. We don't know how to do any of those savage dances where you move your hips." A smile danced playfully across her lips.

Blake extinguished a flame of desire that flickered up. Now

wasn't the time. "You seem to move your hips just fine from what I've seen."

Amanda blushed even through her red-from-dancing face.

Blake laughed. "But I think you have the potential to move your hips well enough to learn some of the savage dances as you call them, without being yanked off the floor for improper technique."

"Blake."

But her response was drowned out by a collective yell from the dancers around them as the tempo abruptly picked up and the lines reformed around them. They had no chance to talk until the set finished with a loud whoop from the crowd and a promise from the band that they'd return shortly for another set.

"Do you want that drink now?" Amanda asked as she weaved them through the throng of dancers leaving the floor, most of which headed for the bar for some much-needed rehydration.

Blake wiped the sweat from his brow. "Only if they've got Gatorade. I don't want alcohol. It'll only dehydrate me further.

"Mike doesn't keep Gatorade on hand, although I'll suggest it to him. He might be able to sell quite a bit of it, especially to the designated drivers and non-drinkers like me. So, do you want to get out of here and find some then?"

"Yes, Gatorade and a little quiet."

"Chicken. Only one set and you're ready to call it quits."

"How many do you usually stay for?" Blake asked as he opened Amanda's car door.

"All of them," she smirked.

He sank into the passenger seat and Amanda started the engine. "And how many is that?"

"Four," she answered. They pulled out of the parking lot and headed away from Trudy's.

"Four? Are you in it for the punishment?" Blake couldn't imagine doing that all night without being carted away in an ambulance.

Amanda laughed. "No. I just like dancing, plus it's a great

work out and a good way to meet lots of different kinds of people."

"And yet, you don't go home with any of the guys."

"No."

"Why?"

"What do you mean, why?" Amanda pulled into a gas station and the conversation was momentarily suspended as they got drinks and gas, and then hopped back into the car. She handed him a blue Gatorade. "Take a swig of that, then wait for the rest until we get there."

Blake took his one swig.

Amanda put the car in gear and pulled out of the gas station and soon onto the highway.

"Where are we going?" Blake looked out the window at the lights and signs they passed.

"To that quiet place you asked for. Although sometimes, it isn't all that quiet."

Blake tried to guess where she was taking him but only kept coming up with some Lover's Lane-type quiet place and somehow he didn't think Amanda would take him anywhere like that in a million years.

Finally, they turned off the highway and drove a little further onto a tree-lined gravel road. Blake looked sideways at Amanda and nearly missed seeing the sign outside his window. All he caught was the word "park" on it.

The trees opened up onto a grassy field where cars were parked randomly away from each other. Amanda found a wide open spot where they couldn't be heard by the other cars and parked. She grabbed her bottle, a blanket from the back seat and opened her door. She put her foot on the seat and heaved herself onto the roof. She poked her head back in. "Come on." She shut her car door.

She'd already spread the blanket out, without managing to fall off of the roof, when Blake grabbed his bottle of Gatorade and joined her. "Okay, what are we doing? And why are there other people here doing it?" he asked

She gave him a mysterious smile. "You'll see." She tapped his bottle with her own. "Cheers."

"Cheers." Blake gulped down half his bottle.

Amanda lay down on the blanket and looked up at the stars. "I love it here."

Blake lay down next to her. "Where exactly is here?"

"Brinker Park."

"Okay. Am I supposed to know anything about that?"

"Nope."

They lay there and listened to the sounds of the night: bugs, an occasional bird call, and faint strains of songs playing on other cars' radios. Then a rumble sounded.

Blake checked the sky. No clouds. The stars were bright. "Mandy, what's the rumbling sound?"

"You'll see."

It grew louder by the second until they could feel the car vibrate beneath them and their chests along with it.

Blake propped up on one elbow to see what was happening and his eyes grew wide at the sight of the bottom of a huge aircraft flying directly overhead. It was so close he almost felt as if he could reach up and touch it. "Mandy!" he shouted, but his voice was drowned out in the roar. He looked down at her.

Amanda opened her mouth and screamed at the top of her lungs, but Blake couldn't hear it. He could just see her mouth and eyes wide open with complete euphoria.

And then it felt like the air was suddenly sucked out of their chests and put just as quickly back in as the plane passed directly over them on its ascent to cruising altitude.

The last sound of Amanda's scream faded as the plane pulled up into the black sky alight with stars.

"What was that?" Blake's whole body shook from the near miss of being hit by a plane.

"Hmmm, judging by the vibration and rush, I'd say a Boeing 797." Then Amanda laughed until she cried.

Bewildered and shaken from the adrenaline rush, Blake stared down at her and wondered if he really knew anything about Amanda at all. "I thought we were going to die."

She shook her head back and forth as she struggled to get her laughter under control. "You should see your face." She hiccupped.

"I can see now why the guys don't take you home." He swung his legs over the side of the car with his back to her. "With you it's always a near death experience or a trip to the ER."

Amanda grabbed at his hand. "Wait, wait. I'm sorry. I just wanted to see your reaction."

He looked back over his shoulder at her. "My reaction?"

She nodded. "I wanted to know if you'd like it as much as I do."

"Like the feeling of very narrowly escaping being crushed by an airplane?"

"Oh, for goodness' sake, don't you have airports near where you live? Haven't you ever done this before or at least seen Wayne's World?"

"Yes, to the airports. No, to the last two. What exactly is this we're doing?" His temper was up.

Amanda sat up and noticed the curl just at the base of his hairline. It was obvious he was due for a haircut soon. Amanda stretched one hand out to touch it, but then pulled back. "Brinker Park is at the end of the airport, more specifically at the end of the runways. It's a great place to get a safe adrenaline rush and just cut loose a little."

Blake hadn't missed the heat of her hand so near his skin even though she hadn't touched him and turned around. "Safe adrenaline rush?"

"Well, some people like to bungee jump or sky dive or river raft. I'm not that adventurous. This way I can let go and scream my head off and still feel in control."

"It's always about control with you, isn't it? Even with the fun."

Amanda lay back down on the blanket and looked back up at the sky. "Yes," she said quietly.

Blake lay back down too.

"When I was younger, I used to lay here and wonder where the planes were going, what fantastic adventures the people on them were headed for, and I used to wish I was up there soaring through the clouds and stars off on my own adventure."

"Do you still feel that way?" Blake asked.

"No. The first time I flew on a plane I had an anxiety attack and discovered I get airsick. I spent most of the flight using up the supply of barf bags. Flying wasn't what I'd hoped it'd be."

"You did pretty well, getting to and from Texas," Blake pointed out.

"I've had four years to work on my fear of flying and my air sickness. Now, I can keep it boiling just below the surface, and I keep medication on hand. Plus, it depends on the length of the flight and whether I'm flying over land or the ocean. I nearly didn't come home for Christmas my freshman year. It was all I could do to put one foot in front of another and make myself walk onto the plane; mostly because I wanted to see my Mom so bad. School wasn't what I had imagined it would be, and I needed her so much."

"I'm guessing I was part of that last remark."

"Yes."

Blake waited a moment before he propped up to look at her and asked, "Am I forgiven for that yet?"

Amanda's brow furrowed as she concentrated on the stars. "Yes, I think so."

"Well, at least I've wiped out that past grievance. I'm pretty sure I'm still in the red for the marriage though."

"Yes." Amanda turned her eyes on him. "To answer your question from before, I don't go home with the guys from Trudy's because I can't afford to get involved with someone and mess up my plan."

Blake looked down at her as his fingers itched to trace a line across her cheekbone. "Your plan?" he murmured.

"Yes. Get my nursing degree, graduate, make a difference in a third world country, and then if love decides to show up, I'll consider it."

Blake frowned. "It's a very tidy plan you've got there. Sounds like fear drives it."

"Fear?"

"You don't date because it would open the door to being vulnerable, to putting your heart in someone else's hands."

"Well, yeah, exactly. I don't have time for heartache and pain. I've been working my butt off for the past four years to keep my grades up so I could keep my scholarship. Something you didn't have to worry about. Dating, heartache, those were distractions I couldn't afford, especially after I got a taste of them from you. So, yes, I've kept guys at a distance to stick to the plan." The sadness in Blake's eyes confused her.

"So, you've wasted four of the best years of your life all because you stubbornly stuck to your plan and put love at the bottom of your list."

"Wasted? I ranked near the top of our class, graduated, got the job I wanted and am on my way to Africa to make a difference and save lives. How is that wasting my life?" Amanda tugged at the hairband holding her ponytail and yanked it out. Her hair fell around her shoulders, momentarily distracting Blake.

"Because you didn't live it in the meantime."

"What did you say?"

He could see his words had acted like a slap in the face. "Your plan is admirable, Mandy, but if you don't agree to deal with the misery and mess that can come with a relationship, then you can't know the joy and euphoria that come with it either. You can't dismiss one without leaving the other behind too. Life is meant to be full of highs and lows. It's the lows that make you appreciate the rest and not take it for granted. That's what I mean when I say you wasted the past four years; that you haven't really been living."

Amanda lay back and threw one arm over her face. "That's what Alison said."

"What?"

"She said it was time to let go of the plan and live a full life and get messy. That life and love have their own timetable and it doesn't always sync with 'the plan'."

Blake couldn't help but smile. "I've always liked Alison."

Amanda removed her arm to see him. "Then why didn't you marry her?"

"Because I don't love her." The words tumbled out before Blake could stop them, and inwardly he cursed himself for making that mistake again. Amanda had made it clear she wasn't interested in his declarations of love or in returning them, yet he kept throwing the words out there and giving her yet another reason to distance herself from him.

"There's another one coming. Do you want to scream with me this time?"

Surprised that she hadn't berated him for his blunder, Blake lay down. "Sure. I could do with a good scream."

The rumble came first, then the vibration. The plane passed over them just as before and they screamed at the top of their lungs then laughed until their sides hurt.

"I see what you mean about the safe adrenaline rush," Blake finally got out.

They stared up at the stars and after Blake had pointed out a few constellations, Amanda said in a soft voice of confession, "You're the first guy I've ever come here with. Until tonight, I've only ever come with my sisters or friends or even sometimes alone when I just needed to think."

"Well, I'm honored," Blake replied sincerely.

"But I don't want you to get the wrong idea. I still want –,"

"The marriage annulled, I know," he finished for her. "You want to stick to the plan and not get messy."

"I don't know how to live any other way. I'm not sure how to try to, even if I wanted to."

Her voice was filled with an emotion Blake couldn't put his finger on, so he rolled onto his side to see her better.

Tears flowed out from the corners of Amanda's eyes and made their way toward her ears. "It's not easy for me to talk about my emotions and especially not with you." She tore her gaze away from the safety of the stars to look into his eyes. "I can't afford for you to break my heart again. I don't think I can recover from it a second time. That's why we have to annul this marriage and go our separate ways."

"Amanda," he said in hushed tones and wiped at her tears with his thumb. "I don't want to hurt you."

"I know." She made a sound that was half laugh and half cry. "I know, and I know that you mean it. You are making it so hard for me not to give in."

Blake had never seen Amanda unglued. Angry, yes. Icy, yes. Smiling, yes. But never at war with herself. She was always so assured. He watched her uncertain of what to do and decided he was better off doing nothing as he tried to shove down the hope that tried to blossom in his heart. "You want to give in?" he whispered.

"I can't." Her voice broke and so did the bubble of hope in Blake's chest.

Suddenly, her hand wrapped around the nape of his neck and caught hold of the curl at the bottom of his hairline, then tipped her head up to meet his lips.

That was all the encouragement Blake needed. He melded his lips to hers. For a few blissful moments everything else faded away.

Amada tried to break off the kiss, and got out a very quiet, "no" before Blake's lips found hers again. She broke contact again and said forcefully, "No."

Blake pulled back. "What's wrong?"

"Nothing. Nothing's wrong. Well, I mean, this is." She rubbed at her eyes.

"You don't like the way I kiss?" Blake asked.

"No, I mean yes, that's just the problem."

Blake desperately tried to follow her train of thought. "Mandy, most married people enjoy each other's kisses. That's one of the reasons they get married. So how is that a problem?"

"We're not most married people. You're Blake Worthington. I'm Amanda St. Claire. We got married because you got me too drunk to think straight, and I said yes. We're not supposed to be together. You're supposed to marry some rich socialite, and I'm, I'm..."

"You're what?" Blake said softly. "Supposed to live your life alone? Where is your happily ever after in the plan? When does he come in? When does that happen?"

That was the one piece of the plan Amanda had never been able to map out, when and where she would meet her husband. In the remote areas of Africa? Hardly likely. Graduate school, maybe? If she went. In a hospital somewhere? And now Blake had zeroed in on another one of her fears, that maybe she wasn't meant to be loved and cherished by someone in that way. "I don't know," she got out weakly.

He put a hand on top of hers. "Why can't it be now? Why can't it be me?"

"Because," she looked up at the stars as if they had the answer, but, of course, they didn't. "Because I have to go to Africa. I have to make a difference."

"Why can't you be married and go to Africa?"

"Because being married means settling down, having kids, and making sandwiches and mowing the lawn, not saving lives and not seeing the world and all the things I want to do before turning my life over into someone else's hands and never having control of it again."

Blake let go of her hand. "Is that what you think marriage is? What being married to me would be like?"

"What being married to anyone, including you, would be like."

Blake shook his head. "Haven't you paid any attention at all to your parents' marriage?"

"Of course I have."

"Is that what you see between them? Your mom a slave to her husband and family with no life and passion of her own?"

"Well –,"

"Have you ever asked you mom if she's happy with her life unfolding the way it has or if she has any regrets?"

"Well, no," Amanda admitted.

"Then maybe you should." He turned away and swung his legs over the side of the roof. Over his shoulder he said, "And while you're at it, you should know that I would never treat you the way you just described. I would never take away what makes you Amanda St. Claire in any way by killing your passions and interests. And if you think I would, then maybe we should go our separate ways." He jumped down to the ground and pulled open the car door. "Thanks for the date, Mandy. It's been enlightening. But it's late, and we should get home." He sat down and shut the door.

Amanda remained on the roof for a moment with a tornado of emotions whirling around inside her and at the heart of them the most terrorizing emotion: fear. Then she slowly slid off the roof, taking the blanket with her and the certain knowledge that the ride home would be one of uncomfortable silence as they both bit back the words to describe the emotions tearing through their hearts.

# Chapter Thirty - One

"Rise and shine," Amanda announced from the side of Blake's bed. "I made you breakfast for your big day."

Blake sat up and rubbed his eyes.

Amanda held a tray out toward him in what he thought was a peace offering. It had been a very tense and polite couple of days since their date.

"Just a minute." He grabbed his t-shirt from off the floor next to the bed and threw it on, but not before he caught Amanda admiring the definition of his chest and abs. Inwardly, he smiled to realize she wasn't completely immune to his appearance. He propped up the pillows behind him, and she set the tray down on his lap.

"I knew you'd need an early start for today. In fact, I'm surprised you aren't up already." She sank down on the bed near his feet.

Blake looked at the clock. It was barely six thirty, yet Amanda was up and dressed and ready to start the day. "You're up early," he remarked and dived into his eggs.

Amanda's hair was down, and she pushed a lock behind her ear as she pulled at a stray thread on the blanket. "I've been having trouble sleeping the past few nights," she confessed.

"Second thoughts?" He attacked the buttered English muffin.

"Second, third, fourth. I've lost track at this point." She gave a brittle laugh. "But my tangled thoughts are mine to sort out and not for you to worry about."

"I'm always willing to listen to you," he said softly.

Amanda skipped over his kind remark. "I meant what I said the other night about sticking to the plan."

"I know."

They sat there in silence, each waiting for the other to break it. Blake ate and kept his steady gaze on Amanda, who picked at the blanket, and refused to meet his eyes.

Finally, Amanda stood up and brushed at her denim capris. "I just wanted to tell you how proud I am of you for putting together this fundraiser and for working so hard to save the animal shelter no matter how it turns out at the end of the day."

"Thanks." Blake set down his empty orange juice glass.

"I have to admit, this isn't what I had in mind when I got you the job there."

"I know."

"You do?" Her eyes flew up to meet his.

"I knew exactly what you were up to after the first day. You got me a menial filthy job, so I would give up and go home to Texas after a few days."

"Yeah, well, that was before I learned what your life was like in Texas." She rubbed a bare foot against the back of her other calf. "If I'd known that ahead of time, I'd have realized the animal shelter would've seemed a total picnic in comparison."

"Doesn't matter. I've learned a lot from the experience of working there and putting this day together. So, before I forget, thank you."

Amanda looked away and blushed. "You're welcome."

Blake wiped his mouth with his napkin and set in on top of the plate.

Amanda picked up the tray of empty dishes. "I'd like to do something for you today."

Blake raised his eyebrows at her. "Besides making me breakfast?"

Amanda bit her lower lip. "Yes. I'd like to ask to be your go-to-girl today."

Blake crossed his arms across his chest. "Go-to-girl?"

"Inevitably, things are going to come up, fires are going to need to be put out, and you can't be everywhere at once. Or you just might need to stop and get lunch or at least a pretzel to hold you until it's over. I want to be the person who does whatever needs doing to keep things running smoothly, and to keep you from falling over from dehydration and hunger."

Blake rubbed his stubbly chin with one hand. "I could use a go-to-girl today. Think you can handle it without one or both of us ending up in the ER? We are a dangerous combination."

"I think we can get through today without a trip there."

"Okay, then. You're hired. You can be the go-to-girl today."

Amanda gave him a grateful smile. "Thanks."

She lingered there holding the tray until Blake said, "Um, Mandy, I'd like to grab a shower before all the crazy starts. So, unless it's on your agenda to catch me in my boxers in addition to being shirtless this morning you may want to head upstairs."

Amanda's cheeks blazed crimson. "I'll go wash up the dishes while you get showered."

"Thanks."

Her feet pounded up the stairs blocking out the sound of Blake's low chuckle. He quickly showered, dressed, then headed up the stairs to the kitchen where Amanda hung a towel back on the stove handle. Blake appeared in the kitchen doorway and with a finger tapped at the clipboard in his other hand.

"If you're going to be the go-to-girl, we'd better go over the itinerary and stations so you know what's going on."

"Right."

"So, look it over while I drive."

"Right."

In the car, Amanda studied Blake's detailed notes and drawings, asked questions and tried to appear at ease. Several cars pulled into the park behind them.

"Good timing," Blake called to her brothers, Madge, and Moose, as they all exited the cars. "Let's get everyone t-shirts, and then I'll pass out assignments." He opened the trunk of the car and everyone slid a t-shirt over their existing ones, except for James and Josh who swapped theirs.

"It'll be too hot in another hour to have on two shirts," Josh explained.

"Right. James and Josh, you're in charge of parking all the vendors and showing them their set up areas." Blake passed them two maps.

"You got it, boss," James said. He and Josh moved off as the first truck rolled up.

"Madge and Moose, we need to mark off the perimeter for the pet parade, bake sale area and set up the adoption center." Blake handed them their papers.

"We're on it," Moose said.

"Moose and I will head to the shelter about ten, to pick up and transport the animals here for the start at noon," Madge said.

"Perfect," Blake said.

Madge gave Blake an impromptu hug. "Thanks Blake."

He patted her on the back. "Don't thank me yet. Let's see if we succeed first."

"I have a good feeling about today," Madge said.

Blake shot a quick glance at Amanda before replying, "Me too."

Madge and Moose moved off to complete their assignments.

"What do you want me to do?" Amanda asked tightening her ponytail.

Blake pointed to the trunk. "First, let's set up base camp under the pavilion, and we can plug those in there." He pointed to the walkie-talkies he'd rented for the fundraiser. "They should be all charged up, but we'll be swapping them out all day as batteries run out and need to be recharged. Then hand out t-shirts to all the volunteers and vendors as they arrive."

"Yes, sir." Amanda saluted. She picked up the box of t-shirts.

"Oh, and you'll need one of these." He pitched a water bottle into the top of the box. "You can't be my go-to-girl if you pass out from dehydration." He hefted the box with the walkie-talkie equipment onto his shoulder, and they moved into the shade of the pavilion.

"How are you going to keep the animals protected from the July sun?" Amanda asked as she sorted shirts by size.

"Tents." He pointed at a truck that had just rolled up marked Eddie's Special Events. "There should be a truck with water coming too, and we've got signs to go up in the parking lot to remind people not to leave pets in their cars. Cheryl should be taking care of those when she gets here."

"You seem to have thought of everything."

"Thought of, called, contacted, and now hoping everyone follows through."

She laid a hand on his arm. "They will."

The rest of the morning left very little time for conversation beyond where to put things or find things or get instructions as the park filled with vendors, vans, and volunteers.

At noon, Madge got on the megaphone at the edge of the pavilion and welcomed everyone to the event. She announced the first pet parade and the opportunities available for pet adoption, games, events, and bake sale through the afternoon. Everyone clapped and then headed off to check out vendors, play games, or enter into the pet parade.

Blake had a minute to step in under the pavilion and grab a bottle of water from the blue cooler next to one of the tables. He took a long swig, poured some on his face, and then shook it off out in the grass before he stepped back in. "How are things going in here?" he asked Amanda.

"Well, so far so good. Here's that pretzel I promised you."

"Good, because I'm starved."

"Yeah, and who knows when you'll get to eat again today."

"If I do, I'll be looking for a snow cone or some of Busco's custard. It's got to be the hottest day of summer today."

"Nope. Wait until August."

"You'll be gone by then," he reminded her.

"Oh, yeah, right." She handed him the salted pretzel in wax paper.

"It's still warm," he said in surprise.

"Can't say I don't deliver." She smiled at him.

"Thanks, Mandy."

"You're welcome."

They stood there with goofy grins on their faces for a moment before Blake's walkie-talkie went off and the twins asked him about a vendor who'd showed but wasn't on the map. "Sounds like I've got my first fire."

"Go get 'em." Amanda waved as he walked away, scarfing down the only food he'd seen since breakfast. "I'll have to see if I can shove a hotdog in his hand later," she muttered to herself.

Blake's voice blared from her walkie. "Amanda."

"Go for Amanda," she replied.

"One of the judges didn't show for this round of pet parade. Either find me another one fast, or step in and do it yourself."

"You got it." Amanda dodged people from the pavilion over to the pet parade. Just as she came to the circle of people there to watch, she spotted Mr. Wiggins and tapped him on the shoulder. "Mr. Wiggins, how nice to see you," she said.

"Nice to see you too, Amanda."

"Are you going to watch the pet parade?" she asked.

"Yes."

"Do you have any family in it?"

"No. I was actually watching it to get an idea of what kind of pet my grandson would like."

"Perfect. How would you like to get a closer view?"

"What did you have in mind?"

Amanda tucked the lock of hair behind her ear. "I am in need of a pet parade judge to round out the panel. Would you do the honors?"

"Sure. That'd be great."

"Thank you, Mr. Wiggins." She led him over to the judges' area to the empty spot, gave him his papers, and then signaled Harriet from 4-H that she was all clear to start the parade. Amanda stayed to watch for a few minutes as the kids walked around with dogs, cats, iguanas, lizards, fish, a ferret, and a few hamsters before she headed back to the pavilion.

"Got you a judge," she radioed Blake.

"Thanks. The regular should be here for the next one." Pet parades were being done every two hours until six.

"Got it."

"Who'd you get by the way?"

"Mr. Wiggins. He and his wife bred Yorkies for years. I figured he could handle the pet parade."

"Great. Thanks."

When he got a moment, Blake hustled over to the pet parade to check on things there. The first ribbons were being awarded, and the smiles on the kids' faces were pure delight. Then he stopped by the adoption center where he hoped most of the animals from the shelter would find new homes today. The July sun beat down mercilessly, and he noticed Madge and Moose had set up some fans to keep the animals and people cool. "How's everything here?" he asked Madge as she finished up some paperwork with a woman and her two kids.

"We've had more adoptions in the last hour than in the last month. At this rate, the shelter will be almost empty by tonight."

"That's a good thing, right? To have all the animals go to homes?"

She wiped a trickle of sweat off her brow. "It is a good thing. I asked Brooke to stay at the shelter to handle any that came to look at some of the more exotic animals that we couldn't bring out here. I called her a bit ago, and she said she's had lots of calls about the fundraiser and that people have been popping in to look at the animals there."

"That's great."

"It's all your doing." She grinned at him.

"Oh, no. All the puzzle pieces were already there, I just moved them into place. You could just have easily done this."

Her expression grew serious. "No, I couldn't. I explained that to you when you first came to work at the shelter. This is your doing. So, take some credit."

Blake held up his hands in surrender. "Okay, Madge. I'll be back to check on you later. Do you need anything?"

"Nope. I just sent one of the volunteers for a jug of water. Once that gets here we should be fine."

"Okay, radio me if you need anything else. I've got some more checks to make."

She waved at him as another family approached asking about which animals were available to adopt. He passed by the food court area and saw the Ladies Aide Society had a cake walk going. The music stopped, a number was called, and a kid that looked to be about five with a ring of bright blue around his mouth, probably from a snow cone, jumped up and down and yelled that he'd won. Blake looked over to see a woman bringing him a cake decorated like a rocket and smiled. He shook hands with each of the vendors and volunteers as he passed them and thanked them for coming and supporting the shelter. The day burned on in a blur of pet parades, adoptions, games, cake walks, and, finally, it was time to bring out Whiskers and make the estimate of how much the fundraiser had actually produced.

He walked into the pavilion. Amanda looked soaked to the skin. Her hair was wet and stuck to her scalp and neck. It struck Blake that she'd probably look like this all the time in Africa and that she'd never looked better. "What happened to you?" he asked.

She looked up at him from her clipboard and calculator. "July," she answered.

"You look like you got caught in a car wash with your clothes on."

"Wrong. Wet t-shirt contest," she teased.

"You won, right?"

"Nah. Runner up. Alison's chest is bigger."

Blake's laugh came all the way from his stomach and a heartbeat later Amanda joined him. "That was a good one," he said, once he'd regained his breath. He pointed at the calculator. "How'd we do?"

"Well, you probably should've gotten someone with more math skills than me to crunch the numbers, but I think overall you've raised about two-hundred thousand."

"That's all?" Blake's face fell into a disappointed crease.

"That's all! Do you realize how much that is for the shelter? What were you aiming for?"

"Like twice that, or at least enough to make it through the next year."

"Blake, with this much Madge should be able to run the shelter for nearly a year with all the food and stuff you've received in addition."

"I was hoping to set them up for two years."

She stood up, grabbed him by the shoulders, and pulled him down to her eye level. "Now you listen to me Blake Worthington, you've succeeded with this fundraiser. You've raised enough money to run the shelter for a year, and Madge told me that all but two of the animals at the shelter were adopted today, including the tarantula. So, don't you begin to feel guilty or like you failed in any way. I won't have it. This is far more than anyone else could've done, and you should be proud." With their eyes locked together and her rant over he realized how close their faces were to one another. All it would take was one little move to bring their lips together, but neither of them moved.

A cough sounded. "Uh, sorry to break up this cozy moment," James smirked unapologetically at them. "But Blake, everyone's gathered on the field for your presentation and announcement."

Blake blinked and stood up. "Uh, right."

Amanda shoved a hotdog into his hand. "Eat this on the way."

"Thanks." Blake took off at a brisk pace.

James linked his arm through Amanda's as they walked toward the field at a slower pace. With a twinkle in his eye he said, "You like him."

Amanda rolled her eyes. "Oh please, James."

"You do," he reiterated. "Admit it," he dared her.

"Fine. I like him. You happy now?"

"Nope."

She bumped him with her hip. "What is it you want me to say?"

"Look, I know it's none of my business –"

"You're right. It's not." Amanda tried to squash the conversation.

"But, maybe Blake wasn't a mistake."

"What?" Amanda stopped, unwound her arm from James's, crossed her arms over her chest, and turned to face him.

"Look, I know when he showed up you were furious about it, and having to tell us, and it was obvious there was nothing like happily ever going on, but you've got to see that things have changed between the two of you."

"I'm still going to Africa." Amanda wasn't going to admit anything to James.

"I didn't say things were perfect. You still have a real love-hate relationship at times, but the way you two fight is so right. Look, we all like Blake."

"And that's a good reason for me to stay married to him." The sarcasm dripped from her voice.

"Amanda, you are so stubborn. All I'm trying to say is, I think you should really give the marriage a try. You might just like it."

"And where will that leave me? Not in Africa. I'll be stuck being some charity socialite in Texas. Well, I have a difference to make in the world and lives to save."

"Yes, but at what cost?"

She glared at him. "You know how much I've saved over the last four years to be able to do this."

"I wasn't talking about money," James said quietly. "I was talking about your heart."

"What do you know about my heart?"

"I know that you don't listen to it nearly as much as you should. A bad St. Claire trait at times. Do you know what I'd give to have Shayna back?"

"What?" He rarely brought up Shayna, and he usually didn't make heartfelt confessions to Amanda.

"I'd give up Josh."

Amanda was ready to scoff at this remark. The twins were inseparable as well as insufferable. But then she read the look of seriousness and pain in his eyes and choked it back. "Josh?" she whispered.

"I was too proud to tell Shayna my feelings. I was too stubborn to even check in with my own heart to know how I felt until it was way past too late."

"I'm sorry," she fumbled.

"I just don't want to see you make the same mistake, little sis."

Impulsively she hugged him. "Thanks, James. I appreciate it. I really do. But, I have to make my own mistakes."

"I know. I'm just trying to give you a heads up. Africa will still be there no matter what you decide. That continent has been there for a while now. It's not going anywhere any time soon. Come on, or we'll miss your husband's big speech."

They put the sun to their backs and walked across the grass to where the crowd was gathered.

"Just remember, it's no good saving lives if you haven't saved your own. Not to mention how many lives you could save with Worthington Enterprises as your backer." He winked at her.

With difficulty Amanda admitted to herself that with Blake and the Worthington fortune, she could indeed save a lot of lives, including her own.

## Chapter Thirty - Two

From the doorway of Amanda's room, Blake waited for her instructions.

"The boxes along that wall are for storage. The boxes on this wall are for stuff I'll want in Africa, and the black trash bags are for donations." Amanda pointed to them.

"What about trash?" Blake asked.

"Can in the hall. Are you sure you want to help me with this?" Amanda stretched her arms over her head.

"Sure. I don't mind. I'll probably need to do it to my own room soon."

"Okay."

"Where do you want to start?"

Amanda pointed to her nightstand. "Let's start there and work our way around the room."

"You really think you can get through the whole room in one day?"

"I already did some initial weeding out with Alison right after I got home from Vegas. Plus, I'm not a pack rat. I'm not overly sentimental about stuff."

"I've noticed."

Amanda raised an eyebrow at him as she swept her hair back into her customary ponytail.

Personally, Blake preferred her hair down. He cleared his throat. "Sorry. Nightstand it is. Today I'll be your go-to-guy." He picked up an old battered teddy bear with a missing nose. "Is this a donation or trash?"

Amanda snatched the bear away. "This is Mr. Hugs-A-Lot. I've had him since I was four. I'm not giving him away. If I could, I'd take him to Africa, but there just won't be room." She sighed and rubbed the spot where his nose had been. "He goes in the storage box for now. But I'll get you back out as soon as I come home." She snuggled the teddy bear one last time and then handed him to Blake who wisely set him gently in a box marked storage.

"The alarm clock and lamp stay. But that reminds me that I'll need my travel one for Africa." She retrieved her travel clock from the closet and set it in the box marked Africa.

Blake grabbed the book next to the alarm clock. "What about this? *Sweet Confections*."

"I'll have finished it long before I leave for Africa. That is one of my problems though. I can't take my Kindle because it's too likely to get broken or stolen and who knows when I'd be able to charge it up if I did take it, and I can't take books because they take up too much room. I really love to read, but I guess I'll have to find another way to spend my leisure time and get myself to sleep at night."

"I bet you can find a bookstore when you land. Probably even a second-hand one and just get paperbacks and leave them in the villages when you finish them. I'm sure they'd appreciate a free book, even if it is a romance novel."

"I don't only read romance."

It was his turn to raise an eyebrow.

"I also read historical romance," she rebutted, and then they both laughed.

Amanda opened the top drawer. "Scriptures go to Africa, but I'll pack them right before I leave."

"Should I write that down?"

"What?"

"Well, do you want a list of last minute items to be packed so you don't miss them?"

"That would be a good idea. Why didn't I think of that?" she murmured to herself as she slid a pen and pad of paper out of her stand. She handed them to Blake. "Here."

He started the list.

Amanda picked up her journal. "I need to grab the one for Africa." Another trip to the closet and she deposited a journal in the Africa box. "Can you also make a list of last minute storage items?"

"Sure." Blake flipped to a clean page on the pad and scribbled away.

"Make sure it's legible or it's no good."

"Yes, Ma'am." Blake saluted her. "Let's see what you've got in the bottom drawer." He pulled it open to find only a shoe box covered in silver wrapping paper marked 'Treasures' in a glittery blue substance. "What's in here?" He started to open the box.

Amanda snatched it out of his hands. "It's none of your business. It goes in storage." She put it in the box.

"C'mon. Show me just one thing or my curiosity is going to drive me crazy. You already told me you're not sentimental, and yet you've got a box full of memories that are special to you."

Amanda tapped one toe nervously. "Just one thing." She picked up the box and opened the lid. She pulled out a perfectly white sea shell and handed it to him.

He looked at her. "It's a shell."

"Yes. I found it on my first trip to the beach. I was eight the first time I saw the ocean and played in the waves. I picked it up on my first day in Corpus Christi."

"It's beautiful." He handed it back to her, but it slipped from her fingers and fell onto the light brown carpet. "Sorry."

They both bent down to retrieve it, cracked heads and Amanda dropped the box full of treasures all over the floor. Ticket stubs, friendship bracelets, pictures, junior high notes, and a dried flower spilled all over.

"Sorry, Mandy. You okay?"

She rubbed a spot along her hairline. "I'm fine."

"I'll help you clean up." He picked up the treasures carefully and deposited them back in the box while Amanda did the same. He paused when he saw a picture. "Is this us?" He turned it to her. It was just of their faces with a bit of building and sky in the background.

Her face paled a bit. "Uh, yeah." Her hand shook as she took it back from him and put it in the box.

Blake's brow crinkled. "When was that from?"

"Freshman year. Our second date. Top of the bell tower." Her voice was strained.

Remembrance dawned on his face. "Oh yeah, I'd forgotten about that."

"I'm not surprised."

"Why'd you keep it? I thought you spent the last four years hating me. Why would you keep a picture of us?"

"To remind me how good a thing can start and how painfully it can end." She put the last item, the shell, in and shut the box. It landed in the storage box with a quiet thud.

Blake reached a hand toward her. "Mandy, I—"

She moved away. "Just don't. We've already had this conversation." She rubbed her hands across the top of her shorts. "Okay, night stand is done. Bookshelf is next."

Blake steadily piled the books into storage and donation boxes until the shelves were bare, which only left the trophies on the top of the case.

"I need to get a step stool to reach those. I'll be right back." Amanda headed for the door.

"We don't need the stool, Mandy. I can reach them." With ease, he lifted one off the end and read it. "Soccer, huh?"

"I played goalie." She shrugged. "I was okay."

"Well, at least that's a skill you'll find useful in Africa."

She gave him a quizzical look. "Soccer?"

He smiled. "Soccer is a favorite sport there and a poor man's game. All you need is a ball and you're good to go. You want to see a kid's face light up, bring a soccer ball." He handed her another soccer trophy.

"Seriously? When did you come across that bit of trivia?"

"Well, you forget that I like history, and I probably watch far too many documentaries and the history channel. I imagine the kids in the areas you'll be going to won't have much, but they're still kids, Mandy. They still like to have fun, and they know how to be happy with what they have, unlike a lot of people in our country." Bitterness crept into his last remark.

"Well, most of the world thinks money can buy happiness."

He snorted. "My family has plenty of money. Do we seem happy to you?"

"No," she answered candidly.

"Yet, your family, with considerably less, is quite happy. Don't you think the impoverished Africans will have the secret to happiness in their smiles?"

"I guess I never thought about it, but I'll let you know."

"You mean you're still going to talk to me after you leave for Africa?" This was the first indication she'd given that they'd have any contact once she left, and Blake wanted to get a promise from her if he could.

"I'll very well have to since it doesn't look like the paperwork will be finished before I leave."

"Right." He squashed down the feeling of rejection inside. He finished handing her trophies, a few dance ones, and the remainder were from swimming.

Silently, she wrapped them in packing paper and set them in the box with the rest.

"What's next?" he asked.

"Desk." She opened drawers and bagged all the pens, pencils and markers. "I'll give these to my mom. She'll know what to do with them."

"Can I take them?"

She looked at him surprised. "What do you want with a bunch of old pens and stuff?"

"Well, if you're not going to use them, the shelter could. They're always in need of basic office supplies, and you know how pens walk away."

"Oh, right. I never thought of that." She tossed him the bag, and he set it in the hall. She handed him a bunch of notebooks. "Storage."

Blake set them in the second box and glanced at the paper-covered trophies again. "I didn't know you were a swimmer," he remarked.

She handed him a stack of stationery. "Storage again. I swam a lot when I was young."

"It looks like you were pretty good, judging from the number of trophies."

She shrugged. "I went to my first J.O.'s my sophomore year of high school."

"J.O.'s?"

"Junior Olympics. We were all pretty excited. My parents didn't want me to know, but my coach was recommending that I relocate to further my training because he thought I just might be Olympic material. Not that my parents could've afforded that. But then I injured my shoulder before my junior year, and they had to do surgery and it was never the same after. End of swimming career."

"You must've been devastated." Blake picked up the stack of papers from the top of the desk.

"I was pretty upset at the time, but it just wasn't meant to be. I don't really think about it much or talk about it either." She pointed to the stack. "Recycle. I don't need those anymore."

Blake looked down. "What are they?"

"Notes from college classes."

Blake put them out in the hall. "Looks like that just leaves your dresser and closet."

"Not really." She pulled open the dresser drawers. Only two of them had clothes left in them.

"What about the closet?"

She opened the door where not much was left either. "Alison and I already went through my clothes, and I've been emptying the rest of the closet over the last few weeks. I didn't want to leave it all to the end and feel stressed." She picked up a roll of packing tape. "Will you hold the boxes shut?"

"Sure."

A half an hour later the boxes were taped, marked, and stacked neatly across one wall of the closet. They hauled the recycling, trash, and donations outside.

Amanda shut the trunk on the bags of donations. "You up for some lunch?"

"Definitely. I was ready an hour ago."

She smiled. "I thought so. You like burgers, right?"

"Just like every other guy."

"Then we'll hit Mark's after we drop off the donations."

It was a quiet drive to Mark's as he contemplated whether to consider this a date, friends hanging out, or something else entirely. With their order filled they sank into some aluminum chairs with orange seats and unwrapped their burgers.

Blake took his first bite and gave a little groan of approval before he proceeded to devour it, at eating-contest record-breaking speed. When he finished, he wiped his mouth with his napkin and stood up. "That was awesome. I need another. Do you want anything else?"

Amanda laughed. "I think I'm good." She pointed down at her half-eaten burger. "One of these is enough for me, but you go ahead."

By the time Blake had polished off his second burger, Amanda had just finished hers.

"So, what now?" he asked. "I thought packing up your room would take all day and maybe even some of tomorrow."

Amanda checked the time on her phone. "How about we go home and surprise the family by cooking dinner and dessert? I know Mom would appreciate having a night off."

"I'm all for doing something to please your mom. She and your dad have been more than generous to me."

"I think my family has been happy to have you around this summer."

"I agree. But, what about you? I know you were less than thrilled when I showed up on the doorstep with my suitcase. Are you happy now that I came?"

Blake gave her the perfect opportunity to open up to him, but could see Amanda still struggled with her feelings toward him.

"It's been enlightening," she remarked.

They sang along to the radio the whole way home.

In the kitchen, she tossed him an apron. "Come on. I'll teach you how to make homemade bread." She tied a blue apron around her waist.

Blake looked down at the apron before he tied it on. "Kiss the cook? Really?"

"That's my dad's. It's very manly. My mom gave it to him on Father's Day one year and he doesn't seem to mind."

"That's because he's more than happy to get a kiss from your mom."

"True." She took a recipe book down from a shelf full of cookbooks and flipped through it. She stopped on a page. "Here we are."

"Are you sure this is a good idea? I burnt the toast, remember?"

"Yes, but you made good progress with the eggs. I think you can handle this, unless you don't think you're up to the challenge." Her eyes dared him.

"I'm in. But don't blame me if it all goes wrong and we have to run to the store for a loaf of store-bought garlic bread."

"I'm not worried about the bread. It's dessert you're going to have to worry about."

Blake looked at her. "Why? What are we making for dessert?"

"Baked Alaska."

"What?"

She flipped a few more pages and tapped on one. She handed the book to Blake who skimmed the instructions.

"You're crazy. I can't make that."

She took the book back. "Not alone, but I think we can do it together. Now quit stalling and get in the pantry. I'll read off the ingredients and you grab them."

Blake saluted her. "Aye, aye, captain."

They spent the rest of the day in the kitchen, measuring, mixing, baking, cooking, and cleaning.

When Jenny walked in from work she asked, "What's all this?"

"Dinner," Blake answered, with flour in his hair as he washed dishes.

Jenny looked at the kitchen in various stages of dirty and clean and then asked Amanda, "Do I want to know?"

"Nope. Dinner will be ready," she checked the clock, "in about fifteen minutes. Go put your feet up with Dad."

"He's home?"

"Got off a little early tonight, and I banished him and the girls to the family room. Tiffany was being an insufferable flirt with Blake, and I was ready to dump the flour bucket over her head."

"Luckily, I caught it before she did," Blake said.

"I see." Jenny grinned. "Well, thanks for dinner."

Blake raced off to shower in order to remove the flour from his hair, while Amanda agreed to set the table. With his hair still damp, he reached the bottom of the stairs, when she called, "Dinner!"

Everyone raced in and took a seat around the table. Blake made it just in time for the prayer. Then it was the endless round of passing bowls, plates, and catching up on the day. Tiffany grumbled about some girl named Katie who'd snagged some guy she'd been racing after all summer named Beau. Missy asked Amanda for advice on some of her college classes for next semester. Blake caught up with Bill and Jenny about work and enjoyed just feeling a part of the family. He knew his days were numbered. Amanda would leave for Africa in just over a week, and while he knew Bill and Jenny were too kind to ever kick him out, he knew he'd have to deal with his parents and his future sooner rather than later. Plus, he had enough to pay for the lawyer now to settle the annulment. Lost in his own thoughts, he didn't notice his phone ring.

"Blake, are you going to get that or turn it off?" Missy ripped off a slice of the homemade garlic bread he hadn't managed to sabotage.

"Oh, sorry." He reached down to silence his phone and return the call later when he noticed it was his mom. "Uh, Jenny, I'm sorry, I know you don't like calls during dinner, but it's my mom." She hadn't called him since the birthday party.

"Sure."

Blake hopped over Missy into the hallway and caught the call just before it went to voice mail. "Mom?"

Amanda tried to overhear Blake's conversation, but Missy and Tiffany were too loud and then she heard the front screen door slam and knew Blake had gone outside. Her forehead puckered as she wondered what the call was about. Blake's parents had continued to give him the silent treatment after their visit, even with the media circus about his domestic dispute and arrest.

"Amanda." Jenny's voice called her daughter back to the present moment.

"Sorry, Mom, what?" Amanda focused on her mother and realized there was just a hint of gray showing at her temples.

"We wondered what you and Blake had whipped up for dessert."

"Oh, we made Baked Alaska."

"Baked Alaska?" her sisters chorused.

"What's that?" asked Missy as she polished off her garlic bread.

"It's a cake, with ice cream on top, that you put meringue on top of then bake in the oven," Amanda explained.

"Sounds weird," said Tiffany as she cleared her dishes to the sink.

"Just give it a try," encouraged Jenny. "Oh, and you and Missy have dish duty as apparently I have the night off and Amanda and Blake did all the cooking."

"Ah, Mom," Tiffany groaned. Doing dishes came in only second to cleaning the shower on her not-fun-to-do house cleaning list.

"No nonsense, Tiffany. You do as your mom says, or I'll

consider confiscating your phone for the night," Bill said.

Tiffany gave a little yelp and turned on the water. "Missy, get over here and help me," she ordered.

"Keep your shirt on, I'm coming." Missy grabbed her dishes and joined Tiffany at the sink.

Blake walked in ashen-faced.

"What's wrong?" Amanda asked.

"It's my dad. He's had a heart attack. They're at the hospital. The doctors aren't sure if he's going to pull through."

Jenny clapped her hands to her mouth. "Oh, Blake," she gasped.

Bill handed Amanda the car keys. "My car has a full tank of gas. Take it and get going. You should be able to get there by morning."

Blake shook his head. "Thanks, Bill, but that might be too late. My mom is sending the plane. It's already in the air. It'll be here in an hour. I just need a ride to the airport."

"Right. I'll take you. How soon can you be ready?" Amanda asked.

"Ten minutes. Fifteen tops." Blake thundered down the stairs.

"Sorry about dessert, Mom. You'll just have to finish it up and eat it without us," Amanda said.

"Don't worry about that now," Jenny reassured her.

"I'm going to help Blake pack." Amanda raced down the stairs after him.

Blake had his suitcase open on the bed and threw his clothes in as fast as he could. He didn't worry about folding or whether they were dirty or clean.

"I can empty the dresser," Amanda volunteered. "You grab whatever is in the bathroom."

Blake just nodded.

Amanda removed the remainder of his clothes from the drawers and got them into the suitcase still folded.

Blake emerged from the bathroom with a small toiletry bag and tossed it into the suitcase. He shut the lid and zipped it up.

"That should be it." He heaved the suitcase to the floor.

"What about the closet?" Amanda asked.

"I did that first." She followed him up the stairs. The family waited for them on the front porch.

Bill shook Blake's hand. "Been good to have you, Blake."

"Thanks, Bill."

"Come back, okay?" Missy gave him a quick hug.

Tiffany's hug took a little longer. "We'll miss you."

Jenny squeezed him tight. "You're always welcome here, so don't be a stranger regardless of how things turn out."

"Thanks, Jenny. I'm sorry to leave like this," he apologized to all of them.

"Family comes first. It's the rule we live by." Jenny patted his arm. "You go take care of your family. We'll be praying for your father."

"Thanks."

"Be back soon," Amanda said to her family.

"I know you're in a hurry, but don't drive too fast. It won't do you any good to wind up in an accident," Bill reminded her as she and Blake went down the front steps.

"Got it, Dad." She shook her keys in a wave.

Blake already had his bag in the trunk and was in the car when she sat down in the driver's seat. "Thanks," he said. His face wore a tight-pinched look.

The drive to the airport was tense and silent. Amanda followed the signs to the smaller private airstrip and parked.

In a flash Blake was out of the car and had his suitcase in hand. He wheeled it into the small lobby attached to the main hangar. Amanda followed him in and lingered in the background while he checked in. When he finished, he turned around. "Follow me. The plane's already landed."

He led them to an adjoining building with another hangar. Inside sat the Worthington company plane. A man waved at Blake as he entered and yelled, "Blake." He approached them and shook Blake's hand. "We'll be ready in about five minutes. Just have to finish the checklist, and she's already fueled.

"Thanks, Fletcher. This is Amanda."

"Nice to meet you." Amanda shook hands with him.

Fletcher looked at Blake. "I thought you were the only one on the flight."

"I am. Amanda drove me to the airport. I'll just say goodbye, and we'll be off."

"Fine. Your mother's in a right tizzy."

"I'm sure," Blake replied.

Fletcher tipped his hat to Amanda. "Nice to meet you. Excuse me." He headed back to the local official he'd left standing on the far side of the plane.

Blake set his bag down next to the steps of the plane and stuffed his hands in his pockets. "I only have a few minutes. Sorry, this isn't the way I planned for us to part."

She gave him a wry smile. "Were you picturing a tearful goodbye as I got on the plane for Africa?"

"Not exactly." His gaze was so intense Amanda had to look away.

After an awkward pause, she said, "Look, Blake –"

He cut her off. "Thank you for letting me into your family and your home this summer, and please thank your parents again for me. If I left anything behind, just ship it COD to my parents' house."

"I will," she answered.

Fletcher went past them up the steps, and the sounds of the plane preparing to start up filled the hangar.

Blake gently placed a hand on her cheek. "Take good care of yourself in Africa. I'll let you know when you're a free woman again."

Surprised to find tears in her eyes, Amanda tried once again to speak, "Blake."

And then his mouth crushed hers with an urgency and passion she was unprepared for, but before she could even process the kiss, it was over.

"I love you, Amanda," he whispered and then sprinted up the steps of the plane and through the door which closed right behind him.

The engines roared to life, and someone tugged on her arm and pulled her backward away from the moving plane into the safety of the lobby she'd entered through. She raced out the door and stood next to her car. As tears wet her cheeks, she watched the plane taxi down the runway and soar into the sky. In that moment she knew that Blake Worthington, the one guy she'd sworn to never love, had just taken off with a piece of her heart.

## Chapter Thirty - Three

Two days after Blake left, the annulment papers arrived. Amanda pulled them out of the envelope, read through the cover letter of explanation from the lawyer, skimmed the document, and signed her name on the line with the red flag next to it, adding her signature to Blake's. In a sentimental moment, she ran her finger over his name. She gave herself a mental shake, placed the document in the return envelope, and then ran it to the nearest FedEx store before she could change her mind. Now all she had to do was wait for the confirmation letter to say that the annulment had been processed and approved. Although, it probably wouldn't come until after she was in Africa.

She'd kept busy over the past two days with serving at the hospital, making dinner for the family, and repacking her suitcase. Her family seemed to intuitively know not to speak about Blake, now that he was gone. The busyness of serving others kept her from examining her own heart, but late at night, when all was quiet, she admitted to herself that she missed him.

After dinner and a movie with her family, Amanda closed the door to her room. She picked up the novel she'd been so into only a few days before and idly looked at the page her bookmark sat on without really seeing the words.

Her phone rang. She looked over at it, expecting it to be Alison with her happy engagement news and dropped the book when she saw it was Blake. She fumbled with unlocking the phone before it went to voice mail and finally said, "Hello."

"Hey, Mandy."

Even over the phone Amanda could tell he was tired. No, not tired, exhausted. "Hey, how's your dad?"

"He's going to pull through, but it's been a very rough couple of days. He'll need some major recovery time, surgery, and some serious life changes to keep another one from happening."

"Oh, I'm so glad he's going to make it. We've been worried here. I mean, I'm sure not the same amount of worried as your family," she stammered.

"I know what you meant, Mandy." There was a pause.

"How are your mom and Cici doing?"

"Mom's a wreck. We have to pry her from dad's side to get her any rest. She's convinced he's going to die at any moment, although the doctors have reassured us that the critical moment has passed, at least for this heart attack. I'd hate to be dad though, once she gets him home. She'll be relentless about him following his new diet and exercise routine. She'll do anything to keep him alive and by her side as long as she can. I think what scares her most is the idea of going through again what she did with Andrew." Another pause.

Amanda could tell Blake was holding something back, but she didn't want to pry or push. "When will he get home?"

"Not sure. I'm guessing a few weeks."

"What about Cici? Did the ice break there?"

"Things are better between us. The attack shook her up pretty good. Kind of woke her up to a lot of things about life."

"I'm glad things are better. I can't imagine still being estranged from any of my siblings if we were going through Dad having a massive heart attack."

"I don't think that would ever happen in your family. How is everyone there?"

"The same, except they've been asking me if I've heard from you yet. It'll be a major relief to mom to hear about your dad." Amanda tapped a fingernail against her front teeth.

"Your mom's a good woman. Remember to tell her I said that."

"I will."

"Are you all set for Africa? We packed up your room and made your lists. Did you return your library books, check your visa for the thousandth time, and get your teeth cleaned? Probably hard to find a good dentist over there." His attempt at levity didn't mask the fatigue behind it.

"I did. Thanks for asking."

"Sure." Another pause.

The suspense became too much for Amanda, and she plunged into the topic they were both afraid to approach. "I got the papers."

"I know."

"You do?"

"Of course. I asked for confirmation on delivery."

"Oh, right." The fingernail tapped again.

"What did you decide to do with them?" Blake's tone was decidedly guarded.

Amanda rubbed her lips together. "I signed them and sent them."

"Well, that's that then. Now we just have to wait for them to be processed and for the lawyer to notify me when it's done. Then I'll let you know. I'm sure that will be a relief to you, make for a day to celebrate."

"Blake, I –"

"Sorry. I was rude. I'm just tired." He yawned through the last word.

"I can tell. What will happen to the company?"

"The company. Now there's a mess and a half. They want me to run it, of course."

"Will you?"

"I don't have much choice. Dad can't, Andrew's gone, and Cici's too young. That just leaves incapable, incompetent me."

Her heart twisted at the bitterness of his words. "Blake, you do have a business degree. I think you can do this." Amanda tried to bolster his confidence.

"I can do it. That doesn't mean I should, or that I'll succeed. I certainly can't run the lab. It's all gibberish to me."

"I'm sure your dad has someone to run the lab."

"Well, yes. There is Walt. He's been there forever and is the only one who knows this stuff as well as dad, so he can do it. But, Mandy, I'll fail. I know it. I can feel it. I've failed at almost everything I've touched or tried. I couldn't even keep our marriage together. I can't let the company go down because of me. Already the stock went down because of dad's attack, and the board seems to think that a press release naming me as the CEO interim, or something like that, will bring it back up. I just can't do this. There's too much at stake. It should be Andrew here, and me that went down that mountainside, then everything would be fine." Blake sniffed.

Amanda could tell there were tears he was trying to hide from her on his end of the line. A rivulet of moisture wet her cheek. "Blake, please don't say things like it should've been you instead of Andrew. It won't bring him back, and it disgraces his memory and the love you have for him to speak like that. And you can do this, you can run the company, and you will succeed. You won't fail yourself, or your parents, or Andrew. It will be okay. You might even discover you like it." She gave a small forced laugh.

"You really believe I can do it?"

"Yes."

"Will you do me a favor?"

"What?"

"Will you come down here and see me before you go?"

Amanda hesitated. "I can't."

"You can't or won't?"

"I can't, Blake. I get on a plane for Africa in two days."

"You could just come down for the day. I'll send the plane for you. Please, Mandy," he pleaded. "I need you."

"Blake, you don't need me. You already have everything there you need. It's all inside of you. You're just tired and overwhelmed, and in a week or so when things have settled down a bit, you'll see you don't need me and that you're fine without me." Tears flowed fast down her cheeks.

"Which one of us are you trying to convince of that? You or me? Because right now, I'm not entirely sure it's just me."

"You, definitely you." Her words came out too fast.

Blake tried again. "Please, Mandy, I need you."

Amanda held her ground. "No, you don't."

"Fine, then. I want you."

Amanda knew she had to end the conversation or her heart might just win out over her stubborn side. "Blake, just stop. You have a responsibility to your family to run the company, and I have a responsibility to go to Africa and save lives. That's what has to happen now. Not me running down to Texas."

"Is there anything I can say or do to convince you to come down here?"

"No." She brushed at the tears that dribbled off her jawline.

Blake gave a long sigh. "You can't say I didn't try."

"No, I can't." An awkward pause followed.

"I'd better go to bed. I think you're right. I just need some rest." He cleared his throat. "Thanks for the chat. I'll let you know when things are ended. Have a safe trip to Africa."

His attempt at normality undid her more than all the rest because she knew how much she'd hurt him. "Blake, I'm –"

"Goodnight, Amanda." He said her name like a soft caress, and then the call clicked off.

Amanda stared down at the phone. The screen went black. Part of her wanted to call him back, and the other part wanted to throw the phone against the wall. He'd asked her to come, wanted her to come, and she'd refused. She was running again, too afraid to listen to her heart and breaking his in the process. Hurting Blake for breaking her tender heart four years earlier was something she thought she'd wanted for a long time, but now it felt wrong, and worse somehow because she knew she was injuring her own all over again.

Trance-like, she pulled a box out from under the bed and slipped away through the hall to the deserted family room. She set the disc in the Blu-ray player and watched the screen as the images slid past. She left the sound off. Beautiful women in gorgeous dresses, handsome men in tuxes, and the looks on their faces floated across the screen. She replayed the vows and kiss over and over again searching for the moment of doubt that should be there. But it wasn't, just her blissful face next to Blake's. Sometime during the replays, Jenny slipped into the room and joined her daughter on the couch and held her hand. Finally, Amanda turned off the screen and looked at her mom. The room was vaguely illuminated by the kitchen nightlight that filtered through the hallway.

"Blake's dad will be okay," Amanda whispered.

"I'm glad to hear it for both Blake's sake and his family. But I don't think that's why you're sitting here alone in the dark watching this, is it?"

Amanda shook her head. "I wanted to see if I made the wrong choice like I thought I had at the time."

A smile played at the corner of Jenny's mouth. "And?"

"I don't know." Amanda shook her head. "It's all so confusing."

"Anything else?"

Amanda pulled at a loose thread on her t-shirt. "The papers came today. I signed them and sent them back." She sniffed and wiped her nose with the hem of her tee.

"Oh, I see."

"That's been my plan all along, but then Blake called and asked me to come see him before I go. He said he needed me, that he wants me. I told him no."

"Why?"

"Because we weren't meant to be."

"And you're so sure about that, so you've been sitting watching your wedding over and over again."

Amanda bit her bottom lip in a vain attempt to keep it from quivering. "Mom, I have to go to Africa. I have to."

"Do you?"

"Yes."

"Blake won't stop you. He loves you."

"I know."

"You do?" Jenny seemed surprised by this.

"Yes."

"I see. Then what's the problem?"

Amanda's heart swelled to the bursting point as she wrapped her arms around her mom, rested her forehead on Jenny's shoulder, and let the tears flow. "I don't know."

"I do." She smoothed Amanda's hair. "Despite all your plans, stubbornness, and fears, you've fallen in love with him."

## Chapter Thirty - Four

Amanda finished her last class of the day and shook hands and bowed to each of the women in the room. They were truly grateful to know how to save the children born into their families and tribes. She'd taught three classes that day in a structure that barely earned the name of hut. It was built from some scraps of wood, and dried grass made up the roof. She gathered her items together and put them back in her bag. At the door, she dipped her bandana in the basin of water, wrung it out and wrapped it around her neck. This was the only source of air conditioning available in such a remote area, but over the past two weeks, she'd grown accustomed to it. Out here in rural Africa, water truly was life. Well, that and mosquito netting.

"A good day?" Jahad, her interpreter, asked. Amanda had long since given up trying to determine his real age, but she guessed he was in his fifties. His gray wiry hair stood up in all directions, so he kept it cropped short. A few gold caps covered some of his teeth making his smile all the more brilliant against his dark skin.

"Yes, a good day."

"But you are looking forward to a shower, yes?"

"Yes."

He picked up her bag and threw it into the back of the rusted out jeep. The children of the village came out to wave and run after them as they rumbled across the unpaved road back to the main city.

Amanda idly watched the landscape as she turned over the past two weeks in her mind. The days before she left for Africa were sort of a blur because she was so turned up, second-guessing all her decisions about Blake. The plane ride had been long, but uneventful thanks to a pressure point bracelet her parents had given her just before she left. It seemed to be the cure to her airsickness woes. Her arrival in Africa had stunned her. She really hadn't been prepared for the vibrancy of the people, their clothes, or the amount of noise in the city. Even with the training videos she'd watched, she'd still been unprepared for the poverty of many of the areas she'd seen, especially the refugee camps she'd taught at. What amazed her even more was the happiness the majority of the people expressed when they had so little. Not because they were ignorant of what they lacked, but because they had found the secret to being happy with what they had, and anything beyond that was truly a blessing. She should make Tiffany come out here and visit. Maybe then she'd straighten out from being a bit of a spoiled brat. Thinking of Tiffany turned her thoughts to home.

Tonight she'd sleep in a real bed for the first time since she'd left the city nearly two weeks earlier. She'd slept mostly on a pad on the ground with a mosquito net tucked tightly around her. The first few days she'd been stiff but then her body adjusted. She imagined she'd be stiff tomorrow after sleeping in a proper bed again. The city also meant a hot shower. Out of town, she'd been lucky to grab a sponge bath every few days. She also looked forward to a good meal, but she was most excited about a telephone call home.

Hours later, the jeep pulled to a stop in front of the building where she stayed in the city. The program had a room available for their volunteers to use and had set up the rotations so that rarely were any two in the city at the same time. It was cleaned in between volunteers by a little old woman named Vima. A little peace and space were just what Amanda craved after being out in the wild, as she thought of it.

"Thanks, Jahad." Amanda climbed down from the jeep and grabbed her bags out of the back.

Jahad climbed down too. "Do you want me to carry them up for you?"

Amanda shook her head. "I'll be fine. See you in two days?"

This time it was Jahad's turn to shake his head. "I think Karma has you for the next round."

"Karma?"

"There are a lot of dialects out there. We can't speak all of them. Don't worry. She'll take good care of you. Just check your e-mail for your next assignment. Your pick up and interpreter will be in there. Get some rest. Your next two weeks out will be even rougher." He smiled and the light from the building lamps glinted off his gold teeth.

"Rougher? You're kidding, right?"

Jahad just laughed, swung into the still running jeep, and waved as he pulled away to go to wherever his home was in the city.

Amanda watched him go, then hauled her bags upstairs. After a shower, she dropped her clothes off at Vima's to go to the laundry. She wandered the streets until she located a respectable-looking window counter for her dinner, then searched out the internet café she'd found on her first visit to the city. She checked her e-mail. A few from her family, one from Alison, one from the program, giving her instructions for the next round of teaching, which she printed out, but disappointingly, nothing from Blake. She'd hoped to have heard something from him, but he'd been silent ever since she'd refused to come see him.

Her last stop on her way home was a phone booth that made international calls. She pulled out her prepaid phone card and dialed away. A few tense moments later the line picked up.

"Hello?" Missy said.

"Hey, Missy, it's me," Amanda replied.

Missy didn't quite cover the phone all the way as she yelled, "Mom, it's Amanda!"

Amanda winced at the volume.

Missy came back on, "How's Africa?"

"Hot," Amanda replied, fanning herself in the booth.

An extension clicked in and Tiffany said, "Good one. Do you

have a dark skinned boyfriend yet?"

Another click and then Jenny exclaimed, "Tiffany!"

"No, Tiffany. I don't have time for guys right now. Although, I met a man with gold teeth you might like."

"Ew!" Tiffany shrieked. "Bring me back something exotic to wear for winter formal. All those bright-colored clothes will be totally eye-catching."

"I'll see what I can do," Amanda laughed into the phone. "Better yet, get a job and come get the dress yourself."

"That'll be the day!" Tiffany snorted.

Gently, Jenny said, "Girls, hang up now, so I can talk to Amanda."

"Have fun," Missy and Tiffany said in chorus, then their lines clicked off.

"The boys will be here soon. We just got your e-mail and texted them to get over here on the double. Now, how are you? Are you eating well? Did you get malaria yet?"

"Mom, I'm fine. I've adapted to sleeping on the ground, eating local food, and keeping my mosquito net tightly tied around me at night."

"Good. Just be careful there."

"I am. Thanks for worrying about me."

Amanda could feel her mom's smile over the phone. "That's my job, dear, to worry about you. Now, here's someone else that worries about you."

Amanda's dad came on the line. "Hey, sweetheart, how's it going over there?"

"Good. I'm doing lots of teaching and saving lives."

"Good, that's what you went to do. You tired of it yet and want to come home? Because I'm sure as proud as your mom is, she'd be all too happy for you to come home earlier."

"No, dad. I'm good. I'm not coming home early. Try to console mom for me."

"I will, sweetie. Oh, just got a text from the twins. They're going to miss this round; stuck under a car at the shop. But Richard just walked through the door. Here he is."

"Love you, dad," Amanda slipped in just before Richard came on.

"Hey, little sister," he said.

"Hey, Rich."

"I've got some exciting news for you."

"Really, what?" Amanda imagined it was a new car for Rachel, or that he'd booked them a vacation to Disneyland or something.

"You're going to be an aunt!"

"What!" Amanda screamed so loud into the phone that a few passersby turned their heads in her direction. "Are you serious? Why didn't you tell me before I left? You must've known by then." If she'd had Rich in front of her, she'd have lightly pummeled him with her fists.

"Actually we didn't know. Rachel had been feeling run down lately. We thought it was from working so much or maybe she just needed some time off to rest. But then she pulled a muscle in her shoulder at work, and when she went to the doctor, she explained about what had been going on, and he ordered a blood test to check her levels and thyroid and stuff and that's when she found out."

"When was that?"

"The day after you left the city, so we've been sitting on this news for nearly two weeks waiting to tell you. Rachel is sorry she didn't get to tell you, but she got stuck at work, again."

"You're going to have to get her a new job."

"Actually, if things go well at work this month, I should be getting a raise. Then after the baby is born, Rachel can stay home if she'd like to. Her health insurance is better for now than mine, although I hope to change that next year."

"Richard, that's wonderful. All of it. I'm so happy for you both!"

"Thanks. We're looking forward to you being here when the baby is born."

"I'll look forward to seeing you all when I get there." Amanda purposefully left her remark truthful but non-committal. She didn't want to lie to her brother about her return plans, and she was really going to miss meeting her niece or nephew as a baby.

"Hey, Alison just ran in and she wants to talk to you too. Take care!"

"You too."

Alison's voice came through the line. "Isn't it awesome about Rich and Rachel?" she asked.

"I'm really excited for them."

"I don't know how much time you have left, so I'll just be quick. I'm engaged!" Alison squealed into the phone.

Amanda pictured Alison jumping up and down on the other end of the line. "I'm so happy for you!" Amanda knew it had only been a matter of time before Alison and Sheff got engaged with all that had been happening this summer. But the reality of it washed over her and brought up a major stab of sorrow at letting her own happiness go when she'd let Blake slip through her fingers.

"And of course I want you to be my maid of honor. Will you? Please say yes."

"I'm so honored."

"Now you have two good reasons for coming home when your program is over. You'll be an aunt, and I'll need you to help me with all the wedding arrangements. You can also slap me upside the head when I get cold feet a few minutes before walking down the aisle. We're also excited for you to come home."

Amanda laughed. "I've only been gone for about two weeks. How can you all be so desperate for me to be home already? It sounds like life is moving along quite well without me."

The phone beeped and Amanda checked the time left on her card – three minutes. "Hey, Alison, my card is about to run out, and I need to talk to mom real quick before it does. Send me a picture of the rock!"

"I will. She's right here. Bye."

She heard the shuffle of the phone changing hands. "Mom?"

"Yes, dear. Now you've heard everyone's happy news, and I

didn't spoil any of it by telling you. They were a little worried about that."

"Yes, Mom. I'm really happy for all of them. Mom, I've only a got a minute left. Has anything come in the mail for me?" Amanda knew she could count on her mom to understand what she was referring to.

"No, honey, I'm sorry. Nothing yet. I'll let you know when it does."

"Thanks, Mom."

"Have you heard from him at all?" Her mom's voice was considerably quieter.

"No, and I don't expect to. I think that ship has sailed, and I'm pretty sure I'm the one who cast it off."

Ever the optimist, Jenny said, "Well, life is full of the unexpected. Maybe the ship just took a detour around the Straights of Magellan."

The phone beeped in earnest now. "Thanks, Mom. I love you!"

"I love you too, dear!"

The line went dead.

Amanda looked down at the receiver, sighed, and hung it back in its cradle. She'd been so caught up in the conversations that she hadn't noticed how warm and stuffy the booth had gotten. She pulled the used phone card out of the slot and took in a breath of city air as she exited the booth. She stopped in at a corner shop to refill her card on the way back to the apartment.

She readjusted the mosquito netting one last time before she climbed into bed. The program advised sleeping with them every night no matter where you were, even if it was the Ritz Carlton. After all, it only took one bite.

Amanda stared at the netting without focusing on it. She replayed the phone call home. How could she tell her family and Alison she wasn't coming home at the end of the program? That she wouldn't be there for the birth of the baby or Alison's wedding? That she had plans to stay in Africa much longer than the few months of the program, and based on the way she felt now, she didn't think she ever wanted to come home to Iowa. She would be the perpetual globe trotter. Maybe that way she could outrun her broken heart. Maybe someday she'd meet someone who would make her feel the way Blake did, but right now that seemed like a delusional fantasy. Despite all her plans and precautions, she was right back to where she'd started with Blake four years ago, heartbroken. Only now, it was her fault, and this time she knew it hurt on both sides, not just hers.

She turned her face toward the pillow to catch the tears and vowed this would be the last time she'd ever shed tears over Blake Worthington. She'd made her choice and insured that happily ever after was gone.

## Chapter Thirty - Five

The hot sun glared down on Amanda's little work space, which today was just a blanket spread across the dirt. She looked at the doll that represented a new-born baby and thought about Richard and Rachel's upcoming baby, the one she wouldn't see. At least in the States she knew the chances of their baby's survival were high, whereas this little village had seen more than its share of infant mortality. She ran her hand over the top of the smooth plastic head. How it hadn't melted in the heat over the past four weeks she couldn't say. She felt like she melted several times a day. She was in awe of the women who carried the vessels of water for miles each day from the well just to have water in their villages. Certainly she had greater appreciation for the daily comforts of her life back in Iowa.

A light tap on her shoulder pulled her from her reverie. A lean woman in an orange dress spoke, but Amanda didn't understand. Jahad had been right when he said there were many languages and dialects. Amanda tried to just learn "please" and "thank you" in all of them. She'd acquired a few more words on her short visits to the main city, but she pretty much had to rely on her interpreter, who was Karma this go around.

Amanda held up one finger to the woman, which seemed to be a universal sign for one minute, and looked around for Karma. She was on the far side of the hut circle engaged in a rapid conversation with the tribe leader, and from their expressions, Amanda couldn't tell if it was going well. She was on her own to muddle through this time. She looked back at the woman and smiled.

The woman repeated her request, but this time she picked up

the doll and blew on its face, then handed it to Amanda.

This time Amanda understood and gestured for the woman to sit down. She did somewhat awkwardly and that's when Amanda realized the woman must be expecting. Then she noticed the child that hid behind the mother. Amanda couldn't tell if the child was male or female, but he or she looked to be about three years old. She smiled at the child, who ducked behind the mother's shoulder and peeped out at her with its round brown eyes.

Amanda went through the resuscitation routine with the young mother, showed her how to suck out the fluid, blow air into the lungs and give compressions if necessary. The mother followed Amanda's example and then asked her to repeat it twice more by handing back the doll and blowing on its face. After the third time, she smiled and laid the doll down on the blanket. Amanda stood and offered her hands to the mother who gratefully accepted the help up. She embraced Amanda and turned to retrieve the little one holding onto her skirt, but not before Amanda saw her eyes glistened with unshed tears.

Karma and the tribe leader arrived just as the young mother left.

"Who was that?" Amanda asked, pointing to the mother's receding back.

Karma interpreted the tribe leader's answer. "She is Anola. You saw her son, and she is expecting another baby later this year."

"Why was she crying?"

Again Karma interpreted. "She has already lost two children at birth. She was either crying because she wished she had the knowledge you've given her to save them or from joy that she may be able to save the next one."

"So, that's why she wanted me to show her over and over again," Amanda mused.

"Very likely," Karma agreed. "And she's not the only one in this village to have lost a baby. Most of the women here have." She shot a glance at the head tribesman and then back to

Amanda. "Uruku is very grateful for your teaching here today, but I think it's time to get back to the city." In an undertone, she added, "This guy's giving me the heebie jeebies."

Amanda laughed. "I haven't heard anyone here say that before. Where did you even learn that expression?" She gathered up her supplies, including the blanket, and stowed them in her black duffle bag, which was coated in dust and looked gray after a month of traveling around.

"Television, Three Stooges, maybe?" Karma said something Amanda guessed was along the lines of gratitude and made a deep formal bow to the tribesman.

Amanda attempted to copy her, but didn't quite get it right. The tribesman gave her an amused smile and waved them off. As usual, the village kids shouted and chased after them as they drove away.

Amanda closed her eyes and let her mind wander as the jeep rumbled along. Karma wasn't much of a conversationalist and the roar of the jeep made conversation difficult at best. It would be hours and nearly dark before they reached the main city again. The breeze created by the moving vehicle, while still warm, felt good against her moist skin. She adjusted the beach towel that ran the length of the seat so none of her skin stuck to the vinyl.

As usual in her quiet moments, Amanda's mind turned toward home and her family. Tonight she'd be able to check her e-mail and talk to them. She was anxious to hear her mother's voice again and ask the question that burned constantly at the back of her mind. Had she heard from Blake? Was the paperwork done? Was it over? Ah, Blake. Somehow her mind always wound its way back to him, even though she kept trying to vanquish him to the vaults of her mind and heart.

Amanda forced her eyes back open and located the romance novel in the backpack at her feet. She spent the rest of the ride focused on the story and steadfastly ignoring reality.

Karma pulled up to the curb and let the jeep idle. Amanda shut the book and looked up at the building in front of her, then back to Karma. "This isn't where I'm staying," she said confused. "Why are we here?"

Karma shrugged her shoulders. "A text came through just as we hit the city limits that said to bring you here." Karma carried a cell phone with her for emergencies and her time in the city.

Amanda had decided it wasn't worth the bother or the cost to keep one since her interpreters were required to have one. Amanda looked up at the building again. It was a posh hotel, probably the finest one in the city. The program didn't have money for this kind of place. What was going on? Amanda hoped out of the jeep and assembled her three bags. "Did the text say anything else?"

Karma checked the message. "Oh, yeah. There's a room key waiting for you at the front desk."

"What?"

"Hey, don't complain. It beats the apartment and where I'm staying tonight. Call me if you get into trouble. See you later." She shifted the jeep into gear and peeled out into a narrow space in traffic.

Utterly bewildered, she picked up her bags. The doorman opened the door and tipped his hat at her. She nodded and walked across the marble floor to the front desk.

An impeccably dressed young woman greeted her. "Good evening. May I help you?"

Amanda shifted her feet. "Uh, I was told to pick up a room key?"

"Name, please?"

"Amanda St. Claire."

The woman's red fingernails tapped on the computer keys. "Welcome, Miss St. Claire. Your room is ready and waiting. Please let us know if there is anything you need." She passed Amanda a gold key, not one of those key cards she was used to seeing.

"Actually, I'd like to know who is paying for the room," Amanda said.

The woman gave her a professional smile. "Everything has been taken care of. Order whatever you wish and let us know if there is anything we can do to make your stay comfortable."

Sensing the woman wouldn't give her any further information on her mysterious benefactor, Amanda thanked her and stooped to pick up her bags, but a bellhop already stood at her side with bags in hand.

"This way, Miss." He led her to the elevator, up to her floor, and into her room. He deposited the bags on the floor inside the doorway. Amanda scrambled through her backpack to find money for a tip, but he said, "It's already been taken care of," and pulled the door shut behind him.

Amanda looked at the door for a moment, wondering if she should run for her life or just enjoy this luxurious gift. Thankfully, the last four weeks had taught her to ease up on being in control all the time and enjoy the beauty of the moment. She turned around and looked at the room. The floors were a warm mocha marble while the walls were a peaceful cream. Bold splashes of colorful artwork adorned the walls. She stepped over to the balcony at the far end and opened the French doors. Below looked like a smaller version of Central Park, and the noise of the city around her faded away. She took in a deep breath of the night air, then hightailed it into the shower, which turned out to be equipped with massaging jets that came out from three walls. She dried off, wrapped herself in the robe she removed from the hook on the back of the door, then checked out the bedroom. On the bed lay a white short-sleeve sweater and white linen pants including clean underwear and bra, all in her correct sizes.

The idea of who might be behind all this had been in her mind since she pulled up in front of the hotel, but she still refused to believe it might be possible even with all the signs telling her it was the most likely answer. She ditched the robe and put on the clean garments, relishing in their smell and softness. Then she stepped back through the sitting area, opened the doors to the balcony, and there he was silhouetted against the starry sky.

Blake.

Her heart leapt in her chest.

He turned and smiled at her. "You always look beautiful in white," he said softly.

She checked herself just in time from flying into his arms. She knew once she let his arms wrap around her she'd never let him go again. Instead she replied, "Thanks and thanks for the room too."

"You're welcome."

They stood there for a moment, neither one quite knowing how to begin.

Blake pulled a piece of paper out of his jacket pocket. "I brought you this."

She took it and quickly read it. It was the annulment from Las Vegas. Finally. But what she'd wanted so badly to hold in her hand so many weeks ago now left a cold feeling running through her. She looked up at him. "You came all the way to bring me this? You could've just sent it to my parents or called or even e-mailed me."

He cocked his head to one side. "Even with everything I've done to show you I've changed, and how much I care, you think I have the bad manners to tell the woman I married that it's over through an e-mail?" He took one step toward her and she stepped back. He stopped.

"No, I mean, I don't think you have bad manners," she stammered. "I just meant it would've been simpler, less expensive."

"What good is having all this money if I can't use if for a good cause?"

"Is that what I am? A good cause?"

"No, yes." He shook his head and chuckled. "You can be so difficult and infuriating and stubborn."

This got her a bit rankled. "Then why would you want someone like that for your wife?"

"Because you are so sexy and desirable and beautiful when you are mad and trying to resist me." He took another step toward her.

With the French door at her back Amanda had nowhere to go. Her heart hammered in her chest. "That doesn't seem very reasonable."

He stroked her cheek just once. "Love isn't reasonable."

Amanda's legs shook. If she didn't get him out of here soon, all her resolve was going to crumble away. "Blake," she whimpered.

"I brought you something else." He reached into his pocket and pulled out a ring.

Amanda instantly recognized it, and her eyes widened as she raised her lashes to meet his gaze. "Why are you doing this?"

He ignored her question for the moment. "Mandy, will you marry me?"

The shaking traveled from her legs through the rest of her body. "I can't," she whispered.

"Why?"

"We don't belong together. We're too different. I have lives to save and you have a company to save."

"We can work through all that, and we're not too different, and we do belong together. There's only one reason left for you to give that I'll accept. You don't love me. Look me in the eye and tell me you don't love me, and I'll leave you alone for good this time."

Amanda fixed her eyes on him and opened her mouth, but she only got as far as, "Blake, I –," before the lie stuck in her throat. A tear slipped down her cheek. "I can't say it," she gasped.

"I love you and you love me."

"How do you know?" Amanda tried desperately one last time not to give in, but felt the last of her shattered remains of resolve melting away the longer Blake looked in her eyes and leaned in toward her.

He paused. "Because I can see it in your eyes." His eyes took on a distinctive twinkle. "Not to mention your mom mentioned your feelings had changed after our last phone call."

Ratted out by her mom! If Amanda hadn't loved her mother so much she might've considered shaking her hard by the shoulders.

Blake grinned impishly. "But, I want to hear you say it."

She inhaled sharply. "Oh, Blake."

"Here, I'll go first, again." He put his arms around her and peeled her from the door, which sent warmth spreading through her body and her stomach doing the tango. "I love you."

She inhaled the smell that was pure Blake, and in a voice that was barely a whisper said the hardest three words she never thought she'd say, "I love you."

Blake drew her in even closer. "Sorry, I didn't hear you. Say it again a little louder."

"I love you." This time her voice had a bit more volume.

"Just to be sure I heard you right, one more time."

"I love you!" That shout burst her heart into a million carefree butterflies.

Blake picked her up and twirled her around until they were both dizzy and gasping for breath. He set her back down on the ground without letting an inch come between them.

"I'm going to ask you this question again, and this time, Mandy, don't think about it, just follow your heart." He held up the ring between their faces. "Will you marry me?"

"Yes."

He slipped the dazzling ring on her finger. "And this time will you stay married to me?"

She moved to try and punch his arm even as she said, "Yes," but the word never quite made it all the way out because Blake's mouth covered hers, and she abandoned herself to the rush of sky-high emotion brought only by Blake's kiss.

# Chapter Thirty - Six

When they both got their breath, Blake said, "Come on. We haven't got much time, and I'm trying to give you more than an hour if I can." He took her hand and tugged her to the hotel room door.

"Blake, what are you talking about?"

"You need to get ready."

She blinked. "For what?"

"The wedding, of course." He kissed her on the cheek and pulled her through the door and into the hallway.

She grabbed onto the doorframe, and the door handle struck her in the hip. "Now? No. No way. I'm not getting married again without my family."

"Who said you had to?"

"What?"

"You didn't think I'd make the mistake of marrying you a second time without your family, did you?"

"They're here?" Amanda let go of the doorframe and fell against Blake, who caught her.

"Yes."

"You mean just my parents, right?" She tried to get her breath.

"No, I mean all of them."

"All of them? Including Rachel?"

"Including Rachel."

"I need to sit down."

Blake laughed at her reaction and picked her up. "No time. I'll just carry you."

She twined her arms around his neck and gazed adoringly

at him and then a thought struck her. "But, what about your family? Your dad?"

"They're all here too."

"Seriously? They're not exactly my biggest fans. How did you do it?"

They got on the elevator and headed down as Blake explained.

"A lot has changed in my family in the past few weeks. Things are different and a lot better. Dad's brush with death was probably the best thing that ever happened to us, except for maybe you." He nuzzled her neck.

"Stop," she protested half-heartedly. "Are they really okay with us?"

"Yes. In fact, dad told mom that if she left him behind to miss the wedding that he would eat nothing but doughnuts, pork rinds, and fried chicken until she returned. Mom had him packed in short order after that."

"Wow!"

"Yeah."

The elevator door opened.

"Think you can walk now?"

"Yes."

He set her lightly on her feet, took her hand, and walked her toward the salon.

Amanda pulled him onto a sofa in the lobby. "Hold on for just one minute. I need a few answers. What about running your dad's company? What about my work here? Are you expecting me to give it up and fly home tomorrow? Where are we going to live?"

Blake laughed. "Slow down, Mandy. It's all taken care of. I'm still running the company, and I'll be going back and forth until you've done what you came to do in Africa."

"Even if it's years?"

"Yes, but Dad will get back into things once he's well recovered. I may work on running the African division for a while once that happens."

"Do you have an African division?"

"We do now." He grinned at her. "So, I'll take care of our living arrangements here."

"What about everything else?"

"We'll sort it out along the way. Now, stop planning and get ready." He pulled her to her feet and led her into the salon. A matronly woman with too bright red lipstick met them. "Amanda, this is Claudia. She and her team will take care of your hair, make-up, and nails."

"But what about my dress? And where is everyone?"

"I'll see you in about an hour." He kissed her on the cheek and headed for the door. "It's all here, and so are they." He pointed to the far side of the room.

Five salon chairs turned around in unison.

"Ahh!" Amanda screamed as her mom, Tiffany, Missy, Rachel, and Alison descended upon her with hugs and kisses. "How did you all get here?" she demanded.

"Blake, of course." Jenny hugged her.

"Isn't it amazing?" Tiffany squealed.

"It's so romantic. I can't believe we're in Africa!" Missy twirled around and the dress she wore registered in Amanda's brain.

"Wait!" Amanda looked at Alison. "Are those the same dresses as in Vegas?"

"The very same and all the accessories too. Blake had the stores ship them to him and then they flew with us."

"I seriously need to sit down."

"Good," Claudia chimed in and steered Amanda into a salon chair, "Because we need to get to work." She clapped her hands. The women parted to let the team of technicians in. For the next hour Amanda chatted with the women she loved most in her life while Claudia's team worked their magic. Finally, Claudia spun the chair around so Amanda could see the result.

"You like?" Claudia asked.

Amanda stared at her reflection. "You did it just the same."

"Oh, yes. Mr. Worthington sent pictures ahead so we could

get it just right."

"It's beautiful. Thank you," Amanda said with heartfelt gratitude.

"We better go," Jenny said. "Girls, go take your places. This last bit is mine."

"Mom," Amanda began as the girls trailed out of the salon.

"Just follow me." Jenny led them across the hall to the boutique and into a large fitting room. On a bust hung Amanda's wedding dress while a turquoise table held all the accessories including her shoes.

"Oh, Blake," Amanda breathed.

Jenny had Amanda fully outfitted in short order then turned her around to face the three-way mirror. "Oh, Mom," Amanda said again. "It's all so magical, like a dream, but better because it's real, and you're here." Tears sprang to her eyes. She hugged Jenny.

"Now, don't start all that. I'm not sure either one of us is wearing waterproof mascara and I wouldn't ruin the way you look for anything in the world." She air kissed her daughter's cheek. "Are you ready?"

Amanda took one last look at the two of them in the mirror. "Yes. I'm ready."

Jenny led them through the main lobby and soon they were outside in the garden Amanda had seen from her balcony. Her mother stopped just before a break in the hedge. "Stay here. I'm going to take my seat. The girls and Dad will be here in just a moment to take you down the aisle. Don't peek." She smiled and disappeared.

Up the path came the Worthingtons. Danyelle reached her first and pulled her into a hug. Surprised by this greeting, Amanda simply patted her back.

"We have a lot to apologize for," Danyelle said.

"Most especially me," Rex added. "I hope you will forgive all the horrible things I said to you in Texas. They were undeserved and an inexcusable way to speak to Blake's wife."

Danyelle shot a look at Cici and cleared her throat.

"I'm afraid I have an apology to make as well. Will you forgive us?" Cici asked.

"Of course," Amanda replied graciously. "Our first meeting was under very unusual circumstances, and I understood why you were so upset."

"We're looking forward to getting to know you better," Danyelle said. "We'd better take our seats now." She and Rex moved forward.

"Cici," Amanda said. "Are you wearing one of the bridesmaid gowns?"

Cici blushed. "I am. I hope you aren't mad."

"No, I'm not mad. Why weren't you in the salon with the rest of us?"

Cici fidgeted with an earring. "I thought it would be awkward to be there. I should go take my seat with my parents." She turned to follow them around the hedge.

Amanda put a hand on her arm. "Aren't you in the line up?"

"Oh, no. I thought you wouldn't want me there, and it would mess up the numbers. You only have three groomsmen."

"Cici," Amanda said gently. "You are Blake's sister. I wouldn't have you miss being in the lineup for anything. We're family." She squeezed Cici's arm.

Cici's eyes lit up. "Really?"

"Yes. You can walk down with Josh, and I'll have Alison walk solo. She won't mind. Just wait here."

Cici nodded.

A moment later the crew rounded the hedge along with all her brothers on the opposite side. They grinned at her.

Bill took her arm. "You look beautiful," he said softly.

"Thanks, Dad. I'm so glad you're here." She squeezed his arm.

"You can thank Blake for all that's happening." He returned her gesture.

"I will."

The music started and the women and men paired up to walk down the aisle. Alison was the last to disappear around the corner, and then it was Amanda's turn.

"Right foot first," her father said.

They rounded the corner of the hedge, and Amanda's breath caught in her throat. The garden looked like it had been made by fairies. Hedges, topiaries, fountains, and endless strings of twinkling lights adorned the greenery. Jenny sat in a chair to one side of the aisle with Blake's parents opposite. They all smiled at her. She smiled back then turned her focus to Blake. She'd always loved his smile, but tonight it took on an ethereal quality.

Amanda floated down the aisle by her father's side. The look in Blake's eyes confirmed that he knew this time he'd gotten things right. This was the way to start their life together, with family at their side. Happiness radiated from her head to her toes.

Once Bill handed Amanda to Blake the priest dismissed the attendants to sit down except for Alison and Rich, who had duties to fulfill. It was a small audience and a relatively short ceremony but Amanda didn't mind and it seemed like Blake didn't either. It was perfect for them. They exchanged vows and Blake slipped the matching wedding bands into place on her finger before she placed one on his. The priest pronounced them married and invited Blake to kiss the bride.

"With pleasure," he said low in her ear.

"The pleasure is all mine," she purred back.

He raised an eyebrow at her, then kissed her soft and slow.

Her brothers gave a hoot, and they broke apart while everyone clapped. The music began and Blake whisked her down the aisle. When they rounded the corner out of sight of their families, his mouth descended onto hers once more for a swift kiss. "How was your wedding this time, Mrs. Worthington?"

She grinned at him. "Well, while I appreciate the fact you had it recorded, I won't need the video to remind me what happened tonight. It's etched in my brain forever, just like you are etched onto my heart." She held up her hand with the glittering diamond rings on it. "And these are never coming off again."

♥ ♥ ♥

**Want more sweet stories full of heart?
Join my newsletter for an exclusive gift!
http://eepurl.com/cfX_TP**

**Get all the books at:
www.lisaswinton.com**

If you enjoyed this book, please LEAVE A REVIEW! Word of mouth is a huge way of thanking an author and helps readers find more works by the author. It only takes a few minutes of your time and can be as simple or as gushing as you want to make it.

# Acknowledgments

Thanks to my writer's group in Kansas: Regina Sirois (*On Little Wings*), Danyelle Ferguson (*Sweet Confections*), John Ferguson and Karina Fuggett. They are my supporters and champions!

To Kathleen Brebes, Eva Call, and my sister, Alison Love, who did marvelous edits on my book to make it sparkle and shine like a diamond ring. This book is fabulous because of you!

To Danyelle Ferguson, Alison Love, and Jenny Wirt who contributed their names for characters as winners of my blog contest.

NaNoWriMo is the reason this book is here. I wrote 50,000 of the 85,000 words in 22 days thanks to their challenge! The whole book took me a mere three months to write!

Thanks to LDStorymakers, LDStorymakers Midwest and Authors Incognito, who gave me incredible knowledge and insight regarding writing and publishing. Thanks!

Thanks to the McDonalds on 7th St. in Frederick, MD, where I spent many hours editing

Thanks to Ashley Johnson for creating a beautiful cover!

My final thanks go to my family and friends. My husband, who quietly supported me, watched our kids so I could attend conferences, and encouraged me to publish. My kids, for being cool when I forwent making dinner or cleaning the house (both rare exceptions for me) to write. I hope they see you can pursue new things at any age. My parents and extended family, who constantly asked how my writing was going and supported me. THANK YOU ALL!

## About the Author

Award-winning author Lisa Swinton loves romance, travel, Disney, Jane Austen, and tidying up, not necessarily in that order. When she's not writing and being a mom, you might find her singing onstage.

Connect with me:
Website
Amazon
Instagram
Facebook
Newsletter
Blog
Goodreads
BookBub

Made in the USA
Monee, IL
24 May 2023

34511556R00157